A God for Lions

A God for Doubters

by

Lucien Gregoire

© 2002 by George Lucien Gregoire. All rights reserved.

No part of this book may be reproduced, stored in a retrieval system, or transmitted by any means, electronic, mechanical, photocopying, recording, or otherwise, without written permission from the author.

ISBN: 1-4033-5452-9 (e-book)
ISBN: 1-4033-5453-7 (Paperback)
ISBN: 1-4033-5454-5 (Dust Jacket)

Library of Congress Control Number: 2002093967

This book is printed on acid free paper.

Printed in the United States of America
Bloomington, IN

1stBooks – rev. 07/05/03

This is a book for old and young alike who are not certain of their immortality. It is for those who have doubt, either great or small, that *the rose can, indeed, grow on the other side of the wall*. This is not a book of theory. Rather it is a book of reality, one of fact.

Some names have been changed as to protect the privacy of persons living and dead. All quotations from Christian, Judaea, Muslim, Hindu and Buddhist scripture are actual. The quotations from these scriptures, including the *Bible*, the *Torah*, the *Koran*, the *Vedas* and the *Tripitaka* have been *italicized* as to differentiate them from the regular text. All references to Hebrew, Egyptian, Greek, Minoan, Mesopotamian, Sumeric, Scandinavian, Hittite, Syrian and other cultures are historical fact. The references to the book '*Sequel of Relativity*' are the author's own creation and are not a part of any existing work. Opinions of psychiatric and medical associations are current and the author extends his gratitude to those members of these professions who have contributed to this book. Albert Einstein's *Theory of Relativity* provides much of the underlying framework of the thinking herein and for this reason the early part of what follows focuses on establishing a simple practical understanding of Einstein's work on the part of the reader.

The MidEast is considered a part of the Western Hemisphere in this book as it recognizes the same God as do those in the west. Words actually written or spoken by persons living or dead have been *italicized* as to differentiate them from the regular text.

Comments or gift and signed copies of this book or the authors other books, Email: yourangel@att.net or 410 625 9741
Books can also be ordered on www.1stbooks.com

A sampling of the three dozen plus stories in this book:

Sam
The Little Girl in the Attic
General Patton at Milan
The Moth and the Butterfly
The Bike
The Birds and the Bees
Major similarities among the world's religions
Major differences among the world's religions
The Scientific Case for Reincarnation
Just What Are We Trying to Save?
    The Case for Saving Ones 'BODY'
    The Case for Saving Ones 'MIND'
    The Case for Saving Ones 'SPIRIT'
    The Case for Saving Ones 'SOUL'
Explicit Descriptions of the hereafters:
    The Taoist heaven
    The Hindu heaven
    The Buddhist heaven
    The Muslim heaven
    The Jewish heaven
    The Christian heaven
    The Sure Bet
Evolution of belief in God from the caveman to the present
Complete Genealogy from Adam to Christ

NOTE: the stories must be read in order as they are all integral parts of the overall narrative

A God for Lions

I came upon a common?

as tiny as a mouse,

I saved him from the bitter cold,

and took him in my house.

I wrapped him in some swaddling clothes,

and lay him in his bed,

you'll never guess what Santa did,

when down the chimney he slid,

and under the tree was a miniature shed,

and a surprise that lay in its crib!

Lucien Gregoire

The Story of Sam

Baltimore Harbor, Christmas Eve,

It was the coldest night of the year. No, it was the coldest night of the century. As I passed by the boarded up carousel that sat at the southern end of the harbor, I could still see its lights, I could still hear its music, I could still see its stampede of lions, and tigers, and pigs, and horses, and sheep. And I wondered what was their destination? Wondered where they were going? Wondered what was their dream?

As I looked up I could see the great nineteenth century house that I called home. Fronting on a cobblestone street, its rear with its snow covered decks looked out at me. Looked out, hopelessly, over the harbor.

And icicles all over, some masquerading as daggers and others as spears, as if they had gotten their dates mixed up and witches and goblins, not Santa, their aim.

An icy rain was falling. So icy, that as each drop reached the pavement it added to the stalagmites that were hanging there upside down from the sidewalk. As I proceeded up the walk that ran aside my house, I stopped, thinking that I had seen what could be a small animal, a small ball of fur, huddling at the side of the walkway. Turning back, just at that point at which the walk intersected the alley that ran behind my house, was a small gray mouse. Then, noticing the length of its tail, I surmised that it was, indeed, a baby rat. And I thought of the large rat that my carpenter had killed in my cellar the week before. Could this be one of her babies?

It was breathing heavily. Obviously, near death. Even its tail was frozen to the ice. "There is nothing I can do," I thought. So,

A God for Lions

with a somewhat weighted heart, I proceeded up to the house. Opening the door, I went immediately to the fire, and stoking the coals, added a couple of logs. Then to the bookcase, and picking up a book, I curled up in the overstuffed chair that flanked the fireplace.

The light and the warmth of the fire felt good. The tree, which sat at the other side of the fireplace, told its tale, of light, of tinsel, of angels, of balls of silver, of crystal and snow. Soon the chill that I had picked up out on the harbor was gone. And as I turned a page, I thought of the creature, God's creature, that I had passed on the way. "Perhaps it's over," I said to myself, "Yes, it must be over by now. It's best, he's with his mother now."

Soon I proceeded up the stairs and entering the bedroom, I again went first to the fireplace, and stoking the coals, added another log. Then changing into my pajamas, I climbed under the covers, still with book in hand, I proceeded to read myself to sleep.

But sleep was not going to come easily that night. For, suddenly, one of those things one calls tears came up out of my heart and started from the crevice of my eye and ran toward its lid, and I looked first to the right, and then to the left, and then again to the right, and then to the left, once more, and *not quite, yet, a man*, I let it slip out onto my cheek. And in my heart, nothing, not a thing was left in its place.

"Well maybe," I thought, "he could still be suffering. Got to be sure." So getting up, I proceeded down to the living room, and still in my pajamas, I donned my boots and mackinaw and proceeded out into the night. The freezing rain had now made its transition to snow. Silent white flakes drifted down softly as if to sleep. But a brisk wind crept about on the ice-covered ground, keeping them very much awake.

As I proceeded down the walkway, I hoped that it would all be over. And coming to the spot where he lay, I saw that he was, indeed, punishing me for what my carpenter had done to his mother. His breathing was more labored now and even some of his hair was now frozen to the ice. Tiny petals of snow had begun to cling to his whiskers. He seemed to be looking up at me, a sad look, one that said, "Please help me."

I proceeded back to the house and again I entered the living room, this time going directly to the door that led to the cellar. Down the steps I went, and I opened the door to the workshop. I gathered up a putty knife, an old rag, a small box and an old birdcage that was there.

I moved back up the steps and leaving the cage in the living room I went back out into the cold and returned to where he lay. I first chipped the ice around him and then very carefully that which was beneath him, and having freed him from his prison, I picked him up with the rag and with great care I placed him into the box.

Taking him into the house, I set the box down near the fireplace and went about readying the cage. I lined it with paper, added a jar cover filled with water, a small piece of carrot, and, of course, a crumb of cheese.

Then I went up to the medicine cabinet and then back down to the refrigerator. And returning to the chair that sat beside the fireplace, I reached over and picked him up. Now, his tiny body trembling nestled in the rag. I first warmed the milk with the heat from the fire. Then taking up the nose dropper, I began to nourish the baby rat.

His labored breathing started to abate and I wrapped him in the rag, "His swaddling clothes," I thought to myself. I put him inside the cage and locked its door. Then, carefully placing it under the tree, I proceeded up the stairs. And going to the fireplace, I stoked the fire once more. And with my book in hand, I climbed back into bed,

and images of Santa soon danced in my head,
and even Dickens could not guess what he did,
when under the tree was a miniature shed,
and a surprise that lay in its crib!

When I rose the next morning, Sam, as I would come to call him, was already up. And although still very slow from his experience, he seemed to be none the worst for it. The small piece of cheese was gone and he had already made some inroads into the carrot.

As I sat there in the dining area sipping my coffee, I looked out over the harbor, and wondered what I could do now. The long winter was still young. If I were to put him out now it would not give him a fighting chance. After all, his mother is gone. Then thinking of his mother, I wondered to myself, "What if he has some brothers and sisters?" And looking out at the alley that ran behind the house, I realized that now I was beginning to toy with my very sanity, itself. After all, these were wild animals, animals that were outcasts to society, to everything that was civilized.

But, nevertheless, knowing that I was dealing with nature's creatures, God's creatures, I must do whatever I can. So putting on my coat and boots, I proceeded down the cellar stairs and out the rear of the house and across the frozen garden. Unlocking the gate, I proceeded into the alley. And sure enough, I came upon another one, and then another. But, too late, for the night had taken its toll. God's tiny creatures, each one frozen in its tracks. I checked up and down the alley once more, and my next door neighbor opened his window and called out to me, "What did you lose, what are you looking for?" And I told him, "Rats, baby rats, baby rats that might be suffering from the cold!"

From that day forward, my neighbor, whenever we met on the street, seemed to keep me at some distance. I've never understood why? Perhaps you know why?

Lucien Gregoire

Going back into the house, I, unfortunately, couldn't bring Sam good news. I tried not to look at him, so as to spare it from him, that he might see it in my eyes. For this terrible blast of winter had, indeed, dealt him a severe blow. And, going to the cage, I took him out, and sitting by the fireplace I stroked his back so as to console him in his great loss, hoping, all the time, that he wouldn't notice the tears that were forming in the corners of my eyes.

And, indeed, it was a long harsh winter. Each time I looked at Sam in the cage, I knew that I had done right. And as spring approached I thought I could keep him there all his life. And now he was all full of life. Yes, I would want to keep him there for he was now my friend, my pal. But to do so I knew would deprive him of life. Deprive him of the opportunity to fall in love and possibly bring others into the world, others that would perpetuate his kind.

So the winter had finally passed and the day had finally come when I had to say goodbye to Sam. Taking the cage in hand, I proceeded out the door. This time the day was glorious. The four golden federal stars, which adorned the weather-beaten brick facade that fronted my house, sparkled in the sun. The air was brisk, and a slight breeze was trying to charm the leaves on the trees. I crossed the street toward the great park that overlooks the city's harbor and I set the cage down on the ground near some bushes that ran in a row up a slope.

When I had first put him in it, I had some question that, perhaps, because of his tiny size, that the cage might not hold him. That he might squeeze out through its ribs. Now he was so big that I feared that he might not be able to get out of the door. But when I opened the door, he ran out of the cage and up along the edge of the bushes and then, suddenly, he stopped. And he looked back at me with his eyes, the same eyes that had looked up at me from the ice, as if to say, "Thank you, thank you from the very bottom of my heart," and he was gone.

As I passed my neighbor's house, with the cage still in hand, he asked, "Out looking for rats again?"

And unlocking the door to my house, I replied, "No, just sending one off to college."

And, going in, I closed the door behind me, and one of those things one calls tears came up out of my heart and started from the crevice of my eye and ran toward its lid, and I looked first to the right, and then to the left, and then again to the right, and then to the left, once more. And, *not quite, yet, a man,* I let it slip out onto my cheek. And in its place, in my heart, was left something that would be with me all the days of my life.

And later that evening I went down to the harbor. As I passed by the carousel, it was now all lit up. And now all could see its lights, and all could hear its music, and all could see its stampede of lions, and tigers, and pigs, and horses, and sheep. But I still wondered what was their destination? Wondered where they were going? Wondered what was their dream?

And my neighbor? Well, after that, whenever I saw him he avoided me, he avoided me completely. I've never understood why? Perhaps, you know why?

Lucien Gregoire

the little girl in the attic

It was the first day of spring in the year nineteen hundred and sixty nine when the train pulled into Amsterdam Central Station. I realized that finally, for the first time, I was truly in Europe. Following my friend's advice who had been there before, I quickly found my way to the travel services booth and landed a room. The clerk handed me a small slip with an abbreviated map spelling out directions to the hotel. He had written on the slip what was obviously the room rate. '395 NLGs'. Not being familiar with exchange rates, I was totally unaware that I was, indeed, splurging this very first night in Europe.

As I stood on the sidewalk in front of the hotel, I saw that it was, indeed, a five-star hotel. "One, two, three, four, five," I whispered to myself as I counted the stars on its marquee. And thinking of my friend back home that had given me the helpful hint, I thought, "You really messed up this time." The clerk at the railway service desk must have noticed my *Rolex* watch that I had picked up for ten bucks on Times Square. But thinking that I may have already paid the bill, as I remembered that the clerk at the railway service desk had taken my credit card, I walked up to its grand entrance.

As I entered the hotel with my ragged jacket, my knee-torn Levi's, my molded pack on my back, and my wear-and-tear sneakers, I had an uncomfortable feeling that I was being watched. And as I walked toward the check-in counter, I realized that I was, indeed, being watched. For a uniformed sentinel just to my right was surely evaluating what he saw. Trying to reconcile the measurement between a bum off the street and an eccentric American millionaire, one of the most difficult judgments one can make. And very carefully, without touching it, I shuffled my sleeve up above the *Rolex*. And having successfully evaded the guard, I reached the counter and the credit card did the rest of the trick.

The room was magnificent, with a four poster bed, a small well-stocked refrigerator and an all marble bath. The bath seemed to have two johns and I surmised that the funny looking one must be one of those things they call a bidet. I've been to Europe many times since and I still have not figured out what they use them for? On the marble vanity, which enclosed the sink, were lined up a half dozen or so miniature bottles, like soldiers at attention. As I started to read them, I, quickly, realized that I couldn't read them at all. "I might end up gargling with the shampoo," I thought. "Maybe, they'll take them off of the bill?" Then, I wondered what this was all costing me? And taking out my Dutch-English translator and checking the conversion table, I exclaimed out loud, "Wow!"

The following morning I had a remarkable breakfast. Crepe suzettes with a memory built into them. I thought that I must be in a French hotel in Holland. Needless to say I checked out. I could write off one night at these rates over five years or so but two nights might put me under, forever.

I spent the day as a tourist. Starting with the art museums.

I went first to the Van Gogh, which synchronizes classical music with the great master's art. The music is tailored to the mood of the art on each level. One starts at the top. Here, are the artist's lighter works, the daisies, the wheat fields and the thatched roofed cottages. The music is light and airy. Mozart, Mendelson and Debussy make their rounds. And as one descends both the art and the music like two great stallions in their quest for the roses run even with each other, all the way down to the ground floor. And here the starry skies are foreboding, the people, the cows, the oxen, even the flowers are brooding. The light is gone and darkness reigns supreme. And Beethoven, Wagner and Faust have their time.

Then to the Riiks Museum and Rembrandt's masterpiece the *Night Watch*. As immense as it is beautiful and enticing. Here, only here, among all of God's creation does quality and quantity end in a tie.

And finally to the Rembrandt Museum. As I wandered from room to room I came to realize that this man, this master, knew of man's greed better than any other before or after him. For in a few short minutes I would see more gold than adorns all the great Christian domes of the world.

And when I had completed my tour of the museums, I realized that I had, indeed, seen that day in Amsterdam more money on canvas than I would see in all of my professional career, on all of the balance sheets of all the corporate giants I would have the privilege to work for.

And later that afternoon I happened upon a street that ran down along one of the city's great canals. And midway down the street I came upon a house. An old man stood at its front door. And he beckoned me into the house. And going up the front steps, I followed him in and then up the stairs again.

At the top of the stairs he led me to a bookcase. And much to my surprise he opened the bookcase and I followed him up some stairs, some more. And finally, reaching a landing, I found myself to be in a simple room, an attic, one end of which was a some kind of a kitchen and at the other end, a kind of parlor.

And the one with me handed me a small book with a picture of a small girl smiling with dimples on its cover and told me in a quiet and reverent voice almost as if not to wake her, "This is what she was," and, moving to the center of the room, he added still more silently, "This is where she lived," and taking me to a window he added, "This is what she saw," and taking me to a chair that sat in a corner, "This is where she spoke of things that used to be," and taking me to a small table set against a wall, "This is where she wrote of things that were," and taking me into a tiny room off to one side he said, his voice now edged in solemnity, "This is where she thought of things that had never been and dreamed of things that were to be," and finally, taking me back to the doorway of the room, "But the things she dreamed of were not to be," he whispered almost hopelessly, "for this is where she was no more."

He pointed to a black and white photograph of a factory with its chimneys smoking. A factory that could be any factory, except for a single thing, a swastika flag flying from its mast!

I tucked something into his hand. The action was quick. That is all I can remember of it. Just that it was quick. Then I moved toward the landing, staggered down the stairs and like some kind of a ghost I emerged from the bookcase, and slipped down another flight of stairs. I stumbled out of the door and down the steps to the walk, moving hurriedly from the pursuit of it all. Like one who has just robbed a bank. Escape, escape was my only desire. My only end, my single destination.

Shortly, I came to a bench that sat to one side of the canal. And sitting down, I gazed for a moment or two at a mother duck with a half dozen or so of her children following her down the canal. And then I heard it. I heard it for the very first time. From the pounding on the door, to the hoofbeats on the stairs, to the opening of the bookcase, to the scurrying in the attic, to the manacles being fastened, to the clanging of the boxcar doors, to the bedlam at their destination. Then, to the shouting of the guards, to the waving of the hands, to the chambers on the right, to the ovens on the left, to the smelling of the flesh, and witnessed the end of a lifetime, the end of a little girl's lifetime.

I glanced first to my right, and then to my left, and again to my right, and finally to my left, once more. So as to assure myself that the coast was clear. To assure myself that no one, not even the great one above was watching. Then, only then, did I roll the tear back into the corner of my eye.

I rested awhile and opened the book the guide had given me, *The Diary of Anne Frank*, and I read,

Lucien Gregoire

"I still believe that people are really good at heart ... when I look up to the heavens, I think that it will all come right, and that peace and tranquility will return again."

"Not really what most people would call a vacation," I thought to myself, "Not exactly like lying in the sun with a Pina Colada by your side somewhere in the Caribbean. But it is necessary," I reminded myself, "It is necessary for her, it is necessary for me, and it is necessary for all humanity. That what she dreamed of, those things that were to be, will come to be, for her, and for me, and for all humanity."

Still reeling from the blow, I looked up and on the other side of the canal I saw a 'coffee shop'. And getting up, I followed the rail that guided one around the edge of the canal to the shop. As I ordered a cup of coffee, the waiter muttered something in Dutch and offered me a cigarette. I had never smoked a cigarette in all my life. But I took it, I took it, I needed something desperately. I lit it up and started puffing on it.

The shop was of a rather eye catching, unique design. It was a little like being in a disco back in the states. I noticed that a couple of people were actually dancing in the next room to psychedelic lights and blaring music. "This was certainly a strange coffee shop," I thought. Then, I began to feel a little dizzy. It seemed that the deep aroma that the cigarette was giving off was making me light-headed. I thought I'd better go back out into the fresh air. I left enough on the table to cover the waiter's congeniality and I proceeded out of the shop onto the street.

I started to look for a hotel and as I passed by a small side street, halfway down on the right I could see a small red sign that blinked, "Hotel". I proceeded toward the hotel and as I approached its entrance I, suddenly, stopped dead in my tracks. I had just passed a large display window. As I turned back to look, there in the window was a half-naked girl. A nervous sweat immediately formed on my brow. I looked back to the hotel sign that continued to blink down on me. Then back to the girl who was even more naked and now beckoning to me. And then I muttered to myself, "I'm not really ready for this kind of thing, yet." And I proceeded to hurry on past the hotel to the main street where I quickly moved up the avenue and checked back into the hotel where I had splurged the night before.

And that night I dreamt not of the girl in the window, but of the little girl in the attic, the one with the dimples. Once again, did I endure the pounding on the door, to the hoofbeats on the stairs, to the opening of the bookcase, to the scurrying in the attic, to the manacles being fastened, to the clanging of the boxcar doors, to the bedlam at their destination. Then, to the shouting of the guards, to the waving of the hands, to the chambers on the right, to the ovens on the left, to the smelling of the flesh, and witnessed the end of a lifetime, the end of a little girl's lifetime.

And I hoped that what she dreamed of, those things that were to be, will come to be, for her, and for me, and for all humanity!"

General Patton at Milan

The next day I took the train to Utrecht, Holland's big college town. I went out of the railway station with my backpack on my back and found my way down the street to a 'coffee shop'.

It was of the same décor as the one I had been in the day before in Amsterdam. "Must be some kind of a chain," I thought to myself. And, again, I was offered a cigarette. But this waiter spoke English and I knew what he was offering me. It was then that I realized that the day before I had not been in a coffee shop at all. I had been in a drug store. Not a drug store as one sees in the states, but a real drug store. One that sells real drugs, street drugs. "No wonder I got so dizzy," I thought. I would come to know that in Holland drugs are more in control of the government rather than is the case of the states where the cartels are in control and that these 'coffee shops', as they called them, were a way of controlling distribution and use of drugs.

I went out of the shop and found my way further down the street to an outdoor restaurant with the intent of sipping on some wine and doing some people watching. The restaurant was quite crowded.

Unfortunately, what can be best described as a farm boy showed up at my table. I was shortly to learn that he was, indeed, a dumb Dutch farm boy. He mumbled something to me in Dutch and I reached quickly into my pocket and drew out my miniature Dutch-English translator.

Flipping rapidly through the pages, I said, "Wijn. Wijn." And then turning to another page, I said, "Wit. Wit." And flipping a couple of more pages, I said, "Fles. Fles." Then I repeated all three in Dutch, "wit - wijn - fles." And then very articulately I repeated again in English, "white - wine - bottle."

And all the time I was supplementing my dissertation with a rather sophisticated assortment of sign language. From drawing the shape of a bottle with my hands, to lifting an imaginary glass to my lips as if to drink, to pulling my handkerchief out of my pocket so as to confirm the color white. I even gave quite a fairly good impression of what one could only interpret as a drunken man. And all the time, the farm boy's expression told me that all this was far too much for him. Certainly, one of the most strenuous challenges one can face in life is to try to make any kind of sense out of a conversation with a dumb Dutchman. And with a slight and mischievous smile blanketing his confusion he headed back into the restaurant.

And as I waited there I started to plan the strategy that I would use when he would show up with a bowl of soup and a cheese sandwich. But it was a wasteful effort for in a couple of minutes he showed up with a bottle of white wine. He carefully, with a certain hint of professionalism, uncorked the wine and without a word he started to pour my glass very slowly at first and then quite suddenly before I had the slightest chance to stop him, he filled it right up to the brim. And he gave me a pleasant smile and turned and went back into the restaurant. And I said to myself, "At least he got the order right although he doesn't know a thing about pouring wine, particularly white wine."

Much to my astonishment two girls in their twenties sat down at my table. Both girls were blond of exact shades as if they both worked out of the same bottle. As if to give me something to tell them apart, one had brown eyes and the other had blue eyes. I, unaccustomed to the European practice of sharing tables, thought, "What am I going to do with two of them?" One of them laid on the table what was obviously a Dutch newspaper and much to my surprise asked me in English, "Where are you from?" And I told her, "Baltimore, Maryland." And she replied, "I'm from Darien, just outside of Stamford, Connecticut." And the other one added, "I'm from Wellesley, just outside of Boston."

And I thought, "rich girls." I knew both these towns and they were loaded, I mean really loaded. And I said, "You sound like you've been here for awhile?"

And the brown-eyed one answered, "Yes, we live here. We both married Dutch boys."

"How did you come to meet them?" I asked.

"We work for an American bicycle company, comfort bikes, and were transferred here a couple of years ago." "You know, Bowden?" the other added.

And just then, before I had the chance to offer them some wine, the waiter showed up with another bottle of white wine and very rapidly unstopping it he filled their glasses properly halfway. Then giving each of them and then me a glancing smile he moved away through the restaurant.

"I didn't even hear you order," I said.

"He knows us," said the blue-eyed one, "We come in here whenever we are in town."

I knew of Bowden. It was the Mercedes Benz of the bicycle world. I didn't think you could buy one for under a thousand dollars. Then I asked, "When are you going to move back to the states and settle there?"

"Maybe when the children are grown?" said one, "Maybe never," added the other.

"You have children?" I said, somewhat surprised.

"Not yet. But that's why we intend to stay here, in order that we can bring up our children here." "Where they have a better chance at life," added the other.

"How could they possibly have a better chance here than in the states? Why the United States is the Promised Land," I shot back.

And the brown-eyed one took up the challenge. "Not in our book. The day is coming, and it is not far off, that an inevitable part of every teen's life will be drugs. That is, in the states.

A God for Lions

Here we have a chance to bring up our children in a drug free society."

"What are you crazy? Yesterday in Amsterdam I went into a coffee shop and the waiter put a reefer in my mouth. You call that drug free?" I said, quite agitated.

"Well, maybe I should have said, drug controlled society," she corrected herself.

And she went on. "What is really important is that here in Holland you will rarely hear of a child, anyone under eighteen, who is involved in drugs at all. In the states, as you know, the cartels control the market. It is almost as if the policy in America was designed to make drugs available to young children. It permits drug dealers to target young children, eleven and twelve year olds, to peddle their wares for them. First they get the kids hooked and then they have them where they want them. The kids have to do whatever they are told in order to get more. And this sometimes extends to sexual favors. And this often results in teenage pregnancies and eventually abortions.

"Here there is no substantial black market. The cartels have no incentive to use our children as their salesmen. The government is more in control of what's going on and as long as the government controls the market our kids are relatively safe. In the states it is the cartels that control the market."

"Just think," the other intervened, "If you were not a regular user and wanted to buy a certain drug where would you go?"

"I guess I'd just ask some kid," I replied.

"Yes," she agreed. "But here in Holland teens are not involved in drugs. If someone wants drugs, they know where to go. And what's most important is that it is somewhere that teens are not permitted to go. Here we make it more difficult for a teen to get drugs and easier for an adult to get drugs. But in America you make it easier for a teen to get drugs and more difficult for an adult to get them."

And I thought to myself that what she was telling me made some sense. Certainly in the states the growing drug situation was rapidly becoming one of, if not the greatest problem in American society. That it was not only becoming a way of life, it was fast becoming a way of growing up. That the cartels were targeting our youth, even young children and were, indeed, using them to sell their wares. Yes, the cartels certainly did control the market. I wondered if this would work? If the government were to take more control of the market?

And the blue-eyed one interrupted my thoughts. She kind of chuckled and said, "You look like you just got off the boat. Your first trip to Europe?"

"Yes," I replied.

"Visiting friends?"

"No. Just sight seeing," I replied, and my eyes drifted out to the street. The café was obviously in the tourist section of town. There were all kinds of people. Tall ones and short ones, mostly white ones, some oriental ones, a few mid-eastern types, and even some black ones. "And Amsterdam seemed to have no shortage of them either," I thought to myself, "gay ones." The wine was fairly good, and as my attention turned back to the table I mumbled my thought aloud, "You don't seem to have any shortage of them here in Holland."

And she asked me, "Shortage of what in Holland?"

"Fags," I told her, "Gays."

"Oh," she replied, "You say that as if they weren't human beings. That they shouldn't have any rights. They fought for their freedom too," she reminded me.

"That's not true," I corrected her, "In the United States the military application has a box one can check if one is a homosexual."

"Yes," she agreed, "but that box wasn't added until fifteen years after the Great War that won for all of us this thing we call 'freedom'. And to begin with, the box you refer to is rarely checked. Believe me the gays have been fighting along side their straight brothers right along."

I fell silent. I really didn't want to get into this. I was interested in getting into something else. So I decided to change the subject, "I don't even know your names. My name is Lucien." And just as I introduced myself I was interrupted by the waiter who taking the girls' bottle in his hand pulled the cork out and filled their glasses again quite properly, just halfway. And much to my contentment he took my bottle and also filled my glass properly halfway. But then, suddenly, once again, before I had a chance to stop him, he brought my glass to the very brim. And as I started to burn he gave me a darting glance that was again housed in a mischievous smile despite the fact that I had given him a look that could have killed an elephant. And I thought to myself, "Why is he doing this thing to me? Why is he torturing me so? Certainly he must know that if he fills a glass to the top with white wine it will get prematurely warm? I don't understand this?" I struggled with the thought. He then said something in Dutch to the girls and he gave me another broad prankish smile as he moved away from the table.

And the one with the blue eyes started up, "The reason I know a lot about the military is that my uncle was in the army during the world war. He held two purple hearts and a dozen other enviable decorations. In a heroic action he was hit in North Africa and was hospitalized for six months with serious liver damage. He was nominated for the *Congressional Medal of Honor*, but instead received the military's third highest award for gallantry in action, a *Silver Star*.

"Anyway," she continued, "a year later he was hit again and this time he was paralyzed from the waist down. He was hit by friendly fire when he placed himself between his own troops and two dozen or so Italian school children so as to alert his men that they were about to fire on the children. Since it occurred toward the war's end it helped to heal the wounds of war and since the action was witnessed by so many he was awarded the *Congressional Medal of Honor*, the honor that had escaped him in North Africa.

"Well, to make a long story short, my uncle was gay and with his life then seemed wasted he felt he could be a martyr for the gay cause. Foolishly, he announced that he was gay while he was still in the military hospital. He once told my mother that his admission as to his homosexuality took much more courage than when he had placed himself before the 'firing squad' to protect the children. He hoped that he could attract national attention but he didn't attract a fly. What he overlooked was that at that time there was no gay cause."

And she went on, "At that time, homosexuality was not exactly the type of thing that his family wanted to talk about, much less see spread across the front page of the local newspaper. In fact, as you know, it still isn't today."

"So, the Army threw him out?" I queried.

"No", she replied, "at that time as I mentioned there was no box to check, no policy, so although they didn't like it, there wasn't much they could do about it. Yes, if it had happened after Eisenhower added the box during his presidency my uncle would have been court-martialed, would have lost all pension and benefit rights and would have been discharged.

"As a matter of fact when I said that he didn't attract a fly is not entirely true. For he did draw Eisenhower's attention. He drew an official reprimand directly from Ike. A reprimand that General Patton, my uncle's commanding officer, tried to block.

"Actually," she continued, "my uncle relished in it. He saw it as a victory. That his action was able to draw the attention of Eisenhower, himself."

"So how is he now? Certainly he could do something now. Especially being one who holds the highest military award," I offered.

"He isn't," she replied, "A couple of months after making his declaration he died quite suddenly from a liver infection related to his earlier injury that was brought on by his confinement to bed.

"Only his father flew to Italy for the funeral. His mother was too distraught. His father told my mother that the army provided full military honors for him, that there was some speculation that General Patton himself who happened to be in the area at the time would attend. And although several hundred villagers attended, he didn't show up. In fact, not a single officer of rank showed up despite the fact that my uncle held the *Congressional Medal of Honor.*

a different kind of courage,

"On the day following the funeral, on his way to the airport, his father stopped by the cemetery to bid his final farewell to his son. As his cab approached the gravesite, he noticed a large dark olive green military sedan parked nearby. One of those with the large steel bubble fenders that one sees so often in the movies. A young soldier stood next to it at attention. And at my uncle's grave, kneeling on one knee with his head bowed, was General Patton.

"As my uncle's father approached the grave Patton got up and introduced himself as if the rows of stars on his shoulders could not have conveyed the message. A light rain was falling from darkened skies and one could imagine hearing the firing of artillery shells in the distance although there was nothing there. It was then that the great general told my uncle's father in his low, rasping but powerful voice, speaking very decisively, and pausing on every syllable as if he were addressing Congress, 'At West Point, there are many courses. One learns many things. One learns the history of war. One learns the purpose of war. One learns the strategy of war. One learns the struggle of war.

One learns the noise of war. One learns the horror of war. One learns the victory of war. And one learns the hopelessness of war. But the most important course one takes is taken on the great battlefield itself. And that course is called *courage*.'

"Then he went on and said, 'As you know there is a great difference between Ike and myself. For Ike has never taken this course. Not once in his lifetime has he carried himself into battle. Into the pit. Not once in his lifetime has he pulled the boy out of the mud and searched for where the mud left off and the blood began. Not once has he reached for the final pulse of this thing called life. Not once has he given himself the opportunity to realize this great prize we know as *courage*. His only experience in battle has been in his reading. In his textbooks and in his toy soldiers and in his toy tanks and his toy ships that he moves about on his great table of war. Like the preacher in the pulpit whose only time in battle has been in the atrocities of the ethnic cleansing wars in his scripture.'

"Then with a great tear forming in the corner of his eye, Patton said to him, 'I apologize to you for Ike's action. That his action does not speak for me. Does not speak for those who fought along side your son. Does not speak for America. Does not speak for freedom.'

"'Your son,' he went on, 'has won for you and all of us, this thing called *courage*. This thing called *courage* that I, too, have sought many times. That, I, as a commanding general, would expose myself upon a tank at the very forefront of my ranks, in open line of enemy fire. And with artillery shells bursting all around me, I too have craved for the taste of this thing called *courage*. But even I have yet to realize its dream.'

"'Yesterday,' he went on, 'I should have been here. I intended to be here. For it was my sacred duty to have been here. But I didn't have the *courage* to be here. For it required a different kind of *courage*. Perhaps, even a greater kind of *courage*. I was afraid of what the press might do to me. I didn't want to give

Ike another stone to cast at me. I was afraid of what my family might think of me, what America might think of me.'

"'Your son had that kind of *courage*. He was not afraid of what the press might do to him. He was not afraid of what the army might do to him. He was not afraid of what Ike might do to him. He wasn't even afraid of what his family might do to him. He didn't even care what America might do to him.'

"'Believe me,' he went on, 'after this war is won America must fight a new kind of war. And that war will be fired by the same kind of *courage* that your son, and others like him, have given birth to.'

"The general stepped a few paces to the left and placed his hand on the 'shoulder' of one of the adjoining tombstones, one marked 'Anthony Jackson, 7th Army, 1st Battalion, Company A, Silver Star'. 'For even today your Christian right continues to persecute southern blacks many of which have also shed their blood on the great battlefields of this war. This boy's courageous deed ranks equally with that of your son, but the nation's highest military award is not engraved on his stone. So the gay has a better chance, as Ike can't tell which white soldier is gay and which is not. For had Ike known of your son's homosexuality before he was awarded the medal, the coveted medal would not be marked on his stone today.'

"'And this kind of bigotry extends even to women,' he placed his hand on the 'shoulder' of the adjoining stone, one marked 'Jane Mitchell, Bronze Star and added, 'The world will never know of her valor. Never know of her bravery. Never know of her courage. Never know of her gallantry. Never know of these things that had won for it its freedom. All that evidences that she had ever been is this small white granite stone and the marks upon it.'

He then stepped back a few spaces and spoke to the small row of stones as if they were the once living beings that they represented.

Lucien Gregoire

"'*After this war is won. After the final volleys are fired. After the smoke clears and the tears begin, America must fight a new kind of war. And that war will be fired by a new kind of courage.*

Yes, this war will win for America and all mankind this thing we call 'freedom'. But that war, the war within, will someday win for America the great prize of 'equality' for all men and women, something that this war cannot do. For freedom without equality is not what it pretends to be. The diamond would be made of paste.

It is our differences that have made us into this great nation of one that we are. And the day will come when men and women of good conscience will no longer heed the words of those politicians and preachers who choose to use them to divide us.

And when that day comes, all children will be born into a world of equal opportunity. Only then will America and the world be truly free. Yes, today, men and women of great courage are engaged in this great war which will soon crush the enemy from without, but it must take many more men and women of still another kind of courage who must rise up and crush the enemy from within. Only then would these brave men and women not have died in vain. Only then will the diamond, this thing one calls 'freedom', be real.'"*

"And as he climbed into his vehicle, Patton told my uncle's father, '*It is the soldier who shed his blood on the field of battle, and not the preacher who cowers in his pulpit, who should determine who should and should not be free.** I have been proud to have had your son serve in my army here,' and looking upwards toward the sky, 'and I am sure that He is proud to have him in His army, today,' and letting a tear drop onto his cheek, he nodded to his driver, and they were off."

* George S. Patton at the gravesite of a homosexual *Medal of Honor* winner near Milan, Italy, March 29, 1944.

24

A God for Lions

And she went on, "It is the great regret of my family, that in order to save themselves some embarrassment, they intentionally kept the whole situation quiet. Intentionally kept it from the press. They intentionally kept him, kept my uncle from making his mark. His Mom and Dad still live with this, their inaction. Which they now know was an atrocity on their part. Which was an atrocity on all of our parts. But there is now no remedy. It is too late. Their lives are now broken. They have aged two lifetimes in one. Even I, though only a child at the time, have great regrets about it.

"But, you're right. If he were alive today he could do something. Perhaps not much, but something. In fact, all the other gays who hold the *Medal of Honor* and other awards could do something. But they remain in hiding. For even today this is not something one wants one to know about."

"Others?" I questioned.

"Yes," she replied, "others. In the Great War there were over four hundred congressional medals awarded. If one plays the percentages, that would mean that between twenty and thirty medals are held by truly homosexual men. But, of course, like my uncle most of them did not survive. But if one or two of them who did survive were brave enough to come forward, it would stop much of the preacher's bigotry in its tracks. But, as my uncle said, that would take more bravery today then did his action in 1944 when he stood before the children. Actually, today, in Vietnam, there are a disproportional number of gays versus straights serving and giving their lives for this thing we call freedom, as the draft law exempts men who are fathers of young children. Keep in mind that during wartime homosexual policies are suspended. Homosexuality does not exempt one from the draft. Gays are only harassed during peacetime when there is no blood to shed. You must have done your time in the military. Tell me," she asked, "did you ever meet a WAC who was not a dyke?"

And just then the waiter showed up at the table with our checks. Evidently one of the girls had signaled him. "We have to get back to work," they said almost in unison. And having paid their check and said their ado's they were on their way.

As the Dutch farm boy stood over me with his leering grin, I thought to myself, "So now the time has come for revenge." But instead I over-tipped him, as to confirm that I was an American tourist in the event he had missed the point earlier. Plus I hoped that it would drive him out of his mind. He was obviously in the wrong business. He should have stayed on the farm. And without saying a word he gave me my receipt and, again, a kind of mysterious, somewhat hypocritical smile. And he was off. And as he turned away from my table with his back to me I shot him another look, this time one that could have brought down a herd of elephants.

a couple of stops on the way,

Later that afternoon I took a place at another small café and I sat there for awhile people watching. There were some white ones, some black ones, some yellow ones, some mid-eastern types, and, of course, some gays ones. And for the first time in my life I didn't see any difference among them at all. And with the wine starting to hit me I left the café and started to look for a room. I wandered down an avenue and as had happened the day before I noticed a hotel sign blinking halfway down a small side street. As I headed down the street toward the hotel I suddenly stopped dead in my tracks. Just to my left was a very pretty girl sitting in a window. And I looked first to my right, and then to my left, and again to my right, and finally to my left, once more. Then I heard a door buzz. And I will not tell you what happened after that. After all, my mother might get her fingers on this book.

not so dumb after all,

As I checked into my hotel room that evening, I emptied out my pockets of the records of the day. Half a ticket stub from the toy museum. A stub for the train trip to Rotterdam. And another stub from what I guess one would call the local trolley, a receipt for lunch, another for dinner and, of course, the one for the wine. One thing that puzzles me about Europe is how it uses its available resources. When one goes into a store, most any store, one has to bring ones own bag. The stores don't provide bags. This would seem to evidence that Europe suffers from a shortage of paper. But when one gets a receipt in a restaurant, rather than getting a cash register tape that could do the job, one gets a large rather fancy card. And I was a few seconds away from finding out why this is so.

As I reached for my backpack that held the record of my trip, I noticed a small note written in perfect English on the receipt for the wine,

"Dear Lucien,

Forgive me for calling you by your first name, as I do not know your last name.

And, also, please forgive my sense of humor. Sometimes I let it get away from me.

When I started to pour your wine, I noticed a look of great anticipation on your face, and having only a split second to make my decision, I decided to go for it. So I poured it to the very top. And forgive me, but I relished in your pain.

And as I saw you deeply involved in your discussion with the girls, I decided to go for it again. And, here, I ask that you reach deep

Lucien Gregoire

into your heart to forgive me. For this time I had much time to plan it. The act was premeditated. And as I, again, brought your glass to its brim, I, once again, saw pain in your face. And, once more, did I relish in it.

But as I moved from your table, I realized that what I had seen was not pain, but hate. And this is why I am writing you this note. For I do not want to bring any more hate into this world than is already in it.

I trust that you will forgive me.

Thank you much for the generous tip. It will help me pay my way through graduate school where I am majoring in English.

And, incidentally, thanks for the lesson in Dutch. It will help me in my work!

your mischievous waiter,
Hans"

Comparative drug statistics the United States vs. Holland

DRUG ADDICTION RATE*	percent of population	
	Holland	U.S.
ages 11-15		
1969 beginning of U.S. drug war	0.2%	0.2%
2001	0.3%	5.9%
high school seniors		
1969	3%	4%
2001	4%	27%
adults only		
1969	7%	6%
2001	9%	17%

*use of an illegal drug on a frequency of at least once a month per Statistical Abstracts of the United States 2001 and De Feiten von Nederland 2001

the Moth and the Butterfly

I would like to tell you of Audrey, of my friend Audrey. She was in my class in high school. As homely as they come. Horned rimmed glasses and all. Not a hint of a personality. Seemed to be born without the instinct to smile. Nothing, no not a thing that could attract a single friend let alone a boyfriend. Simply a sad state of affairs. One that each time I saw her would touch my heart, as when one sees a sad faced dog.

On the other hand, I had no trouble attracting friends. Although I was no Cary Grant, I was one of the smartest kids in the class and a four-letter man in the field. Even the nuns were in love with me.

And I will remember my junior prom for all my life. For as long as I live. Everyday of my life. Not so much for what was there, but rather for what was not there.

On my arm was the prettiest girl in the class. And we danced all night. And, later, after I had dropped her off, I drove home and sat in my car for a bit. And I thought not of the prettiest girl in the class, but of the homeliest. For I realized that Audrey had not been there. That no one, no not a single soul, had made it his responsibility to let her, too, have her time.

And one of those things one calls tears came up out of my heart and started from the crevice of my eye and ran toward its lid and I looked first to the right, and then to the left, and then again to the right, and then to the left, once more. And *not quite, yet, a man* I let it slip out onto my cheek. And in my heart, nothing, not a thing was left in its place.

So the winter had come and gone and it was the week of the senior prom. And as I came down the walk, as was very often the case, she was coming the other way. And where normally we would pass with a downcast "hi", this time I walked right into her as to block her path. And she, frightened, said, "What's wrong, I don't understand?" "I was wondering," I said quickly, "I was wondering if you would go with me to the dance this Friday?"

And with her lips starting to quiver, she asked, "Why, why me?" And I told her, "I just thought that I would start at the top, this time."

And we went to the prom and we danced all night. And I still have with me, today, one of the fondest memories of my life. And taking her home, I kissed her, not a real kiss, but a noble kiss, as if we were sharing some great honor of some kind. And afterwards I drove home and sat in my car for a bit. And I thought not of the prettiest girl in the class, but of the homeliest.

And one of those things one calls tears came up out of my heart and started from the crevice of my eye and ran toward its lid and I looked first to the right, and then to the left, and then again to the right, and then to the left, once more. And *not quite, yet, a man* I let it slip out onto my cheek. And in its place, in my heart, was left something that would be with me all the days of my life.

The next year she went off to the university. And I, at the beginning of a rags-to-riches story, went to work for a year to save for school. So when I arrived at the university she was a class ahead of me. And the first time I saw her I didn't even know her. Now she was, no, not pretty. She was beautiful. Even the horned rimmed glasses were gone. And her smile was now relentless, as if she were not born with the instinct to frown. It was as if the fairy godmother had done her work. As if she had touched a common moth and there appeared a magnificent butterfly.

Except for a few "hellos" when we would pass each other I never really got to talk to her as she was forever surrounded by friends. Now she was the four-letter girl and I only another spectator in the stands.

And in her senior year at the big dance, the prior year's homecoming queen opened a small envelope, and I, like the rest of the onlookers, waited anxiously for the name. And it was 'Audrey'. And she was handed two scepters, one for herself and the other for her king. And in a crowd of ten thousand it took her an hour and a half to find me.

And as she led me by my hand to the stage, I asked her, "Why, why me?" And she told me, "I just thought I would start at the top, this time."

And that night I kissed her, not a noble kiss for the great honor we shared, but a real kiss. And she kissed me back.

So for me my dream had come true. And it can, too, for you.

All you need do, is to take a chance, and have on your arm, the homeliest girl at the dance!

Lucien Gregoire

an interplanetary dignitary

I remember the first time that Audrey told me of him. She spoke of him as if he were some sort of foreign dignitary. Some sort of interplanetary dignitary. That, early the day before, he had boarded a giant spaceship and that although he would be traveling at the speed of light, it would take him several months to get here.

And I remember the day he arrived. I remember all seven pounds of him. Each and every one of them. And I remember his first frown. His first smile. His first tear. His first laugh.

And I remember his first step. His first word. His first bruise. His first day at school. His First Communion. His first baseball mitt. His first home run.

But of all the things I remember of him was his first hug. It came from deep within him. An electric communication of some sort or other. One that could have only come from royalty. Perhaps divinity. And it has never left me. His first hug. For it was heaven, you see.

And then there were the many talks I had with him. My many conversations with Johnny. And here I want to share some of them with you.

From *his first question* to that time we visited the *New Jerusalem* together for the very first time. Where we checked into the *Golden Hotel* that sits at the crossroads of *Faith* and *Reality*.

his first question

He was just six years old when he asked his first question as to what goes on in the world around him.

"Daddy, what is the difference between the *right* and the *left?*" he asked, "Why is it that they are always fighting with each other? Is it that one believes in God and the other doesn't?"

"No Johnny," I corrected him, "they both believe in God. It's just that those on the *right* believe firmly in religion. They believe that scripture, what someone is supposed to have said to someone else many thousands of years ago, should guide the way one lives ones life."

"Then," he asked with kind of a puzzled expression, "what do those on the *left* use to guide their lives?"

I thought a moment and guessed, "I would suppose, their conscience."

"Oh!" he replied.

I should have known then that I was in for quite a ride.

Lucien Gregoire

the bike

By the time of his tenth birthday biking, hiking, climbing, swimming, baseball, basketball, football, hockey, tennis and a somersault or two had claimed half of him. And, perhaps, one would call it curiosity, scrutiny, intellect, impulsiveness or just simply the need to know had taken over the other half. That had at this very early age made him into the Sherlock Holmes of our household. But, unlike his celebrated predecessor of the nineteenth century, his investigation was not of this world, but of the next.

It was late in the afternoon when I went down the steps into the family room to see what the little rascal was up to?

As I entered the room, he exclaimed, "I sold my bike! I got two hundred dollars for it!"

He was sitting there at the table hunched over reading a book and I took it as being something that was written in the book. And, I asked, "Who sold his bike?"

"I sold my bike!" he repeated.

Suddenly, it struck me that he was, indeed, talking about himself. "Johnny, you sold your bike for a couple of hundred dollars? Are you crazy? That bike cost your mother and I almost a thousand dollars."

"That's the most I could get for it. I tried to get more. But that's the most I could get for it. It makes no difference how much it cost you. All that counts is what I got for it," he replied quite adamantly.

A God for Lions

"But you don't have any right to sell your bike," I replied, raising my voice just short of a shout.

"Yes I do," he replied, "It says right here, '*Sell all that thou hast...*'"

"What do you mean right here?" my tone took on that of an interrogation.

"Here, here in *Luke*," he answered, reading from the text, once again, "'*Sell all that thou hast...*'"

And as I peered closer I saw that he was reading from the *New Testament*. "What did you do with the money?" I questioned this time with a tone of anger, "Where is the money?"

"Mrs. Jackson has it," he responded.

"Mrs. Jackson has it?" this time I shouted, "What is she doing with it?"

"I don't know," he replied, "but she needs it. Much more than we do. As you know her husband died a couple of months ago, she is losing the house, and she has four young children to bring up."

"But you don't have any right giving her that kind of money," I continued my grilling.

"Yes, I do," he replied, and he completed the sentence that he had just read, "'*Sell all that thou hast and give to the poor!*'"

"But," I continued my onslaught, "but she shouldn't have taken it from you. You're just a child."

"She doesn't know where it came from. I sealed it up in an envelope and slid it under her door," he replied with a somewhat mischievous smile.

"You put it under her door?" I exclaimed, now more frustrated than ever.

"Yes, it says here," he went on more confident than ever, "'*Take heed that ye do not give your alms before men, to be seen of them: otherwise ye have no reward of your Father who is in heaven. Therefore when thou doest give, do not sound the trumpet before thee, as do the hypocrites in the synagogues and in the streets.*'

"Just think," he added, "if anything should happen to me, God forbid, then I will have a bike in heaven. I will be able to get around. I will be able to go over to Grandma and Grandpa's place and visit them. I might even be able to visit with Mr. Jackson and will be able to tell him that his children did not go hungry.

"It says here," he continued, "'*Lay not up for yourselves treasures upon earth, where moth and rust doth corrupt. But lay up for yourselves treasures in heaven, where neither moth nor rust doth corrupt. For where your treasure is, will be your heart also...*'"

And he summed it all up, "And this is from *Matthew*, '*If thou wilt be perfect, go and sell all that thou hast, and give to the poor, and thou shalt have treasure in heaven.*'"

And he trumped all that he had to say with, "'*It is easier for a camel to pass through the eye of a needle, than for a rich man to enter the Kingdom of Heaven.*'" and he added, "even if he makes it, he will have nothing there. He won't be able to get around and visit all his friends who have gone before him!"

By this time my head had begun to spin. "I must go up to the cabinet and get a couple of aspirin," I thought. "Perhaps, a dozen of them."

Then I thought again, "This was just another one of those tough days, one of those very challenging ones. I must keep calm," I reminded myself.

So regaining my composure and lowering my voice, as I had done so many times before when dealing with this little man of so many surprises, I went over to the table and putting my hand on his shoulder, I said somewhat to his astonishment, "What you have done, Johnny, was a good thing to do. Doesn't make a lot of sense, but, nevertheless, a good thing to do.

"Yes, you have a bike waiting for you in heaven. But chances are you'll never have to use it. For you have your whole life ahead of you. But, maybe it will be there for me and your mom some day."

And I added, "But in the future when you read something in a book, any book, discuss it with us first before you take any kind of rash action. You have to learn to do these kinds of things together with us. Do you understand? Your mother and I helped give you life and at least until you are an adult we have the right to share it with you."

And he looked at me and replied, "I understand, in the future I will talk to you about these kinds of things first."

"Good," I said. And going to my desk in the corner of the room, I unlocked a drawer and taking out a box, I removed four crisp fifty dollar bills and sealing them in an envelope, I handed it to him, and said, "Now take this over to Mrs. Jackson's house and slide it under the door. Make sure no one sees you. It would be tough for both your mom and I to get around on a single bike."

And taking the envelope he slid it into his pocket, and winked and said, "Do you think, do you think, at Christmastime we will be able to send Grandma and Grandpa a bike too?"

"Why wait for Christmas?" I replied. And going back to the desk, I peeled off eight more crisp fifty dollar bills and enclosing them in another envelope I handed it to him. "Here," I told him "your grandmother and grandfather could use them now."

And sliding it into his pocket with the other, his eyes widening in a smile, he moved quickly up the steps.

And as he went out of the house and into the snow, I felt fortunate that he had missed the parable of the widow's mite. And opening the *New Testament,* which lay on the table before me, I fanned through the pages to *Luke 21,*

"And He looked up, and saw the rich men casting their gifts into the treasury. And He saw also a poor widow casting in thirter two mites. And He said, Of a truth I say unto you, that this poor widow hath cast in more than they all: For all these of their abundance cast in unto offerings of God: but she of her penury had cast in all the living that she had."

The paragraph had been filled in with a 'pink' magic marker. As I flipped through the pages I noticed that he had filled the book with a wide range of colors. Different paragraphs highlighted in different colors. Yellows, blues, greens, pinks and what have you. But mostly pinks and yellows. And as I scanned through those that were filled in with 'pink', I found that among them were the very same ones he had just read to me. There were many others like the times that Christ instructed His disciples to give up all of their worldly possessions if they would come follow Him. And he had also filled in with 'pink' the only thing that Christ felt so strongly about that He committed the grave of sin of anger. He had filled in the story of Christ throwing the moneymakers, the Pharisees, the republicans, out of His Father's temple. I kind of cringed at this. After all, I was a staunch republican.

And when I came to the last one, 'the widow's mite', there was a single wide stroke at the bottom of the page of the corresponding color 'pink'. And, within it, was the word, 'COMMUNISM'. And beside that was written the word 'TAOISM'.

And my mind drifted back to my college days when I had first learned what the word meant. This word 'COMMUNISM'. Commune. It meant 'commune', that all of God's wealth belonged to everyone. That it be shared equally among all people. That it dictated a redistribution of wealth society. That Christ, in fact, had dictated a redistribution of wealth society. And I had also learned in those days that this is also the basic philosophy of TAOISM. That ancient Chinese scripture which underlines China's culture, today.

And suddenly it struck me, "My God," I exclaimed to myself, "now he has me practicing communism!"

And then I noticed that just below the 'pink' stroke was another wide stroke. This one in 'yellow'. And within the 'yellow' stroke was the word 'SOCIALISM'. And I quickly flipped back a few pages until I came to a paragraph that he had outlined in

A God for Lions

'yellow'. And there he had highlighted in 'yellow' Christ's words "*Love thy neighbor as thyself.*" And I quickly flipped back a couple of pages and there, again, he had highlighted in 'yellow' a similar command of Christ. And as I went back through the book, I found that it was filled in with 'pinks' and 'yellows'. All highlighting these most basic principles of Christ.

"My God," I repeated to myself, "Socialism too. He's got me practicing socialism, too."

And I knew that this was also the basic thinking of the democrat in American society, the philosophy that dictates a redistribution of wealth society. That Christ was a democrat. Perhaps, even worse, a communist. "No," I thought to myself, "Christ must not have been thinking too well on the days He said these things." And as I flipped through the book I found that almost every page was highlighted in 'pink' or 'yellow'. "It must have been the evangelists that have added these things," I thought, "Christ could not have been delirious that often."

"Mostly 'pinks' and 'yellows'. How much easier it is for us today than if we had lived in Christ's time. For in His day one would have to give up all of ones wealth to reap eternal salvation. Today we can lead sinful lives to our heart's content as long as we repent. A much better deal. What Christ required would be far too much a price to pay for simply a *chance* at an afterlife. Yes, He is behind the times," I thought to myself.

I remembered having once read Pat Robertson's memoirs in which he spoke of having once lived his life according to this most fundamental requirement of Christ in the *New Testament*. That he had once sold all that he had to help the poor. But evidently he must have found a loophole somewhere in the scriptures, for I knew that today he was among the most wealthy men in the world. I wondered what it could be? "And then again," I thought to myself, "this could be why Ghandi once said, '*I love Christ, but I hate Christians.*'"

the Birds and the Bees

"I'm getting married," he shouted. He had just come in out of the snow and his cheeks were still red and some flakes still clung to his nose.

And Audrey smiled at me and asked laughingly, "Have you set the date? Where are you going on the honeymoon?"

"You don't understand," and he repeated himself, "I'm getting married and I'm getting married, tomorrow!"

And then he went on, "It happened today, today in the snow. I don't know how it happened, but it happened. It's real, I know it's real, and that's the beginning and the end of it."

Continuing he said, "I was playing with Jeannie and we slipped on the ice and she went down and I almost on top of her. And as I raised myself up, I saw it in her eyes. And I knew it was in my eyes too," and pointing to his heart, "and furthermore, it's in here, and it's in hers too."

"So we are getting married, and that's all there is to it!"

Seeing that he was, indeed, serious, I said, "But Johnny, you're only ten years old. Your mother and I didn't get married until we were in our twenties."

But he shot back quite adamantly, his voice rising with every word, "You were brought up in a slower generation. Things are different today. The pace is fast. If you don't grab on to it when it comes by it's not going to come back and get you. It's going to leave you, leave you behind, forever. And I'm not going to be left behind. Particularly not this time."

Realizing that we were faced with something more, a feeling of great dread came over me. That feeling that comes to all fathers when they are faced by the great moment of truth. That time when one has to give the most difficult sermon one has to make in life. In my case, unfortunately, it was coming a few years ahead of time. I had always hoped that maybe if I let it go long enough, that it would go away. That maybe the schools or his peers would take care of it.

"Johnny, we have to talk," I said seriously.

"I don't want to talk about it, I'm getting married," this time saying it with even greater conviction, "and let there be no doubt about it!" And he headed for his room.

I decided not to follow him. Not that he seemed too upset and this might not be the best time to talk about it. But rather I needed time, time to figure out what to say. And I had no idea what to say. And I turned to Audrey with that expressive look I'd used so many times before, that says, "Help me, please help me?" And, Audrey smiled, a smile of rejection, and said, "All boys, sometime during their life, not necessarily in adolescence, not necessarily in college, not necessarily while they are climbing the corporate ladder, but sometime, most often only once, get the chance to prove their manhood. This is your chance, your big chance, but it has to be your chance, alone," and she went back to loading the dishwasher.

In despair, "All is lost," I thought. "Maybe there's someone who you pay, someone who provides the service? Handles this type of thing on a professional basis?" I hadn't felt such terror since the time that I had gone to confession to tell the man that I had first touched a girl.

I remember that day when I hesitated on the church steps, and turned and walked around the block, and then walked around the block again, and again and again. In all, thirty five times. I remember, because I counted them, each and every one of them. And each time I came up with another way out of it. Maybe I didn't touch her enough to count? I could always join another church? Perhaps, I didn't even need a church? After all, my conscience told me what was right and what was wrong? And then, finally, already having done my penance, I proceeded courageously up the steps and into the church and then into the confessional box. "What does she mean, prove my manhood? Doesn't that count?"

But I knew I was fooling myself, and I collected my thoughts and I bravely started up the stairs and made my way toward his room. And then, knowing that it might tax all of my mind, I was intent on proving my manhood. I was not aware that it would also tax my heart.

As I entered the room, he was sitting up on the bed. He laid the pad he had held in his hand face down on the bed and closing the pen, he slipped it into his shirt pocket. I sat down at the foot of the bed. "I was just making up a checklist of things we have to do," he said. Then, reaching down and putting his hand over mine, he added, "This doesn't mean that I don't still love you and Mom, just that these things happen, and when they happen we just have to accept them, make the best of them."

I felt it deep inside of me coming up from my heart and it reached the corner of my eye, and moved toward the lid, toward the cliff, so to speak. And staggering like the boxer who comes out of the corner and takes an uppercut on the chin that throws him back against the ropes. I gazed first to his right, and then to his left, and again to his right, and then to his left, once more, all the time trying desperately to keep the tear on the edge of the lid.

Having obviously lost the first round, I decided to change my strategy from one of aggression, to one of trying to stay on my feet until the bell rang. I prayed that if I could only get back to my corner, I would have time to rethink my game and come out fighting again. And then, suddenly, the bell did ring. It was the phone next to his bedside. He picked it up and said, "It's Jeannie."

And getting up I grasped his ankle and smiling I said, "Behave yourself!" And then I walked across the room and closed the door behind me.

As I came back into the kitchen, Audrey gave me a look that one gives a six year old, "I didn't chicken out," I shot at her, "the phone rang and it was Jeannie so I thought I would give him some privacy." Then, I thought how cruel this was of her. I thought how much easier it is for the woman. She only has to give birth to them. Yes, a great effort, but the effort is only physical. Not too challenging. Doesn't take a lot of brains. But the man is stuck with the tough one. The one that might tax the far reaches of the intellect and even, perhaps, break his heart. Reach into his very soul. It just wasn't fair.

In the morning the little man came down the steps and sitting down at the table he brought us some good news and, unfortunately, some bad news. He announced, "We've decided to wait a week or two, we still have some things to work out." He, then, pausing as if thinking for a moment, "We can't decide on whether the first one should be a boy or a girl." For the first time I saw a hint of compassion on Audrey's face in recognition of the difficulty of my plight. For the first time she seemed to understand how tough this job was going to be.

Having loaded him on the school bus, I said to Audrey, "Perhaps, we can handle this together." But it was to no avail. As if she had read my thoughts of the night before, she said, "We are man and woman, and there are some things each of us must do on our own, things that the other can't really help them with. For me, it was having him. For you it is this. Now stop trying to get out of it, stop walking around the block. Go in and get the job done." And she added, "You can do it, I believe that you can do it, and all that it will take now is that you believe that you can do it!"

So that day I lost a small fortune for the firm that I worked for. And I knew that I had to get the job done that night, for if I continued to put it off I would have no job. So that evening when I got home I winked bravely at Audrey and I went directly to his room.

Again, sitting on his bed, I took up the same position I had the day before and asked him, "What are you reading?" And he answered, "*Sequel to Relativity.*" And although I would think that he was joking, the cover of the book told me quickly that he was, indeed, telling the truth. "I am reading here," he said, "of the birds and the bees!"

And as if he could see the anguish in my eyes, the fright of a grown man trying to become a man, the terror of it all, he said with a compassionate smile that only a child of ten could possibly muster, "I'll tell you what I am going to do. I am going to let you off the hook," he followed in almost an authoritative manner, "I am going to tell you about them. This thing we call '*the birds and the bees*.' How this thing called love is supposed to work."

Although startled by his declaration, I breathe a sigh a relief and chose not to head him off.

"This book," he said, "this man Einstein says that all matter has energy, moving energy. He puts it quite simply, here, he says 'that all matter is made up of moving parts and those parts we have come to know as atomic particles, the smallest of which are yet to be discovered.'" And continuing reading from the text, he added, "'Energy, therefore, is the fundamental part of any object, whether it be animate of inanimate. Furthermore, all matter is constantly giving off energy, moving parts, and that when energy leaves one form of matter, it will eventually find its way into some other form of matter. And this is true of all matter, from the air we breathe, to the hardest substance known, diamond.'"

I wondered where he was going with all this. What could this ever have to do with the birds and the bees? But he had left me off the hook, and with great appreciation for that, I let him continue.

"Now I'll show you how this works," he said. "I've been experimenting with it. Bring your two index fingers together about six inches in front of your eyes and hold them just barely apart." And pointing to the table lamp, "There, with the light behind them." And, following his instructions, I did what he asked. "Now," he added, "stare at them for a few seconds." And, again, I did what he asked. And he said, "See them? See them?" And, sure enough I could see some movement, kind of a haze, but definitely movement, between my fingers.

"Okay, now," he said "get up and go over there and stand sideways to the wall. Right up against the wall." And, again, I did what he told me to do. Now wondering more than ever what all this had to do with the birds and the bees? "Now let your arm hang limp and press it hard against the wall." And, again, I did what he asked and held the pressure there for about a minute. Then he said, "Now with your arm still hanging limp, move over here away from the wall." And I did, again, what he told me and much to my surprise my arm rose, without any effort, entirely on its own, to a horizontal position.

Then he exclaimed, "Very good, that proves it." As if he were Einstein, himself, coming upon the great discovery, he exclaimed, "What we are seeing is the effect of the physical energy that was released from your arm but was held just outside the arm and could not be released because of the wall. This proves that Einstein was right. Energy, these atomic particles are constantly moving from one object to another. The force of a few of which is so powerful that they were able to lift your arm.

"Actually," he added, "some of the particles did penetrate the wall, just that it would take centuries for your arm to, in effect, become a part of the wall.

"But," he went on, "the sense of smell can probably better demonstrate what Einstein was talking about. There, on the dresser," he pointed.

And as I looked at the dresser I could see nothing that could possibly smell, just two ordinary drinking glasses. One was placed right side up and the other was placed upside down on its glass-surfaced top.

"Pick up the one that is standing right side up and smell inside it," he ordered.

And I did as he told me and I could discern no smell whatsoever other than the air I was breathing. "Can't smell a thing," I stated.

And then he said, "Now pick up the other one, the one that is upside down and smell the inside of that glass."

And, again, following his orders, I picked up the glass and this time there was a very definite metallic smell.

"What you are smelling," he went on, "are the particles of energy that the glass has been giving up but have been trapped inside the glass for the past couple of weeks.

"And sound," he added, "probably demonstrates this thing called energy the very best of all. When we hear a sound," he continued, "what we hear is actually two and most often several particles of energy bouncing off of each other. Moving parts. Energy. For as you know complete stillness can produce no sound.

"But there is much more to this than just sight and touch and smell and sound," and reading from the text, "'This atomic interchange of parts that is continually going on within the universe extends to human beings. That this phenomenon affects all physical matter is a known fact. That it also extends to mental processes is more difficult to prove. But as a matter of fact there is substantial evidence that the exchange between human beings, the physical exchange of atomic particles, is both physical and mental. In fact, is primarily mental.'"

And the text went on, "'It is also possible for one to exchange physical energy for mental energy.'

"'When one wins a marathon,'" he read, "'one obviously expends great physical energy. But this is usually more than offset by the absorption of great mental energy and the amount of energy one absorbs depends to a great extent on how loud the crowd cheers as one comes down the stretch. To take this a step further. If one were the only man on earth and one were to accomplish the same task one would only spend physical energy but not reap the reward of the mental offset, as there would be no other intelligent being to draw the energy, mental energy, from. Mental energy, therefore, can only come from another being, and this can be either an animal or a human being.'

"Regarding animals, however, the energy draw is primarily physical, whereas for humans it is primarily mental. For example, all carnivorous animals, from the lion to the eagle, evolved special structures to enable them to bring down their prey. Sharp claws, strong jaws and long tearing teeth or beaks. These things evolved through time. For example, as the particular needs of a given specie required it to grasp with claws, succeeding generations developed longer or sharper claws. This is a result of physical energy drawing out the claw to eventually make it longer or sharper.

"And listen," he said as he continued reading, "'In human beings, however, the experience is primarily mental. Our ancestors overcame their physical handicaps by living in cooperative groups and using their hands and brains to use tools and weapons intelligently. Hence we have no claws, no sharp tearing teeth. Our presence, and our energy exchange, has been primarily mental. And, today, it continues to be primarily mental.'"

Still not getting, at all, where he was going with it, I continued to listen. I was certainly learning something, something that had evidently escaped me during my schooldays. Then I began to see the point he was trying to get at. He read, "'When someone in the midst of lovemaking says nice things, then that person transfers his or her mental energy to the other and the reception of this energy can be profoundly felt by the receiver. When someone yells at another then that person is drawing mental energy from the other, and the loss of energy can be decidedly felt by the other. When one tells exciting stories filled with interesting information one gives mental energy to the receiver and the receipt of this energy can be decidedly felt by the receiver. On the other hand, when one tells boring or repetitious stories, one is drawing mental energy from the listener and this loss of energy can be decidedly felt by the loser. Every day, people are giving and receiving mental energy to and from those they come in contact with. And there are some that are primarily energy takers, or probably better put, energy thieves, and there are others who are predominantly energy givers.'

"See," he said, "yesterday when I came in and said, 'I'm getting married', I was an energy taker and you were an energy giver." And I thought to myself, "You're sure right about that." Then he went on saying, "When I said this morning, 'We had put off getting married for a week or so,' I became an energy giver, and you were an energy taker." Then he said, "I took the energy right back with, 'We can't decide whether the first one should be a boy or a girl.'

"And tears, too, demonstrate this energy exchange. When one sheds tears of great joy one is left with great energy in ones heart. But when one sheds tears of great sadness, nothing, nothing at all is left in ones heart.

"Now listen very carefully to this." and he read,

"'There are times at which the energy level of two individuals is on the exact same plane with each other. This is what happens when two people *fall in love*.'" And he continued, "and this is what is important in my case. 'This balance can last for minutes, months or for a lifetime, and sometimes even an eternity. And whether or not it lasts depends entirely on the energy flow remaining relatively equal between the parties. If one of the parties starts to draw too much energy from the other, then the *in love* illusion begins to dissipate and although some kind of a relationship may survive, the *in love* illusion is gone forever. If one or both of the parties become less interesting, boring or augmentative, then it's over.'"

And looking up at me, he said, "Jeannie and I have had our moment, but now it is passed. Yes," he said, "I will always cherish having had that moment, but as you know, as I said in the kitchen, when these things come along, you've got to grab on to them. But what's most important is that you grab onto them at the right time. And our time has not yet come. And this is the most important point of all." And he read on from his book, this *Sequel to Relativity,*

"'So what we know is that both physical and mental energy is transferred between human beings. We also know that subatomic particles, the fundamental units of all of God's creation, are the vehicles of transfer of all energy. And when two people *fall in love,* the energy balance is perfectly even between them. It is reasonable to believe therefore that only God can make this perfect balance of this most fundamental unit of God's creation, energy. And this seems to be confirmed by the fact that this *falling in love* phenomenon is fundamental to the creation of life, the creation of God's children. Sex between two beings can be driven by either of two forces, *love* or *lust.* It is important, therefore, that the act be driven by *love*. That the creation of any of God's children not be a product of *lust*. And only when two people are *in love,* that is, they have *fallen in love,* can the act be driven by *love.*'

"So this is why we have to wait," he concluded, "We must make sure that *love*, not *lust*, brings God's children into the world!"

And glad that it was finally over, that I had at last done my job. I could proudly relate to Audrey that I had taken the tiger in hand and that I had taught him of *the birds and bees*.

And as I got up and moved toward the door he called after me. "One question," he asked, "do they have them in heaven?"

"What's that?" I inquired.

"Penises and vaginas?" he asked.

And, I, lost for words, couldn't utter a sound.

Lucien Gregoire

"There are none in heaven," he instructed. "Yes, the preacher told me so. Only the ones down below have them!"

Then he threw me a combination wink and smile as to leave no doubt that he was, indeed, the master of this kind of thing. And I left his room.

Jeannie,

Yes, I remember you,

the dance in the snow,

the slip on the ice,

the flakes on your cheeks,

the look in your eyes,

the thud in my heart,

the dream of it all,

the loss of it all,

that for you,

and for me,

it was not to be.

Johnny

Joshua

It was the middle of July. The whole world was roasting to death and Audrey and I were enfolded in our overstuffed chairs in front of the fireplace trying to keep warm. Snug as a couple of bugs in a couple of rugs.

Like most good Christians, I had always dreamed of being filthy rich someday and this certainly was the manifestation of that dream. For there we were in the middle of summer with the air conditioner clambering toward zero while at the same time smoke was shooting up out of the chimney. Yes, the great air machine of tomorrow and the great log fire of yesterday both roaring off in different directions, as if each could win this race to nowhere.

And he? Well he was quiet as a mouse as he sat at the table behind us all wrapped up in his book. He reading his book and we engulfed in the total peace, solitude and happiness of the moment. Only the crackling of the fire and the occasional turning of a page broke the stillness of the moment. But it was not to be for long.

"This makes no sense at all, listen," he said, "listen,"

"*And the Lord said unto Joshua, See, I have given into thine hand Jericho. Take all ye men of war and go around the city seven times, and the priest shall blow with the trumpets. And when ye hear the sound of the trumpet, all the people shall shout with a great shout; and the wall of the city shall fall flat, and ye are to enter and take to the sword all of the inhabitants thereof, every man and woman and child. Let none remain!*'

'*...and going to the wall of Jericho, Joshua said unto his people, Shout; for the Lord hath given you the city of Jericho. And all the silver, and gold, and vessels of brass and iron, and* *treasure thereof. So the Israelites shouted when the priest blew the trumpets: and it came to pass, when the people heard the sound of the trumpet, and the people shouted with a great shout, that the wall fell down flat, so that the people went up into the city, every man straight before him, and they took the city. And they utterly destroyed all that was in the city, both man and woman and child and ox and ass, with the edge of the sword.'"*

I looked over at Audrey and although I didn't say it she understood it. It was her turn. So she scrambled out from under her blanket and took her place on the firing line, which was just opposite him at the table.

And as she sat down Audrey told him, "Yes, this was a holy time, the time that gave birth to the Christian dream, the birth of Christianity. Actually," she added, "it marked the beginning of Judaism and Islamism as well."

"This was the beginning of Christianity?" he questioned. "This doesn't make any sense at all, all of the inhabitants, all of the men and women and children slain with the edge of the sword? You call this holy? Something is wrong here. Very wrong."

"And listen." he went on, "This is the second of the thirty three wars which won for the Israelites the Promised Land. The land that traditionally had been the land of the Canaanites, which

God had promised to Abraham and Moses. The city of Ai." And he read, "'*For Joshua drew not his hand back, wherewith he stretched out the spear, until he utterly destroyed all the inhabitants of Ai. And so it was that the Israelites smote the city with the sword's edge. And so it was, that all that fell that day, man and woman and child, were twelve thousand.*'

"And listen." He went on, "Makkedah." He then repeated it as if to exact his pronunciation, "Mak-ke-dah. '*And, that day Joshua took Makkedah, and smote it with the edge of the sword, and the kings thereof he utterly destroyed them, and all the souls that were therein, every man and woman and child. And Joshua passed from Makkedah, and all of his war people with him, unto Libnah and Lachish, and smote them with the edge of the sword, and slew all the souls that were therein; he let none remain.*'

"And it goes on and on," he said, "thirty three cities in all. I counted them, each and every one of them. Including Kadesh and Jerusalem. And, what's more, I counted up the victims, hundreds of thousands of them, hundreds of thousands of helpless men, women, and children. You call this unprovoked atrocity holy?" He said it in such a way as to question her sanity.

I saw immediately that Audrey was in over her head. But snug by the fire I ignored her plight and let the slaughter continue.

"You don't understand," she replied, "these were evil people, these Canaanites. That's why God instructed Joshua to kill them all."

"You mean," he asked, "that these people had done the same thing to the Israelites? That they had murdered the men, women and children of the Israelites? That the Israelites were acting in retaliation?"

"No." she answered, "Before that time there had not been any wars that had been inspired by God. Wars that we refer to today as ethnic cleansing wars. Like the Crusades and the Holocaust and the many in between. The Canaanites were a peace loving people. That is why Joshua had such an easy time taking their cities from them. They had never thought of the possibility of war as the Canaanites assumed that all people were like themselves, peace loving people. So they had no defense other than their walls that they had built in order to protect their children and livestock from predatory beasts."

"Why is she giving him more fuel for his fire?" I thought, "She is digging a hole for herself so deep that she will never be able to get out."

"Then they were wrong, clearly wrong. The Israelites must have been a very evil people!" he exclaimed.

"Just the other way around," she corrected him, "the Canaanites were the evil people. They were worshipping false gods." She probably hoped that this would put an end to it once and for all. That she would be able to return to the comfort of her chair by the fireplace.

"What do you mean, false gods?" he quickly asked.

"Some of them worshipped idols and statutes. Others worshipped things like the sun or thunder or other parts of nature. They were evil. They were all evil," she asserted as if he would have missed the point had she not repeated herself.

"Oh," he replied, "then they must not have had freedom of religion in those days. I guess those that were the most powerful just killed all the others who didn't believe in the god or gods that they, themselves, believed in."

"That's not exactly right," she came back at him once again. "It is God that ordered Joshua to kill them all and take their homeland from them. You just read it, yourself."

"Just because He didn't like the other gods?" he questioned more than asked. "He was afraid of the other gods? He didn't want the competition?"

"Well," she added, "there was more to their evilness than just worshipping false gods. These people, these Canaanites, were engaged in sexual activities."

Although I decided not to look around, I could imagine the expression on his face. I knew it was one of total confusion, probably a mixture of incomprehension and surprise. And, then again, I thought that it was more likely to be a pathetic look of compassion that he gave her. As one gives to any 'sick' person.

"You mean God ordered Joshua to kill all these people simply because they were having sex?" and I couldn't believe it when he said it out loud, "No wonder dad was so scared to death to talk to me about it. He must have thought that God would strike him down too. No wonder your generation is so hung up on this thing we call 'sex', this natural biological function of the human body. This God given function of humanity."

And although he paused in anticipation of some kind of a follow-up by Audrey, she remained quiet, absolutely quiet.

"This God, this God," he decided to pick up the conversation once again, "that ordered these atrocities could not have been the Father of Jesus? Or to put it another way, the same God that Jesus claimed to be the Son of?" he seemed to state it, much more than ask it.

"Yes, He was. This is the same God. There is only one God." she replied.

"Then, Jesus was this same God?" his tone demanded confirmation.

"That's right," she agreed with a slight tone of frustration as to the way he had asked the question, as if there could possibly be more than one God.

"He has got her exactly where he wants her now," I thought to myself. "It won't be long now."

"Then Jesus ordered these atrocities," he exclaimed, more than asked.

"No," she responded, "God the Father did. Jesus came along later."

I started to chuckle silently to myself. For I could tell immediately by his follow-up that he was setting her up for checkmate.

"You mean that Jesus isn't infinite? That He wasn't always there?"

"Of course He was always there. He is God." she corrected him again.

"Then He had to have been there at that time. So this makes no sense at all, absolutely no sense at all. This horrific thing that you call 'holy'. This murderous deed that you call the birth of Christianity. For Christ could not have been a part of this God who ordered these atrocities. Because it is quite obvious that Jesus would not have done such a thing."

"Remember," she said, "these were evil people. They were having sex and worshipped false gods," she struggled to justify God the Father's actions. Actions, which she now had conceded had to have been Christ's actions as He was infinite and was one and the same God.

"To begin with," the little man started to go in for the kill, "if people didn't have sex, then just how could humanity go on? Where would the babies come from? And speaking of the babies, why did *Christ*, or the Father as you prefer to call Him, order that Joshua murder all of them too, including the infants and children. Were they having sex too? Were they worshipping false gods too? No," he concluded, "there is something very wrong here." And he again repeated it as if thinking very deeply, "There is something very, very wrong here."

And Audrey intervened, "God ordered that the children and infants also be slaughtered because they had inherited the evilness of their parents. That's why they all had to be killed. If you go back in your book a few chapters you will come to the story of Noah. There you will find that all of the descendants of Hamm, one of Noah's three sons, would inherit the traits of Hamm, the evil traits of sexual promiscuity."

A God for Lions

And following her instruction, he flipped back a number of pages and, started running his finger up and down a half dozen of them. "Yes, you are right," he said, "it says here in *Genesis*, '*And Noah drank of the wine, and was drunken; and he was uncovered within his tent, and Hamm the father of Canaan, saw the nakedness of his father ... And Noah awoke from his wine, and knew what his younger son had done to him.*' he paused for a moment and then continued, "And, this must be what you are talking about, '*And Noah said, Cursed be Canaan, cursed be all the descendants of Hamm, Let them be cursed with his abominable evilness for all time.*'"

Then he paused again as if trying to understand what had taken place in this brief passage of the *Bible*. Just what had Hamm done to Noah? Then he started up again, "But what this is saying is that God would create some of his children to be born that way? To be evil? To be promiscuous? To be homosexuals? And then order those that He created to be good to kill them all and to take from them all that they had? I just can't believe that a God could do that to some of his children. For this would make him an evil God. And if this is true, He is not a God that I can accept. That any man of good conscience would accept. For I believe that God is a good God and that He loves all of His children and that He certainly wouldn't want any harm to come to any of them. No," he concluded, "this is not the word of God, at least this part of the *Bible* can't be true!

"And this poses a great problem for me. For I know that unless I believe in this part of the *Bible*, then I certainly cannot believe in Jesus, because Jesus claimed to be the Son of this same God, this God who ordered these terrible atrocities. In fact, since Jesus is infinite, He had to have ordered the atrocities Himself. For He was God."

He stopped for a couple of minutes as if thinking deeply. "Huh," he said, "this must have been the same part of the *Bible* that inspired Hitler when he murdered all those in the Holocaust. For he, too, sent the infants and children to the ovens."

"No," Audrey interrupted him, "in his case he was inspired by another part of the *Bible*."

"Another part?" he questioned her.

"Yes, another part of the *Old Testament*." She gestured to him for the book and she started flipping through the pages. Then she stopped and said, "Here, here in *Numbers*," and she read, "'*And God spoke to Moses. Thou shalt take the blood that is upon the altar, and of the anointing oil, and sprinkle it upon Aaron, and upon his sons, and the sons of the sons of the sons of Aaron. And he shall be hallowed, and his sons, and their sons, with him. And his sons shall go in, and appoint them every one to his service and to his burden, and the sons of Aaron shall be the high priests, and they, they alone will rule at my side forever. Those who breed contempt for my rule shall be annihilated and destroyed.*'

"What God the Father intended by this command was that the Aryan race was superior to all other races. That it was to rule. Actually," she added, "you, yourself, are of the Aryan race. Hitler thought that he was the prophet chosen to lead the great war which is foretold in the *Bible* that would give the Aryan race sole rule of the world for a thousand years. In the case of the Holocaust Hitler was complying with *God the Father's* instruction that '*those who breed contempt for my rule shall be annihilated and destroyed.*' Hitler's intent was to fulfill this great dream of God the Father when he spoke His command to Moses."

He stopped for another moment or so as if pondering all that had transpired and went on, "Nevertheless, something is wrong here." and glancing out of the corner of my eye I watched him as he scratched his forehead as if thinking very deeply. "We must," he went on, "apply some of those little gray cells, those little particles of energy that have worked so well for the great *Hercule Perot*."

A God for Lions

"Who?" she asked as if she hadn't heard him.

"Perot," he responded. "Hercule Perot, the master detective of Agatha Christie fame."

"Oh!" she uttered. And the way she said it gave away the fact that she had never heard of him.

"The question," he continued, "is why? Why would Joshua and Moses make these bloodthirsty aggressions? Do these terrible things? What could possibly have been their motive?"

"Motive?" she repeated. "Motive? God told them to do these things. They didn't need any motive."

"No." he replied quite adamantly. "Every act a human being does has a motive whether it is eating ones breakfast because one is hungry or going to school to learn or going to work to earn. Otherwise one would do nothing." He stopped for awhile as if trying to come up with a way in which he could explain this thing which was obviously over his mother's head.

"Today if a leader of a large nation were to say that God told him that He had given his people the small nation that sits on his borders and that God instructed them to invade their neighbor and slaughter them all, men, women and children, the world would think him to be crazy. In fact, his own people would think him crazy, insane. And if he ever tried to invade and take over the smaller country, the United States together with its allies in the free world would rise up, and excuse my language, and pound the hell out of him. But the mass of the populace of the United States and its allies today, including certain people in this room," and he glanced over toward me as to include me as one of the halfwits, "accept as a matter of fact that these men, Moses and Joshua who they never knew, got the very same message more than three thousand years ago and that in their case the message came directly from God. And they think that this great atrocity was somehow holy. And the most ridiculous part of it all is that they are staking their eternity on it." He looked up at Audrey as if she was out of her mind and glanced over to me as if I had some kind of an explanation for her madness.

"The *Bible*'s explanation as to what took place is, of course, what we have just been discussing. But to this *Hercule Perot* it makes no sense and when something makes no sense to the 'master detective' he must go further. He must think further. He must ponder the possibilities. So, he would ask himself, 'Why else would Joshua or Moses make these aggressions? What else could have been their motive?'

"And there seems to be only one possible alternative," he continued and then paused again as if searching for other alternatives, "Yes, they, Moses and Joshua, wanted the Promised Land for themselves. There is no doubt about it. They wanted the great treasures, the silver and gold and palaces of Jericho and all the other cities for themselves. For it is quite obvious that if God the Father wanted them to have the Promised Land He would have given it to them in the first place.

"So if this is true, and from an intelligence quotient point of view it certainly is true," he said it in such a way as to draw some kind of a line between himself and Audrey and I, "why didn't they, Moses and Joshua, just tell their people to take the cities? Why did they bother to go through all that is said in these pages, here, to realize their dreams?"

I thought to myself that if Audrey were a dog she certainly would be whimpering by this time. But I didn't hear a thing. Except, of course, an occasional spark from the fire.

"And the reason is clear," he began to set the stage for his conclusion. "We know that God creates all of us to be good. We can only choose to be bad. That is, of course, assuming that we ignore the instruction of the *Bible* that some of us are created by God to be bad, to be evil so to speak. In this case the Canaanites.

"So if one were to accept this supposition, that all men are created to be good, then the Israelites had to have been created to be good. So it follows that if Moses and Joshua ordered their people to murder the Canaanites and their children and take their land, treasures and palaces from them, the Israelites would have known that it would be a wrong thing to do and would not have complied."

By this time one could hear a pin drop in the room. I have to say it that way without any originality whatsoever of my own because there is no better way to describe it.

"So Moses and Joshua knew this. That their people would not commit such an atrocity. They knew that the Israelites would only commit such an evil deed if it were the direct command of God. So what did they do? Just what was their strategy?" he again stopped and scratched his head as if searching for the answer.

"They knew that if they were to convince their people that they had talked to God and that God had commanded that they commit these evil deeds, that the action would follow. That God had commanded that they take these cities together with their treasures, their silver and their gold. That they annihilate all those people that God had said were evil. Every man and woman and child. And this is quite obvious in God's alleged instruction to Joshua, *'destroy all that is within the city, both man and woman and child and ox and ass, ... leave only the silver, and the gold and the vessels of brass and iron and palaces thereof.'*

"And why would they kill the children? And that answer is also quite clear. For they knew that when the children grew up they would seek revenge. They would come after Moses and Joshua. So the children, had they lived, would pose a great threat to both of them.

"And since they knew that their people were basically good people that in order to convince them to commit such atrocities the story must be a very convincing one." And, scratching his head once again as to muster up a few more of those gray cells, he stopped for a few minutes, almost as if he had stopped for good. And then suddenly he started up again.

"Yes, there's no doubt about it. The stories of Creation, of Adam and Eve, of Original Sin, of Noah's Ark, of the plague of the lice, of the plague of the frogs, of the deaths of the firstborns, topped off by of the tablet of the Ten Commandments. Yes, they would have done the trick. No, not today, because of what science has placed before us. But, in those days they must have been immensely credible stories, good enough to do the trick. Good enough to convince the Israelites that Moses and Joshua were, in fact, in direct communication with God. After all, there would be nothing else that would convince them that they had indeed been talking to God, as no one saw them. The *Bible* is explicit in the fact that there were no witnesses to the alleged apparitions of God to Abraham, Moses, Joshua or any other of the dozens of prophets of the *Old Testament*. If one were to count them up, and believe me, I have done my homework, there are over three hundred alleged apparitions to these prophets in the *Old Testament*. Don't you find it strange that they were all unwitnessed? Don't you find it strange that God never once appeared to two or more people at the same time?"

He waited for some kind of response from her, but the only thing he got was the clearing of her throat, "And then there is the fact that in just about everything Moses and Joshua had to say they painted sex to be a horrific crime. Whereas the natural biological instinct of man toward sex is that it is good and beautiful. Particularly important in this respect was the story of Noah's Ark as told by Moses. For it tells us that it was sins of the flesh that caused God to destroy the world. Sex." and without so much as turning a page in the *Bible* as if he were reading it from some kind of blackboard that was in his mind, "*'... as it was all flesh who had corrupted his way upon the earth. And behold, I will destroy them with the earth.'*

"But, perhaps, most foretelling of all is the story of the *Ten Commandments* given directly from God the Father to Moses on the mount, more specifically the first commandment. *'I am the Lord thy God and thou shalt have no other gods before thee.'* Why is it the first commandment? Why is it there at all? For if one accepts Christ, all other gods are immaterial. The commandment is unnecessary. Why was this such a jealous God who gave these tablets to Moses? Why would God, who is all-powerful be so fearful of competition? After all, the other gods were not really gods. In fact, they weren't even men. As a matter of fact, they were nothing. Why would God be so fearful of nothing that He would make this His first and most basic commandment?

"And the answer is clear. Moses put it there. And he listed it first as to give it the greatest importance. For he knew that sex and worshipping other gods were the ways of the Canaanites. That if he was to inspire his people to massacre the Canaanites he must convince his people that the Canaanites were breaking God's greatest laws."

And then like the proverbial snowball rolling down the hill he started to pick up speed. "And Moses and Joshua, knew that even if they were to convince their people that this order had come directly from God, that their people would still not have the heart to kill the infants and children. That their people would know that the infants and children were not having sex and worshipping false gods. And knowing that if the children were to survive that they would eventually take their revenge, Moses added the story of *Hamm*, the promiscuous father of the Canaanites, to give the Israelites the incentive to commit this most evil of all deeds. That all the Canaanite infants and children had inherited the promiscuous traits of Hamm and that they too must also be murdered. Only an imbecile would think of such men as Moses and Joshua as holy men," and raising his voice a notch he stared his mother into a corner, "I think of such men as monsters!"

And, he paused and scratched his head once more, "Now, did I miss something? Is there some other alternative?" And several minutes passed and I could almost hear the little gray cells working away with each other. Then finally he concluded, "No that is it. It has to be it. There are no other viable alternatives. It is not the Israelites or Canaanites who were so evil. Rather it was Moses and Joshua who were the culprits in this thing. The only other alternative is to think that God played such a horrific game with His children. That He had set the whole thing up. For as I have said before if God had wanted the Israelites to have the land of Canaan then He would have given it to them in the first place.

"And this is proven quite conclusively in that everything that Moses had to say in his five books: *Genesis, Exodus, Leviticus, Numbers* and *Deuteronomy* cumulates in the taking of the Promised Land."

And he voiced his conclusion in kind of a mumbling tone, "Yes, there are only two alternatives. That Moses and Joshua were telling the truth which means we are dealing with an evil God. Or that they were lying, which means we are today dealing with a good God. One who loves all of His children regardless of how different He makes them. Yes, that's it in a nutshell. This is what one must decide. This is the bottom line of Christianity, so to speak. Is one dealing with a good or an evil God? Were Moses and Joshua lying or telling the truth when they told their people that they had received this message from God?

And he just wasn't going to give up the floor, "And since Christ is infinite, that is He always was and always will be, we know that if Moses claimed that he had received his message from God that he had in fact received it from Christ. Yet we also know as a matter of fact that Christ would have never told him to commit such foul deeds. So we know as a matter of fact today that Moses was lying when he told his many stories that cumulated in the taking of the Promised Land. And this tells us quite conclusively that today we are dealing with a good God, one who loves all of His children no matter how different He makes them."

I could imagine the pain in Audrey's head and I felt somewhat guilty that I had been kind of enjoying what had just transpired. So when she scrambled back under her covers in the overstuffed chair that sat aside me with her overdrawn look, I gave her a look of great compassion and understanding, one that probably helped to annihilate much of her headache on the spot. And, being the master of this sort of thing, I whispered to her, "You could have won, you know," I whispered, "you should have told him that these things are just stories, stories told by Moses and Joshua, simply folklore. Stories that were told in order to make a point. If you had given him that you would have solved his problem. So in a way you would have won."

"Won?" I questioned myself, "well, perhaps, more of a stalemate."

"Yes," he finished as if he had read my lips when I had whispered to Audrey, "we could say that this is just a story, a tale that was once told to make a point, simply folklore. But one must not forget that its source was the very same man who told the story of Adam and Eve and *Original Sin*. To draw such a conclusion, that these atrocities were simply folklore, would be to conclude that the story of Adam and Eve is also simply folklore. That it, too, was told simply to make a point. For the taking of the Promised Land is a critical link in the chain between Adam and Eve and Christ. Between the *purpose* of Christ and the *person* of Christ, between *Original Sin* and the birth of Christ!

And finally silence prevailed. My own head had started to throb. I was glad that it was finally over. Yet, it was not quite over. "But this taking of the Promised Land has its greatest place in scripture in that it links the *Old Testament* to the *New*

Testament in the *Book of Revelations*, the book of rewards for all of those who are to be saved. That if one does not believe literally in the story of the taking of the Promised Land then one cannot believe in the promised day of resurrection. And after all, resurrection is what Christianity is all about. It is why we believe. For, in the *Book of Revelations*, it is the promise of the *New Jerusalem*, the seat of the 'Promised Land', which is at its core.

"So if one is to believe that in the end one will be resurrected, one will be saved, one must believe that *Jesus* said unto Joshua, '*See, I have given into thine hand Jericho. Take all ye men of war and go around the city seven times, and the priest shall blow with the trumpets. And when ye hear the sound of the trumpet, all the people shall shout with a great shout; and the wall of the city shall fall flat, and ye are to enter and take to the sword all of the inhabitants thereof, every man and woman and child. Leave not one alive!*' For *Jesus Christ* is infinite. He always was, and always will be. For *Jesus Christ* is God!"

And he hammered home the final nail in the coffin, "There is only one point to the story of the taking of the Promised Land and that is to make ourselves rich by murdering our neighbors.

"Remember," he concluded lowering his voice a bit, "when things don't make sense. When someone says something or does something that makes no logical sense there is always a motive. And this motive almost always involves personal gain. For the most powerful instinct of man is selfishness and lust for material gain. And according to the *Bible* Moses and Joshua gained for themselves the great treasures and palaces of the thirty three cities of the Promised Land."

He paused for the last time and made his final point. "Don't you think that more people should read the *Bible* and try to understand what it says rather than relying on the word of the preacher who himself has a motive for what he tells us? After all, one of the greatest palaces and, perhaps, the greatest treasures on earth are in Rome." And as if not to leave anyone out, "And some of the great mansions of the evangelists and many of the cardinals are worth millions. Every single one of them built with money intended for poor and starving children."

And finally silence prevailed. Even the flames in the fireplace had gone to sleep. It was not quite the silence, the solitude that we had been engulfed in at the start of the session. It was another kind of silence. This one broken by the rhythmic throbbing in our heads.

He pushed the books that lay on the table away from him. He got up and picked up his towel and sliding the door open he went out to the pool. A minute later we heard a splash.

> and Joshua took his people to the wall,
> and they did, 'shout, shout,'
> and the great wall of Jericho did fall,
> and those within cringed before those without,
> and the sword fell upon man, woman and child,
> as if devoured by beasts from the wild,
> and when the last infant turned cold,
> Joshua had his city of gold.

the "right" and the "left" defined

"See," he interrupted the evening news, "I was right. This man Moses was not the holy man that we make him out to be." Acknowledging his signal I switched off the TV and scrambled over to his table. "Besides," he added, "it proves that you were right too." I couldn't believe that he seemed to be giving me some kind of credit for something, as most of what I had to say to him was usually wrong. At least 'wrong' in his mind.

"Right?" I said it as if I were questioning his sanity, "I was right?"

"Yes," he replied, "that day when I asked you what is the difference between the *right* and the *left*. That is, you were almost right. 'Those on the *right* use the old scriptures to guide their lives. And those on the *left* use their conscience to guide their lives.' Here, it says it here."

And I interrupted him as he had the book open and I couldn't see its title. "Where? Where?"

"Here in this book, MURDER IN THE VATICAN, the story of the life of the only pope in history to have been born into dire poverty and one of only two popes whose death was unwitnessed, the other having been known to have been murdered by Vatican cardinals."

"Who's that?" I asked.

"John Paul I who died under suspicious circumstances in the Vatican. Don't you think there is something wrong there, that he died after only thirty three days in office? Particularly, in that just a few months earlier he had set a speed record for climbing one of the most difficult mountains in Italy?"

I looked at him questioningly, "I didn't know that he was a mountain climber. I thought that he was known to have been very ill in the months before his death."

A God for Lions

Again he questioned my sanity, "You think the *College of Cardinals* would have elected a man that was known to be very ill to the most responsible job in the church?"

"Anyway," he went on, "That's not the subject. This man, John Paul, was an entirely different kind of man than the church makes him out to be, that the church wants people to believe. He had been born the son of a social revolutionary activist that caused him to take his position on the *left* very early in life. He did not believe that a pope should live like a king surrounded by priceless art and architecture and gold and silver chalices in a palace while children are starving to death in third world countries. He was a great supporter of equality of women in the church and even extended his protective arm to homosexuals. And his description of the difference between the *right* and the *left* is the best I've read to date. When he was only fourteen years old he wrote an editorial, the first of many that would plague the church, which was published in a local *leftist* newspaper. And in the editorial he points out the difference."

"What difference?" I asked.

"The difference between the *right* and the *left*. His name, before he took the name of John Paul, was Albino Luciani. It says here that his letter to the press was undoubtedly written in response to an order by Pius XI to all schools in Italy two weeks earlier in December 1926 to enroll all children under the age of sixteen in the new *Fascist Youth Organization* which later served as the kindling wood for World War II. As you know the pope also wrote a similar letter a couple of years later to all Catholics who lived in Germany. As a matter of fact the fascist movement did not begin in Germany, it began in Italy because that's where the church had its greatest influence. Unlike most people want to believe, fascism did not have its origin in Mussolini or Hitler, it had its beginning in Christianity. In fact during the twenties and thirties when it did not have the connotation that it has today the word 'Fascism' was synonymous with 'Christianity'. If you were a Christian and someone called you a 'fascist' no one thought there to be anything wrong with it. Just like if someone called you a communist at the time no one would think anything wrong with that." And he started to read from the book,

"'I cannot accept,' Albino wrote, 'that Moses was the holy man that Mother Church and the motion pictures make him out to be. After all, Moses introduced the concept of FASCISM to the western world, that ideology that is based on a rich and poor society, one in which children are born into without equal opportunity, many of which are born into poverty and starvation. Moses stressed God the Father's dream in which the white Aryan male rules at His side and woman is to be held in servitude to man, and all others who are different are to be either subordinated, annihilated or cast into slavery. Specifically, Moses in his book 'Leviticus' subordinates those he refers to as 'those with flat noses' (Negroes) and 'those who are of physical blemish' (the handicapped). I am quite dismayed that in all of my life I have never seen a black person as black people are not allowed in Italy. We are an entirely white Catholic country as the minds of the voters are controlled by a Vatican that wants to preserve the purity of our Aryan race.

"'I am equally dismayed that many steps must be mounted to enter most churches. It is almost as if their architects had in mind Moses' command, 'those who are lame, blind and are of other deformity are not to approach the altar of the Lord.' Or perhaps it is that Rome had this in mind when it had ordered them built. And if that is not enough there is Moses' horrific taking of the Promised Land in which he puts to the sword all men, women and even children who worshipped gods other than his god. Moses gave birth to what has been more than three thousand years of ethnic cleansing wars which continue to go on even today. <u>The mainstay of Moses' religion is hatred of others who appear to be different.</u>

"'*Yet, on the other side,*' *he continues,* '*we have Christ. He introduces COMMUNISM to the western world, that ideology that is based on the premise that all God's wealth is to be divided equally among all of His children and a world in which every child has an equal opportunity at a good life. A far different world than we live in today. Christ introduces a single commandment, 'Love thy neighbor as thyself'. In all of His life Christ commits only one sin, the grave sin of anger. He so hated the republicans, the money makers, that in a fit of rage He upturns their money tables and throws them out of His Father's house. Christ's most basic requirement in the New Testament is that one give up ones material wealth and come follow Him.* <u>*The mainstay of Christ's religion is love of others no matter how different*</u>.'

"And his paper goes on, '*There are no other philosophies of life, one either believes in the equality of all of God's children or one doesn't. One must choose between COMMUNISM which is the extreme form of socialism on the left, or FASCISM which is the extreme form of conservatism on the right. These are the pillars of society, Communism and Fascism, and they stand at either end of this rope called 'humanity'. And the job of the people is to make certain that neither one of these extremes wins the tug-of-war. For that would result in a one-party system and dictatorship. So it is important that we work out something in-between. Or we will all end up in the drink. Yet, one can choose to be closer to Christ or closer to Moses.*

'*Although you would never get either one to admit it, a good democrat strives toward COMMUNISM and a good republican strives toward FASCISM. That is, the democrat strives toward Christ and the republican strives toward Moses. And despite Christ's overwhelming testimony two thousand years ago Christianity remains deeply steeped in FASCISM today. It is quite obvious that Mother Church in its support of a fascist state has chosen the word of Moses over the word of Jesus Christ Himself.*'

Lucien Gregoire

"So you were right, almost right," he lifted his eyes from the book. "Those on the *right* use the old scriptures to guide their lives and those on the *left* use their conscience to guide their lives. That is, if you assume that Christ is here," and he pointed to his temple.

Then giving me a telltale smile of comprehension he pushed a sheet of paper that he had before him across the table toward me. He got up and went over to the closet and retrieved a basketball and moved quickly up the stairs and out of the house. And I read,

the left	*the right*
Christ	God the Father
Paul, Matthew, Mark, Luke and John	Moses
conscience	old scripture
for others	for oneself
community values	family values
give to the poor	give to the rich
a redistribution of wealth society	a rich and poor society
love all no matter how different	hate those who are different
COMMUNISM ←DEMOCRATS	REPUBLICANS→ FASCISM
looks forward ←PROGRESSIVE	CONSERVATIVE→ looks back
REASON (lions)	(sheep) BELIEF

freedom of religion

I had taken the afternoon off so Audrey and I were relaxing next to the pool taking in the afternoon sun when we heard the drone of the school bus drop him off. As he came around the corner of the house he stopped at the dumpster that was there and unloaded whatever he was carrying in his hand. As he approached us it became quite apparent that he was rampant. I mean fit to be tied.

"Sister Maria Helena gave me a 'D' on my term paper," he shouted from across the yard. And approaching us, "We were asked to write a paper on 'freedom of religion - prayers at football games,'" he added. "A 'D'. I couldn't believe it, so after class I asked her if there had been some kind of a mistake? But, she told me that there had been no mistake. She told me that A's are for the work of angels, and that D's are for work of the devil. And, she said that my paper was very much the work of the devil."

Then he turned and as he headed toward the house he warned, "I think that you'd better lock up the liquor cabinet cause I think I need a drink." And I looked at Audrey that, perhaps, she could handle this one? And getting up she followed him and disappeared into the house. I got up and headed over to the dumpster to retrieve whatever he had discarded there. And returning to my lounge chair by the pool I began to read,

> "*these are good times, these are bad times, these are changing times*;'
>
> "These words, more than any others, pinpoint the genius of Charles Dickens. But more so, they echo the transcending evolution of Christianity. The Christian

world today does not believe at all what the Christian world believed just five hundred years ago. It has been caught up in the social and economic changes brought on by the emergence of the renaissance, modern science and the consequential technical revolution.

"The miracles performed by modern man have reduced in scope the thirty five miracles, said to be performed by Christ, to the level of those that are routinely performed by mere rank and file magicians, today. The raising of a dead man at a time when there was no way to tell if a man was really dead, the walking on water before the time of illusionary levitation, and the changing of water into wine before the introduction of Kool Aid, cannot begin to shine the shoes of the modern miracles of radio, television, telephonic and satellite transmission, heavier than air flight, men on the moon, computer technology and the Internet. And, perhaps the most astounding of all. That medical science is on the threshold of perfecting the Creator's greatest work. That genetic and virus pre-testing of the sperm and the egg before fertilization in the process of artificial insemination will guarantee a perfectly healthy baby every time, something that has eluded the Creator for countless milleniums.

"Five hundred years ago, man lived in a natural world. One of darkness. A world made by God. Man was a creature of nature. He had only *belief* to guide him. When night fell, he went to sleep, because he had no way of controlling the darkness. And, each night, as he fell asleep, he *believed* that, in the morning, light would come again.

"But, today, he lives, not in a world of nature, but in a modern world. One of lightness. A world made by man.

Now he has *reason* to guide him. He is less dependent on *belief*. He is less a creature of nature. For now he can light up the darkness. And, each night, as he falls asleep, he *knows* that, in the morning, light will come again.

"That the thirty five miracles said to be performed by Christ, failed to convince the Romans that He was God, remains a mystery today. Particularly in that several of them involved Roman soldiers themselves. ... *'and the centurion said, I am not worthy that thou shouldest come under my roof: but speak the word only, and my servant shall be healed. For I am a man under authority having many soldiers under me.'*

"And it remains even a greater mystery why His miracles failed to convince the Jews that He was God. After all they were the direct witnesses of His miracles many of which were said to have been performed before great multitudes of Jews.

"But it is no mystery, there is no question, that had Thomas Edison lived at that time, the Romans and the Jews would have known that he was God. For he would have lit up their lives, not one of their lives, but all of their lives. And, he would have lit them up, forever.

"And all of these advancements, all of these modern miracles of man, have taken place since Thomas Jefferson wrote the Declaration of Independence by candlelight. Since Thomas Jefferson had his slaves harness his horses to the carriage for the long overnight trip to Philadelphia. Since the First Continental Congress first heard the words, *We hold these Truths to be self evident, that all Men are created equal, that they are endowed by their creator with certain inalienable rights, that among these are Life, Liberty and the Pursuit of Happiness.*

"And, as we all know today the Constitution was then, and continues to be today, somewhat of a hypocritical oath. For we all know that the definition of 'Men' as set forth in the founding document, was not at all what it is today. For the word 'men' automatically excluded women and slaves who were considered to be property of men and therefore not 'men'.

"That our forefathers intended a different kind of nation. But, in the very next century, the first American lion, Abraham Lincoln and its first lioness, Susan B. Anthony, were to emerge to change forever what was intended by our forefathers.

"Men and women of great courage, who saw it as their sacred duty, to rise up against what was written. Written in the Constitution, which for these things, had their foundation in ancient scripture, the *Bible*. For they knew that if they were to reach tomorrow, they could not live in yesterday. For yesterday is still and only the present is moving and it is moving toward tomorrow. And, today, it is moving very rapidly toward tomorrow.

"And that the most sacred freedom of all is not a freedom at all even today. The individual freedom of religion. That instead of allowing the individual the freedom to choose his or her religion, one makes certain that the child is brainwashed from birth so as to greatly limit the possibility that he or she is free to choose a religion other than that which he or she happens to be born into. That the first thing to be placed before the Muslim child is a picture of a block of granite at Mecca, and the first thing one places before the Jewish child is the Star of David, and the first thing set before the Christian child is a near naked man nailed to a tree. That ones entitlement to an afterlife is ones birthright. One born into one religion will be saved and one born into another religion is certain to perish.

"Like the word 'men' in the Constitution, the phrase 'freedom of religion' needs much attention too. For if one is to be honest in these things, one would withhold religion from the child until he or she reaches the age of *reason* and then place before the child the options, the basic philosophy of each of the world's major religions. But, no, that would be the thought of a madman. So, yes, we go on. We continue to rob the individual of the sacred privilege of being able to make for oneself the most important decision one can make in ones lifetime. Yes, in this nation we call free, freedom to choose the path one might take to eternity, freedom of religion, in truth, is a myth.

"But, nevertheless, these advancements of modern man, therefore, have given him a kind of independence, and this independence has given him the courage to depart from the ancient scriptures, which until a few centuries ago ruled the way he lived. Today, the average Christian belongs to one of more than a quarter of a million different Christian churches worldwide, each based on a different philosophy. And, what is most surprising, most members of each church have very little idea as to what they believe in. They go for the Hollywood version of Christ, the robes and the miracles, but they no longer accept His principles.

"In fact, some don't even have the intelligence, or want to take the time, to really understand His principles, the basic philosophy of Christ's being. The reasons I sold my bike. And, the churches certainly aren't going to tell them, as society is pulling in the opposite direction, away from His principles, and to emphasize the fundamental philosophy of Christ, would be a lose, lose situation. Lose members, and lose funds.

"And this has all evolved into the great mysterious phenomenon of faith. The inability of the believer to relate what he knows to be fact, to exact the position of what he believes in. And this, itself, is driven by the uncertainty of what he believes in. He doesn't want to take a chance that what he believes in might not be true. The risk is far too great. For his very mortality is at stake!"

"So he has started to work on them too," I thought to myself. "It won't be long before he drives them out of their minds. He must have thrown Sister Maria Helena into shock with this one," and pausing, "Yes, a chip off the old block," and my mind drifted back to that day many years before …

… to that day when the nun had whispered a message to me and told me to pass it on to the kid who sat behind me, and for that kid to pass it on to the third, and so forth. Then, I remember, she had both myself and the last student write our messages on the blackboard and there was no similarity, whatsoever, between the two.

And I remember asking, "How about the *Bible?*" I almost recall my exact words, "To believe in the *Bible*, then, one has to assume, that the stories of Creation and Adam and Eve are exactly how Moses told them in 1400BC. This means, that the great number of intermediate hands through which this message was passed on through the centuries have had to have been infallible. That no one, not a single person, misunderstood the stories, or took literary license and embellished or changed the stories. This would include anyone who retold the stories for the first thousand years or so until papyrus had been developed to the point that permitted some of the stories to be written. And this would be true even after they were written."

"Yes, I completely threw Sister Mary Joseph into shock," I thought to myself with somewhat of a leer in my grin. She couldn't believe her ears. And although she avoided my question we at the time did get a pretty good idea of what the word 'heretic' meant.

And later that afternoon she did admit to me that I was quite smart, actually, too smart for my pants. I never really understood this relationship, that is, between my intelligence and my pants? After that, I often pondered it, but I was never to come up with a logical answer. But, nevertheless, that incident left me, it must have left all of us, with some doubt as to the survivability of the true story of creation, and I knew that the accuracy of this story was fundamental to my belief in Christ.

And my pants? I have found since, that in these things the nun was wrong, for they certainly must be smarter than I.

the similarities among religions

"So that's it. That must be it," he exclaimed. He had been sitting there still as a lion in tall grass stalking his prey for the past couple of hours carefully perusing the pages of both the Old and the New Testaments. And, in addition, he had stacked up to one side about a half dozen other books. There was one on Hinduism which I noticed was captioned *The Vedas, the Hindu Scripture* and next to it was the Muslim New Testament, the *Koran*. And had Johnny not come into my life I would have taken it to be the Muslim *Bible* because until he told me so I had no idea that Muslims, like Jews and Christians, also believed in the God of Abraham and Moses of the *Old Testament*. The one that we call 'God the Father' and they call 'Allah'. Then there were the Buddhist scriptures, the *Tripitaka and the Sutras*. And yes, the *Torah*, the Jewish version of the five books of Moses.

"What's that?" I asked, as he had said it as if he were coming to the end of a long journey. That he had come upon the pot of gold at the end of the rainbow. I scrambled out of my overstuffed chair flanking the fireplace and took my place at his table.

"Why we don't follow His *principles*," He replied.

"Whose *principles*?" I queried.

"Christ's *principles*," he replied, "It says here 'that there are three parts of Christ'."

"No," I corrected him, "there are three parts of God. *God the Father*, who is the *Creator*, and *Christ*, who is the *Redeemer*, and the *Holy Ghost*, who is the *Enlightener*, who tells one *right* from *wrong*."

"No," he replied, "I am not talking about God. I am talking about Christ. There are three basic parts of Christ, His *person*, His *purpose*, and His *principles*."

And he responded to my comment, "What you are talking about is God. That is who we, in the western world, recognize as God, three persons in one God. As a matter of fact, the eastern world, also recognizes three persons in its God."

"They have three persons in their God too?" I questioned in a tone that successfully suppressed my surprise.

"Yes," he answered, "and, what's more, they recognized a *Holy Trinity* long before Christ came along. Actually, it was set forth in their scriptures, their stories, several hundred years before Christ's time. In the Hindu case *God the Father, 'Brahma', is the Creator*. And, likewise, Christ has His counterpart in Hindu scripture," quickly pulling the book entitled *The Vedas* forward and opening it to a page that he had previously bookmarked, "in *'Shiva' who is the Redeemer or Reincarnator*. And *'Vishnu'*, the counterpart of the Holy Ghost, *'keeps the balance between good and evil, tells one right from wrong.'* Vishnu, for the Hindu, is the light of wisdom."

He paused and then stood up and went to the desk that sat just to the right of the sliding doors that looked out at the now frozen pool and retrieved a notepad and pen. Returning to the table he sat down and said, "We will be getting into some deep stuff here, so perhaps a brief outline of what we are talking about from time to time will help make things easier for you," he scratched the following on the pad and lay it on the table in front of me,

Holy Trinity	Eastern God	Western God
The Creator	Brahma	God the Father
The Redeemer	Shiva	Christ
The Enlightener	Vishnu	the Holy Ghost

Although he had said it as if he were talking to a six year old, I let him get away with it.

"Yes," he continued, "by the time St. Jerome came along, four hundred years after Christ, and three thousand years after the God Brahma had first made His debut, he had much to work with."

"St. Jerome? Who was he?" I asked,

"Who was he?" he repeated, quite surprised, "He wrote the first *Bible*. He's the one who put it all together. Formalized Christianity."

"That's not true," I countered, "the *Old Testament* was written long before Christ. Moses, himself, wrote *Genesis* and what are commonly referred to as the *Five Books of Moses*."

He laughed, "For Moses to have written the five books attributed to him is absurd. When one says that he 'wrote' the books of *Genesis*, the *Exodus* and the others attributed to him, one means that he told the stories. In Moses' day, one only had two mediums on which one could write, leather and papyrus. To write the five books of Moses on leather would have been an insurmountable task, as it would require the hides of a quarter of a million sheep. So the only real option he had was to write them on papyrus.

"So, yes, he could have written them on papyrus," he went on, "The problem is that he didn't live long enough. When one wrote on ancient papyrus one was working with an extremely rough surface. In order for a single letter to be legible, it had to be an average of more than an inch square. And the letter would be drawn, not written. And drawing letters takes a long time. In those days papyrus was simply reeds pressed together with beeswax. It took much work to produce papyrus and being extremely expensive it was available to only kings and queens. Although papyrus is highly biodegradable, a few papyrus scrolls have survived in the tombs of the pharaohs that lived about

Moses time and these evidence that drawing letters on ancient papyrus was a very painstaking task.

"And, furthermore, for the five books of Moses to have been written on ancient papyrus, it would take a roll of papyrus a meter wide and one hundred and sixty miles long. I know, because I have done the calculation myself.

"Besides this, reducing stories to print in those days had very little purpose as only a very tiny part of the population was literate. And this remained true until the fifteenth century when the printing press was developed. Even Christ, in His day, being a common man, would not have been literate. As a matter of fact, in all of the *New Testament* there is nothing that says that He ever read or wrote anything. Actually, until the twentieth century more than half of the world's population was illiterate, that is, could neither read nor write.

"Actually, those in the east in Christ's time were generally literate. And the reason for this is that they had developed silk three thousand years before Christ's time. And this permitted their ancient scriptures and other teachings to be reduced to writing at a much earlier time than Hebrew scripture. But, of course, Christ was not aware of the Chinese or the Indians, the Hindus, at His time. He did not know that they were there. In fact, He did not even know that the Celtics were prancing about stone idols in England at His time or that the American Indian was looking up at his totem poles at the same time. That's why He never mentions these others in all of His testimony." He reached again for the notepad and scratched something on it and set it in front of me,

2500BC	Hindu stories are first told
1400BC	Hebrew stories are first told (Moses)
950BC	Complete Hindu scripture reduced to text on silk
525BC	Buddhism: Love Thy Neighbor as Thyself
479BC	Taoism: Sell what thou hast and give to the poor

221BC	Qin, Prince Sheng first man to claim divinity
150BC	*Silk Road* is begun connecting China with India
4BC-29AD	Christ claims divinity
50-75AD	*Silk Road* reaches MidEast. For the first time those in the MidEast and those in the East become aware of each others religions
53-96AD	*New Testament* is written
400AD	the first *Bible* is reduced to text on paper
1453AD	oldest surviving *Bible* today (*Guttenberg*)
1611AD	King James version

While I perused what he had put in front of me, his eyes and evidently his mind had drifted toward the fireplace. He was obviously mesmerized by the flames as when I placed the notepad aside he looked up with a start and quickly took up where he had left off.

"So," he summarized his point, "yes, one can safely attribute the five books to Moses, but no one, in ones right mind, could ever say he wrote them. They were simply stories he told, or is said to have told, that have been passed down from generation to generation. And, their accuracy, of course, depends entirely on the integrity of the tens of thousands of people who were involved retelling them. That no one, not a single soul, changed or embellished any of the stories to satisfy their own whims or desires."

And I thought back to that time in school when I had raised the same question to Sister Mary Joseph. That day that she had talked of how smart my pants were, but he quickly interrupted my thought, "But, that Jerome was the culprit who borrowed the idea of a *Holy Trinity* from Hindu scripture is not necessarily so. It is more likely that the evangelists themselves were the culprits as the history books tell us quite conclusively that those in the MidEast first became aware of those living in India and their Hindu culture during the last half of the first century,

A God for Lions

precisely the time during which the evangelists wrote the *New Testament*.

"That the evangelists claimed that Christ was the Son of God required the application of the concept of a *Holy Trinity* as otherwise there would have been two gods, Christ of the *New Testament* and God the Father of the *Old Testament*. Yes, that they incorporated the idea of a third person into the *New Testament*, the *Holy Ghost*, the *Enlightener*, was most likely to bring the western God on an equal playing surface with the eastern God, the *God 'Brahma'* so that their God, too, would find Its divinity in a *Holy Trinity*.

"Yes," he went on, "if the evangelists had stopped with two persons in one God, then the chances of it being a coincidence would be reduced substantially. For as one knows, a Holy Deity is all they required to justify that Christ was one and the same God as was the God of Abraham and Moses. But, in that they choose also to add the Holy Ghost at the very time that the history books tell us that they had first become aware of the *Holy Trinity* of the Hindu culture is overwhelming evidence that the evangelists stole the idea from the Hindus."

"You're talking through your hat," I stopped him. "Christ is the Son that God the Father promised to send to earth to rid the world of Original Sin as foretold in the *Old Testament*. The ideology of a *Holy Trinity* is clearly a product of the *Old Testament*."

He kind of chuckled to himself. I started to get the message that I had fallen into some kind of a trap, "There is no such thing in the *Old Testament*. Nowhere in all of the *Old Testament* does God the Father promise to send his Son to earth to rid it of Original Sin."

He pulled forth the *Old Testament* and opened to the *Book of Isaiah*. "Here in chapter 7 is the most you have, '*Behold a virgin shall conceive and bear a son, and shall call his name Immanuel.*'

"And if you spin forward to chapter 53 '*he hath poured out his soul until death; and he was numbered with the transgressors; and he bare the sin of many, and made intercession for the transgressors.*' Nowhere in all of *Isaiah* or for that matter in all of the *Old Testament* does it say who Isaiah is referring to. To say that he is talking of the Son of God one is reaching for a straw in the darkness as there is nothing there to suggest that he is referring to the Son of God, not a single word."

Now I knew I had him where I wanted him, "But these things come true in the *New Testament*. Christ was born to a virgin and He died for the sins of others. It is that these prophecies come true in the *New Testament* that prove the validity of the story of Christ. They prove that the *New Testament* is scripture, is a matter of fact, and not just a fairytale."

He gave me a look as one often reserves for a child who is a slow learner. One who is struggling with his first words and asked me, "You don't think that if the *New Testament* was a work of fiction that its authors could have made a few prophecies come true? You don't think that they could have stretched their imagination a bit and interpreted Isaiah's words as of he was referring to the Son of God? You don't think that if Isaiah had been referring to the Son of God that he would have said so? You don't think that it was important enough of a point for him to have said so?"

I continued to hold the expression of a young confused child as he wrapped up his case, "To begin with," he said, "Matthew and Luke, the two evangelists who tell the story of the birth of Christ, according to the *New Testament* itself, were both younger than Christ. They were not even alive when Christ was said to be born, so they had no way of telling what had been the details of His birth. All they would have had at hand was Isaiah's scant testimony in the *Old Testament* and the hearsay of others."

He paused as to give his next statement absolute emphasis over everything else he would have to say, "From a scientific point of view one would be talking of a most remarkable coincidence in time. That the descendents of the *Peking Man* dated 1.7millionBC, the earliest hard evidence of homo erectus in the Eastern Hemisphere, and that the descendents of *Lucy* dated 3.2millionBC, the earliest known hard evidence of homo erectus in the Western Hemisphere, first became aware of each other's existence at precisely the exact time that the New Testament was written.

"And from a Biblical point of view one knows that east and west would have never had to meet for they would have always been aware of each other. For Christ was much closer to Adam in His time than we are today to the two thousand year period of Egyptian dominance. And we know all about the Egyptians today.

"And then we have the added coincidence that Qin, Prince Sheng, who built the Great Wall of China two hundred years before Christ, was the first human being in all of civilization to be recognized by a major population as being of divinity, a concept that had never been thought of in the western world. Even the pharaohs, although believed to have intercession with the gods, were not believed to be of divinity. No one had ever thought of the possibility that a man could be God in the west. And as you know this eastern belief in the divinity of Chinese emperors came to an end when China became a republic in 1912.

"And then we have the astounding coincidence that Christ introduced the fundamental philosophy of Buddhism, *'Love thy Neighbor as Thyself,'* to the western world.

"And we have the extraordinary coincidence that the basic teachings of Christ in the New Testament are a combination of those of Tao and Buddha of the east who predate Him by five hundred years. And there is one more coincidence," he added.

"One more coincidence?" I questioned.

"Yes, one more coincidence," he replied, "That the fundamental concept of Taoism, first introduced by Christ to the Western Hemisphere, that spoke of a redistribution of wealth society, was in direct violation of His Father's dictate of a rich and poor society. Not exactly, *Honor thy Father and thy Mother*, was it?"

I had come to know that Johnny rarely ever would leave any loose ends in these kinds of things. That if one had any doubt of what he had to say that he always had the nails in his hip pocket needed to seal any coffin. And this would be no exception. In a heartbeat he pounded the lid closed once and for all, "And as for the Holy Ghost, He doesn't come along until the *New Testament*. There is no mention of Him in the *Old Testament* at all. If He was God don't you think that He was around during the time of the *Old Testament*? Don't you think it is strange that Moses and all the other prophets never heard from Him? What do you think He was doing all of that time?"

"Strange," I thought, "I never knew that the Hindus believed in a *Holy Trinity*? I wondered why the nuns never told us that. I wondered if they knew?" I tried to struggle back to the original question. It was much more than having lost my train of thought, it was more that for the moment that I was losing my mind. And knowing that he had taxed all of my faculties he decided to let up a bit, to take me off the hook so to speak.

in the beginning,

"But enough of the *Holy Trinity*," he stopped himself, "There are many other similarities between the two major scriptures which have survived today. Keep in mind that the *Old Testament* is the foundation of all western religions including Christianity, Judaism and Islamism. And the *Vedas*, Hindu scripture, is the foundation of all eastern religions including Hinduism and Buddhism. And in those cases one can speak with greater certainty, much greater certainty, of plagiarism." He grabbed a hold of the notepad and wrote down what he had just said,

believe in the *Vedas*	believe in the *Old Testament*
	Christians (plus *New Testament*)
Buddhists (plus *Tripitaka*)	Muslims (plus the *Koran*)
Hindus (only the *Vedas*)	Jews (only the *Old Testament*)

"There are other similarities?" I asked.

"Sure," he replied, "for example, the story of creation. In both cases, the *Old Testament*, Hebrew or western scripture, and the *Vedas*, Hindu or eastern scripture, the story of creation is told by a God who did not know that the earth was round. That the physical geographical point at which the story was told was considered by God to be the exact center of the universe. And then we have the fact that both Gods *'created the earth with its vegetation and life on the third day, the day <u>before</u> they hung the sun and the moon and the stars in the heavens'.* Whereas, today, one knows that the sun is the center of its solar system and that nothing, not a single thing, could live without it, that the earth could not even be held in its rotation without it. That it is its sun that controls the balance and harmony of all life on the planet earth. So both Gods got this wrong, terribly wrong. And that they both got it wrong in the same identical sequence of events certainly goes far beyond coincidence. It is the equivalent of an architect having built the Empire State Building on the third day and having added the foundation on the fourth day. Don't you think that it is strange that we believe in a God who knows all things except that it is necessary to build a foundation before one builds a building? Let alone that we believe in a God that did not know that the earth that He had created was round?

"But what happened on the first day, not on the fourth day of creation, is the more problematic coincidence. As both the Christian God and the Hindu God got it wrong. And, again, they got it wrong in identical fashion. For both of them made the assumption that the waters were always there. That neither of the 'Gods' created the waters. That the eastern God according to the *Vedas* in His very first work of creation, *'created the firmament, by separating the waters, that were there, to the heavens above, and to the sea below.'* And the western God according to the book of *Genesis 'divided the waters which were under Heaven from the waters that were above Heaven. And made the firmament. And He called the firmament Heaven. Then God said, Let the waters under the Heaven be gathered together in one place, and let the dry land appear; and it was so. And, God called the dry land earth; and the gathering together of the waters He called the sea. And He saw that it was good.'*

"In those days men thought that there was a body of water above the heavens. This is because the sky was blue, the same color as was the sea. Also, rain came from above. And this point is made explicit in the *Old Testament*, *'That only God makes a channel in the sky through which the rain and the thunderstorm come.'* They didn't know that, in fact, the sea simply reflects the color of the sky and that it is the sun's evaporation of the sea that permits moisture to rise and rain to fall.

"So both 'Gods' messed up on the very first day of creation. For both of them assumed that the waters were always there. Both of them assumed that there was a sea above the heavens. And, today we know that this is not true. As a matter of fact we know, today, that there is nothing but space above the heavens. Nothing at all.

"And, we also know that, although both eastern and western scriptures tell us that in the beginning there was only water, that water made up all of its space, that, in fact, today, all the water in the universe makes up an infinitesimal tiny spec of its space.

Totally insignificant, a drop in the bucket, when one considers the vastness of the cosmos."

"That doesn't prove anything," I stopped him, "it is logical that God would have told the story of creation in both parts of the world, as man saw and thought of the world at that time as not to confuse him."

"You forget that in the Christian case, *that God spoke these things to Moses.* Do you really think that God lied to Moses? That he intentionally misled Moses? That God could not foresee that eventually man would learn that the earth was round? No," he concluded, "you are reaching for a straw. There is far too much coincidence. Overwhelming coincidence. Even woman was a coincidence. Perhaps, the most astounding coincidence of all."

"Woman?" I queried, "What could woman possibly have to do with it?"

"In both cases," he responded, "in their respective stories of creation, both the eastern version and the western version, both the Hindu version and the Christian version, woman was created as an afterthought by the Creator. Someone to keep man company so to speak."

"So that still doesn't prove anything," I interrupted him.

"You didn't let me finish," he countered. And he drove home his final point, another of those *nails* he would keep in his back pocket, "In both cases," he said, raising his voice firmly, "God made her from a part of man!"

And he quickly pulled the *New Testament* in front of him and read from *Genesis*, "'*And the Lord God said, It is not good that the man should be alone; I will make him an help for him. And the Lord God caused A deep sleep to fall upon Adam, and he slept: and he took one of his ribs, and closed up the flesh instead thereof; and the rib, which the Lord God had taken from man, made him a woman, and brought her unto man.*' And then he pulled forward the book of the *Vedas*, Hindu scripture and he read, '*and the God Brahma saw that there was only man, and He said that it is not good that there is only man. So He cut her from man's body and closed up the wound thus caused. And gave her to man.'*

"There are no probabilities here," he exclaimed. "This is absolute certainty, absolute certainty of foul play. And the foul play had to be on the part of the *Bible*, as the *Vedas*, Hindu scripture had reached its formality on silk more than a thousand years before St. Jerome took up his pen to scratch the first line of the first *Bible* in 400AD. And there is also the fact that the original stories from which Hindu scripture was derived, including the story of creation, were originally told a thousand years before Moses was born.

"And this gives us an important conclusion that since East and West did not meet until after the time of Christ that at least a part of the Old Testament, including its most important book, the *Book of Genesis,* was written either after or in unison with the New Testament. And this includes the *Book of Isaiah*. That despite the fact that the so-called 'experts' claim that it was written five hundred years before Christ, no one really knows when it was written, for the oldest known surviving *Old Testament* postdates the writing of the New Testament by nine centuries."

"The problem we have here," he concluded, "is that everyone reads only ones own scriptures. Everyone believes that they are God's chosen few. That ones birthright is ones ticket to Heaven.

"And this is the great pitfall of faith. The inability of the believer to search out the truth. And the truth if it exists at all can only come from comparing religions. As I said in my paper on *freedom of religion,* **'So convinced are we that we are born into the right religion that we don't want to take the chance that what we believe in might not be true. The risk is far too great. For our mortality is at stake. We would prefer to end our life with a question mark?'** "

the Differences among Religions

He got up and walked across the room to the fireplace and stoked the fire a bit. He added a log or two and stoked it again. I took it that it was finally over and started to get up out of my chair but he motioned me back. He was not quite finished. Sitting down, his dark eyes roamed around the room and finally met mine, "Whereas, there are many similarities between eastern and western religions, there are also some major differences between them. For example, in the west, the Christians, the Jews, the Muslims and what have you all believe the human body and sex to be shameful and sinful. And this has its foundation in the stories of *Original Sin* and *Noah's Ark*. *Original Sin* itself is construed by most Bibliologists to have been the first sin of the flesh, and in the case of *Noah's Ark* God destroys the world because of sins of the flesh, '*And God looked upon the earth, and, behold it was corrupt; for all flesh had corrupted his way upon the earth...*'

"Whereas, in the east, the Hindus, the Buddhist, the Shintos, and what have you, all believe the human body and sex to be good and beautiful. For the *God Brahma* views these things in a very different light than does God the Father. And he pulled the book on the Hindu culture, the *Vedas*, in front of him and read, '*And he saw her in her nature. And he saw that she was good and beautiful. And she saw him in his nature. And she saw that he was good and beautiful. And together they knew that they were good and beautiful. And they praised the God Brahma that He had bestowed such a gift upon them that they could come together.*' Whereas in the case of Moses, '*If a man see her nakedness, and she see his nakedness; it is a wicked thing.*' And then we have Genesis, '*And the eyes of both of them were opened, and they knew that they were naked; and they sewed fig leaves together, and made themselves aprons.'* Actually, half of the *Old Testament* deals with the shame and the sinfulness of sex. Whereas half of the *Vedas* deals with the beauty and godliness of sex.

"And, of course, the *New Testament* confirms the teachings of the *Old Testament* as it makes Christ out to be asexual, one without sin. Actually, it goes so far as to make His very conception, His immaculate conception, free from the filthiness of the great sin of fornication.

"And one can see this difference quite clearly today in that many eastern temples have statues depicting sexual acts built into their facades, whereas western churches have only gargoyles and angels protecting their presence. And this difference in scripture has evolved into one of the most basic differences between western and eastern cultures. In the west sex is viewed as being shameful and sinful, whereas in the east it is viewed as being good and beautiful. That in the west consensual sex is a sin, actually the most prolific of all sins, whereas in the east it is not a sin at all. That better than ninety nine percent of all the sins of the western world are really not sins at all. They are simply natural functions of the human body.

"And this is why religion in the west has evolved into the business it is rather than what it is in the east, simply a guidance of ones life. For if consensual sex were not a sin most people would not need religion as there are very few murderers, rapists or thieves among us. It is the masturbator's *belief* that he could burn in hell for all time for his transgressions that drives him to the preacher's table for repentance. Whereas in the east he knows that he has not done anything wrong at all.

"The fundamental premise of Christianity is forgiveness of sin. As a matter of fact there is no other reason for Christianity. 'Repent and be saved', is the mainstay of the preacher's message. But to a good Christian who believes that sex is good and beautiful, as God intended it to be, this makes no sense as one rarely commits any other kind of 'sin'. This is why the preacher stresses the Bible's condemnation of sex, as otherwise he would have few customers." He stopped and looked at me as serious as he had ever looked at me in his life, "You and Mom are not sinful people at all, and neither is Uncle Jack or Aunt Bessie. And neither is President Carter or the Beetles. And neither am I a sinful person. Yes, there are a few bad apples, but not many, a handful one might say.

"Of course, we have the republicans, the *Christian Right*, who through the years have fought against human rights for blacks, women, gays, the handicapped and others. It took a democratic president and a democratic congress to finally overcome republican opposition to a mandate that ramps be built into all sidewalks in the United States so that my friend Tommy and the other four million like him would be able to get around. Not exactly '*Love thy Neighbor as Thyself*' is it?" he asked without pausing for an answer.

"And it is these same people who strive toward wealth and personal gain in defiance of Christ's most prolific instruction, '*sell all that thou hast and give to the poor*.' And it is these same people who think that God's gift of sex is shameful and sinful. And on top of it all they have the nerve to call themselves 'compassionate republicans,' certainly the epitome of hypocrisy. So, yes, they need Christianity, need forgiveness. But we on the *left* who lead our lives in imitation of Christ, who follow our conscience, *that part of us which is a part of Him*, have no need for Christianity, no need for forgiveness. For we are living our lives each day according to Christ's instructions.

"And then there is the fact that the *God Brahma* reveres all life both animal and human. Whereas, in the *Old Testament*, the Christian God requires man to kill helpless animals, '*Every moving thing that liveth shall be meat for you.*' The *God Brahma*, on the other hand, in the *Vedas*, requires man to honor all life. '*That all of nature, that all of the wild and all of the near belongs to*

Brahma and man shall have no offense to what is God's.' The reason why most of the people of India are vegetarians even today"

Then he paused for a minute or two as if lost in deep thought, as if he had somehow gotten lost in the wilderness, as if he were searching for where he was. He glanced over at the fireplace, almost as if to assure himself that the flames were listening, that none of them had lost their train of thought. Then he started up again. This time back on the path that he had slipped from.

the three parts of Christ,

"But, nevertheless this is not the subject at hand. The subject is *Christ*. The three parts of *Christ*. Not the three persons in God.

"The three parts of *Christ*, His *person*, His *purpose*, and His *principles*. That is what we have for discussion, today. So let us look at them.

"As for His *person*, the multitude accepts whatever the preachers, the picture books and Hollywood place before them. A picture of a man as attractive as one can look and still project the image of a sexless human being.

"And as for His *purpose?* If one listens to the preacher, '*Christ came to earth to die for the sins of mankind.*' But for those few of us who have an IQ above the freezing point this makes little sense as someday either in hell or in purgatory and possibly while still on earth we are going to suffer for our sins. No one else is going to suffer and die for them. As a matter of fact, no God, by His very nature, who comes to earth in the form of a man can die for them. For the true pain of death is not the physical pain, but it is the great emotional pain of death, the great anguish of not knowing if this is the end, that this is goodbye forever to ones loved ones, that never again will one see them?

"The great horror of death is that life ends in a question mark? The physical pain of death is immaterial as compared to this great agony of death. And even in that respect Christ suffered only a few hours whereas the great majority of us will suffer many months before death. We know by comparison that Mohammed suffered the excruciating pain of a brain tumor for more than a year before he died, often thrashing about on the ground kicking his feet and grasping his head with his eyes bulging out of their sockets for hours on end. But unlike Mohammed and the rest of us Christ, being God, never experienced the true torment of death, for He as God knew that for Him it wasn't the end. He knew that His dying on the cross was just a charade. For He knew that He was not leaving his loved ones behind. For He knew that He was going to His Father's house. For He was God. And this was true of all of His predecessors."

"All of His predecessors?" I repeated his statement in a question.

"Yes, for example, Zagerus in Minoan or Greek culture long before Abraham's time was the first god who *'came to earth to die for the sins of mankind.'* And he was closely followed by the god Tammus in Sumeric culture who also *'came to earth to die for the sins of mankind.'* And then in Syrian culture we have the god Adonis who *'came to earth to die for the sins of mankind.'* And Adonis was a Canaanite god, one that Abraham, the first prophet of the *Old Testament*, grew up under. And then in nearby Turkey a couple of hundred years later one has the god Attis who also *'came to earth to die for the sins of mankind.'* And even as late as five hundred years before Christ, one has the god Balder in Scandinavian culture who also *'came to earth to die for the sins of mankind.'* And there were many others. So it is only natural that when Christ came along He too would *'come to earth to die for the sins of mankind.'* For this concept was the mainstay of religion in the Western Hemisphere long before Abraham was born. And one can see this quite clearly that throughout history no god has ever come to earth to die for the sins of mankind in all of the Eastern Hemisphere.

"And in that the idea originated with the Greeks who were the first to trade with the Egyptians tells us that the ideology was created in order to avoid the risk of hell. For the Egyptians believed that it is the weight of good versus evil in ones life and not repentance of sin that determines ones place in heaven or hell in the afterlife. So in this case, in determining what would be the mainstay of Christianity, the prophets chose Greek rather than Egyptian ideology. They chose an ideology that was designed to allow one to lead as evil a life as one wanted to and still go to heaven through the loophole of repentance.

"And the record of these ancient gods has survived in stone today. Even the first one, Zagerus, the Greek god, whose claim that he had come to earth to die for the sins of mankind is inscribed on a Minoan tablet dated 2200BC, an archive that is held by the British National Museum in London today.

"Yet we know as a matter of fact that none of these Gods including Christ died for the sins of mankind. For one knows that the only way God can die is to forfeit His eternity. And we know that Christ is still with us today.

"Nevertheless, in the west this ideology had to be the mainstay of all new religions as they evolved through the years, less they could never compete with existing religions. It was necessary to entice the believer to drop his pence in the preacher's box, a good deal for only a few dollars, *'I am going to make it possible that you will never have to pay for your sins no matter how evil you are. All you need do is repent and drop your pence into my basket.'* And despite the fact that Christ tells us quite explicitly in the New Testament that repenting for ones sins alone is not going to get one into heaven, we take the preacher's word for it like all the fools before us and accept this as Christ's sole requirement. But Christ outlines quite explicitly in the *New Testament* precisely what we must do to be saved. And this brings us back to the point at hand.

"And the point is," he hesitated and then added, "the point is, my bike. Why I sold my bike?" and then he hesitated again, "I sold my bike because I believed in His *principles,* because I was following Christ's *principles,* the third part of *Christ*. Actually the most important part of *Christ* for if one is to define the word 'religion', it means most precisely, 'God's way of guiding one in the present life to achieve the afterlife.'

"Why among all Christians, was I the only one to '*sell all that thou hast, and give to the poor*?' Except, perhaps, Mother Theresa. This is the answer I need?" And he looked up at me as if I had what he wanted right on the tip of my tongue. But I remained silent.

And, then, lowering his voice, he said, "I know why. At least, I think I know why. Do you know why?"

And, again, I was silent, holding back in anticipation of what he was about to say.

"Well," he went on, "I have put a lot of thought into this one, and there is only one possible answer. At least I think there is only one possible answer.

"The words '*sell all that thou hast, and give to the poor*' and most of the other quotations that permeate the *New Testament,* that we talked about that day when I sold my bike, comprise *Christ's principles*. As a matter of fact, they are the very heart of His *principles*. His overwhelming instruction in His testimony on how one should live ones life. And these *principles* can be summed up in a half dozen words, '*Love thy neighbor as thyself*.' And this message He gave not only once, but a thousand times, in as many different ways as is possible, so that if one did not understand His instruction in some words, that one could clearly understand it in others.

"And, what's more, these are the very same *principles* that dominate Hinduism." and drawing forth the book on the *Vedas,* he continued, "in the *Vedas, Hindu scripture,* is the word of the *God Brahma, 'Care only for others less I will not care of you. And I mean only for others. For I am the others. This is all I want of you. For you will not see the brightness that lies beyond the shadow of doom unless you care for others. Unless you care for me.'* Dictating a redistribution of wealth society. And this principle, of the Hindu God, which originated in India, is probably best carried out by the basic practices of the Taoist in China, today. And Confucius, in all his wisdom, too, accepted the philosophy of the Hindu God *Brahma* for his followers in his teaching, *'he who profits most in the end is he who has contributed most to others.'*

"And Buddha, too, gave this very same message to his people. *'When all is done there are only two measurements of life. Oneself and others. The first will lead to treasures in this book of fools. In this book of this life. The other will lead to treasures in the true book. The vast book of eternity.'"*

He paused as if he was trying to put some words together. And then he started up again.

"What *Christ* is saying is this. 'So you say you believe in my *person?* That you believe that I was the *person* who actually performed the miracles that the holy scripture speaks of? So you say you believe in my *purpose?* That you believe that I am the *Son of God,* that *God the Father* promised to send to earth to rid the world of *Original Sin?*'"

And what he had to say then, for lack of a better phrase, knocked the socks right off of my feet, "'Now I require only one more thing of you. I want you to accept my *principles.* I want you to live your life according to my instructions. I want you to prove your *belief.* I want you to put your money where your mouth is!'"

And the little man went on, "Why, then, does the preacher tell his congregation that <u>all</u> that is necessary is that one believe in

Christ? Accept Christ as the promised Redeemer? That <u>all</u> one need do is be born again of water and spirit? That <u>all</u> one need do is repent? That one can accept His *person* and His *purpose* and yet ignore Christ's *principles*?

"And the reason is this. The preacher would have no congregation, no followers. He would have no livelihood. For these are words that the typical believer, his customer, does not want to hear. For, for one to ask that one give up ones wealth is too much. Just like right now, you certainly don't want to hear it. One doesn't even want to think about it.

"So the preacher continues to ignore *Christ's principles*. He continues to lie to his prospective customer about what *Christ's* testimony demands of us. He tells him that *Christ* didn't really mean these things that He said so many times in the gospels. That Christ didn't really know what He was talking about when He said these things. That Christ was suffering from a hangover on the days He had said these things. He tells his customer that all he need do is believe. That God made us to be sinful and all one need do is repent. He makes a joke of Christ's most sacred testimony. The preacher makes a fool of Jesus, of His most sacred testimony. He herds his customers toward the *right* where in total defiance of what Christ had to say, they can gather a greater share of God's wealth for themselves. And being the hypocrite that he is, he does this so that he too will get his share."

the greatest philosophical difference,

"And this tells us quite conclusively that a good Christian, that is one who follows the Christian doctrine of sheer belief and repentance, can never reach the Hindu, Muslim, Jewish or Buddhist heavens as he is following the wrong rules. And as I will prove conclusively in what I have yet to say that he will likewise never reach the *Kingdom of Heaven* as promised by Christ in the gospels as he is again following the wrong rules. The Christian reward is limited solely to the *New Jerusalem* as foretold in the *Book of Revelations*.

"All Christian preachers regardless of denomination today preach that the weight of good versus evil in ones life has nothing to do with salvation. That the only thing that counts is that one believe in ones Savior and be in a state of repentance at the time of death. That Hitler and Mother Theresa had an equal chance at salvation. Actually, Hitler having had the greater chance as he had loads of time to plan the circumstances of his death whereas Mother Theresa died suddenly of a heart attack.

"And this points to the greatest philosophical difference between Christianity and all other religions of the world. For in the east Hitler would have had no chance whatsoever as it is the *cumulation of good versus evil in ones lifetime* that counts, that determines ones place in the next life," he raised his voice a notch, "it is a matter of fair and equal justice. As a matter fact, both the Jews and Muslims of the western world share this very same philosophy of their eastern counterparts, that it is the weight of good versus evil that counts toward ones salvation.

"So Hitler was lucky in that of all the religions of the world he was born into Christianity. For had he been born into any other religion we know that he would be in hell today. But, because he was a Christian one can speak with a high degree of certainty that he is in heaven today. For the evil he did in his life does not count. All that counts is that he died in a state of repentance.

"And the bottom line here is that in the Jewish, Muslim, Buddhist, Hindu, Shinto worlds one is dealing with a good and just God whereas in the Christian world one is not dealing with a good and just God. As a matter of fact, in Christianity, one is ignoring what his God has to say and prefers to pay the preacher for his salvation.

A God for Lions

"Every Hindu and Buddhist and Shinto priest takes a vow of poverty. Ironically, they are the only priests in the world that follow Christ's most fundamental command, '*give up all thou hast and come follow me.*' They live their lives in imitation of the God *Brahma*. Even the Dalai Lama lives under austere conditions.

"Whereas on our side of the world rather than living their lives in imitation of Christ, preachers lead their lives in imitation of those Pharisees that Christ threw out of His Father's Temple. The pope, himself, reigns as a king and lives in luxurious surroundings and his cardinals stay at five-hundred-dollar-a-night hotels when they visit Rome. And the immense wealth of American evangelists with their limousines and grand estates make the pope look like a pauper. There is no priest or preacher in all of Christianity who heeds Christ's most prolific testimony in the *New Testament*, '*sell all that thou hast and give to the poor.*' After all, the Christian preacher is in it for the bucks. And this gives us another major difference between the two. In the east religion is solely the guidance of the spiritual life, whereas in the west it is a multi-billion dollar business that preys for the most part on the weakness and ignorance of men. In the west religion is a business. The churches are in the business of a form of psychiatry in that they treat their patients with therapy, brain conditioning. They condition their patients' brains with the promise of miracles and an afterlife for those who are too weak to accept the will of their God.

"Christ's message is emphatically clear. In fact, there is no message in the entire *Bible* that is more explicit or more voluminous," and he opened his copy of the *New Testament* and fanning through its pages he raised his voice three octaves and spoke quite decisively, pausing after each word as to make his point, "These pages are covered with 'pink' and 'yellow' and 'pink' and 'yellow' are the colors of His *principles*. *'Sell all that thou hast and give to the poor'. 'Love thy neighbor as thyself.'* **And although one would want to believe otherwise, there is no substitute for what Christ demands of us!**

"So, today, the typical Christian does not follow His *principles*. He ignores Christ's message and heeds only His Father's instruction as given to Joshua, *'take from them for thyself all that they have, their land, their vessels of bronze, of silver, and of gold.'*

"Like the Pharisees and the hypocrites *Christ* talks so strongly about so often in His testimony, the great lion's share of Christians today, who sing and dance their praises, are hypocrites. So strongly did *Christ* feel about hypocrisy, that He isolated his condemnation of it from the rest of His ministry. For in a fit of rage He *'upturned their money tables and cast them out of His Father's temple.'*

"And the reason He did this is quite obvious. For *Christ* foresaw that most men would not accept His *principles*. He knew that it is easy to believe, whereas it is quite another thing to do, to make the sacrifice, to do what He instructed. He knew that His church would become a haven for *Pharisees*. For *hypocrites*.

"And Christ could not have been more right. For, today, most Christians, those who call themselves Christians, don't feel His *principles* apply to them. Like the *Pharisees* in the temple, they are clustered together on the *far right* in their churches and their chapels. And when they walk away from their churches and their chapels they go out of their way to avoid the poor and homeless in the street. They continue to ignore those pages of the *New Testament* that are soaked with 'pink' and 'yellow'. Where they continue to ignore His *principles*. Where they actually take up arms in the political arena on the *far right* against a redistribution of wealth society. Christians? Hypocrites? Pharisees? Call them what one may, those that call themselves 'Christians' wage a bitter war against the will of Christ. Not a one of them lives in imitation of Christ.

"And as *Christ* said," he reached into his hip pocket for another one of those 'nails', "'*For I say unto you, That except your righteousness shall exceed the righteousness of the Pharisees, ye shall in no case enter into the Kingdom of Heaven.*' And the *God 'Brahma* agrees with him. And he quickly pulled the book on the *Vedas* in front of him and read, '*there is no greater fool than this hypocrite, who fools himself that he is unto the path of my house, whereas he is onto the path of no return.*'"

And he went on, "Not only did *Christ* and *Brahma* emphasize the evilness of the hypocrite, so did Mohammed. For Mohammed, too, separated his condemnation of the hypocrite from all his other teachings. So much so that the word 'HYPOCRITE' is capitalized throughout his *Koran*" and he pulled the Muslim '*Bible*' in front of him, "For Mohammed knew, too, that most of his followers would be hypocrites. Where they would call themselves Muslims, but not feel that God's *principles* apply to them.

"And like *Christ* and *Brahma*, before him, Mohammed set forth hypocrisy as an unforgivable way of life. And he read from the *Koran*, '*By no means will God ever forgive them. These HYPOCRITES. For God hath no guidance for these perverse people.*'

"And like the Christians, the Hindus, and the Buddhist and every other major religion of the world, the Muslim God has the very same *principles* as do all the others. And he read this time from the *Koran*. "'*give all that thou hast to thy neighbor. For I am your neighbor. If the wealth ye have gained, and merchandise which ye fear may be unsold, and dwellings wherein ye delight, be dearer to you than God, dearer to you than your neighbor, then God too will be dearer to others. And you will not reside with Him in His house this day, or for all time!* 'It is as if the *Universal God* has weaseled His message, His *principles* into all of the world's scripture. In fact, the reason I sold my bike is the only message of God that is uniform among all of the scriptures of the world, every last one of them. It is as if it is the only message that truly came from God, Himself. *'Love thy neighbor as thyself.'* It is as if the *Universal God* wanted to give everyone an equal chance no matter where or to whom they are born. That the rest of the scriptures were filled in by the prophets to serve their particular whims and desires."

And I finally stopped him, "Johnny, when you read the New Testament you have to sort out those things that are really important from what is obviously the mumbo-jumbo that the evangelists added from time to time. And I reached over and pulled forward his book, the King James version of the Bible, and flipped a few pages to Corinthians 6.9 and read, *"'Be not deceived: neither fornicators, nor idolaters, nor adulterers, nor effeminate, nor abusers of themselves with mankind, nor thieves, nor covetous, nor drunkards, nor revilers, nor extortioners, shall inherit the Kingdom of God.'* This is among the two or three most important things that Christ ever said. It is why the preacher so often refers to it to condemn the gays. Christ explicitly details who cannot be saved and it is clear that *those who drive for wealth* are not among them!" I said it with an exclamation point at the end as to make the point absolutely clear.

At first he shot me a glance of total defeat and anguish but it was obviously just a front for what was behind it. He got up and strolled over to the bookcase and returned with a half-dozen books, and then with a half-dozen more.

"I thought that you would bring that up," he said, "So like Noah, I have planned ahead."

"Like Noah?" I questioned.

"Yes," he answered, "it wasn't raining when Noah started to build the Ark and now that it has started to rain I have my boat."

I noticed that all of the books were various versions of the Bible, the Catholic Bible, the Eastern Version, the New Jerusalem Bible, the English Version and a half dozen or so of others. "In different parts of the world," he started, "each of these has its privilege to reign as king. The Catholic Bible, for example, is

A God for Lions

prevalent in Latin America, and in Eastern Europe the Eastern Version is prevalent, and in England the New English Bible is prevalent, and so forth. And in America the King James Version is prevalent." He pulled forward the Catholic Bible and read, *"Be not deceived: neither fornicators, nor idolaters, nor adulterers, nor boy prostitutes, nor abuses of themselves, nor thieves, nor covetous, nor drunkards, nor slanderers, <u>nor the greedy</u> shall inherit the Kingdom of God."* He had in anticipation of the question at hand underlined the words, *'<u>nor the greedy</u>'.* "Although the preacher will try to convince one otherwise, that the Bible is based on original manuscripts, he is lying, as no original manuscripts have survived. Yes, there exists some scraps from the second century and a few shreds of letters written by a sixth century pope that refer to some stories told in the New Testament, but there is nothing of the original scriptures themselves that has survived. The preacher tells one this because he knows that there is no way that one can check out his source, as there is no source." He then pulled forward another book, *'The British Museum - Direct Testament Translations'* and he started, "The source of all modern New Testaments is these few scraps that have survived and what is a 4th century New Testament held by the British Museum in London, the oldest known surviving substantial text. So let's see what it has to say about this," and he read, *"'Be not deceived: neither fornicators, nor idolaters, nor adulterers, nor sexually immoral, nor self indulgers, nor thieves, nor covetous, nor drunkards, nor slanderers, nor revilers, <u>nor those who lust for things of this world</u>, nor extortioners shall inherit the Kingdom of God.'"* He paused as to emphasize his next point. "Every single one of these versions," and he ran his finger down the side of those books he had stacked up along side of him, "and all the other hundreds of versions that are in public libraries today have this reference to *'<u>those who greed for more</u>'.* Yes, sometimes they use the words 'grabbers', or 'greedy', or *'lust for material wealth'*, but they all have it. These words, as you say, are some of the most important words of Christ."

I held my breath hoping that he would not capitalize on the very obvious but he went for it anyway. "So why do you suppose that it was left out of the King James Version?"

I decided not to answer him.

"Men of greed left it out. And what's more they did it intentionally. For they intended that the King James Bible be the underlying mainstay of our society, even our constitution was based on it. After all, accumulation of vast wealth is the great American dream, the great republican dream. I am growing up in a Christian society, one driven by greed."

I decided to ignore him.

"I am growing up in a society that is driven by greed," he repeated himself.

"Yes, I heard you the first time," I told him. And sheer silence enveloped the room as if threatening to never go away.

And he finally broke the silence, "I should be growing up in a society that is driven by compassion. Not only compassion for those that we can see about us, but compassion for many that we cannot see. There are more than one hundred million children in the world today who because of poverty, starvation and disease will never see their sixteenth birthday. One hundred million children who will never have the opportunity to take a chance, and have on their arm, the homeliest girl at the dance!"

"So he wins another one," I thought, and he was not quite, yet, finished, "So not only does the preacher quote only those things that supports whatever he wants his customer to believe, and disregards these other things that his Bible has to say, but his forerunners, his forefathers who put his book together for him, intentionally misrepresented what Christ had to say. This thing which you say is among Christ's most important testimony."

I stopped him again, "The preacher doesn't quote things out of context at all. He tells things as they are."

He gave me one of those unbelievable looks again, "You just told me that it is the preacher who quotes this passage because it includes Christ's most important condemnation of the gays. If you take the time to read the New Testament you will find that Christ never said this at all. This is clearly Paul's testimony in his letter to the Corinthians. Christ had nothing to do with it. As a matter of fact Christ, in all of His ministry, in all of the gospels, never once condemns the gays. So not only does the preacher misrepresent those things said by men as having been said by Christ, he completely ignores what Christ actually had to say, the central message of His ministry, the reasons I sold my bike, because it would be bad for business."

I held my breath for more. And he gave me more, "So these things I have told you of, these reasons why I sold my bike, are not just some 'mumbo jumbo' that the evangelists added from time to time as the preacher would want one to believe they are. They are in fact the word of Jesus Christ, His most solemn message on how we are to live our lives. So I am right, I not only had a right to have sold my bike, it was my sacred duty to have sold it!

"And if one takes the time to read them modern Bibles are loaded with this sort of thing. Every single eighteenth century Bible without exception quotes the tenth commandment as, *'Thou shalt not covet or desire to take from thy neighbor his ... slaves ...'*. It is quite clear that Moses intent was to protect the right of one man to enslave another. Yet, in the twentieth century the preacher has changed many versions of his Bible, including the King James Version, to read 'servants' or 'employees', as the word 'slaves' is no longer acceptable to his customers. The word 'slaves' is no longer good for his business."

He paused a moment as to be certain that I had absorbed all that he had said and finished, "So what this tells us is that men in modern times are changing things in the Bible as they go along to satisfy their own whims and desires or to what would be good for business. One can only imagine the massive changes that other men under far less scrutiny through the ages have made. That the preacher tells his customers that as long as they cast their dollars into his box that all they need do is to believe and repent. He tells them that they can ignore that Christ ever said these things, these reasons why I sold my bike. Christ's overwhelming instruction of how one is to lead ones life. And he does this so that he too will get his share. And as I said before, he makes a fool of Jesus in His most sacred testimony."

"So like the Christian hypocrites, today, the Muslim hypocrites, too, and all the other hypocrites of the world, go about professing their so called high morality and belief and faith and live in luxury. Where they, too, remain clustered on the *far right* away from the will of Christ.

And he glanced up toward the ceiling. His eyes seemed to be searching for something there. Although it was midwinter I started to look for a fly and I saw none. And he quickly interrupted my thought, "Why do we think He is up there? Jesus is obviously not up there. For He is somewhere else. For the bigot He is the little girl in the attic, the little black child in the ghetto, the strange little boy in the playground, the nun who aspires to be a priest. For the hypocritical Christian on the *right* He is the welfare mother, He is the beggar, He is the Iraqi child deprived of medicine, He is the imprisoned drug addict, He is the beggar in the street!"

He looked up at me as if to gather my reaction to what he had said. Then he carefully closed the book that he had open before him and stacked it there neatly with the others in the pile. Then getting up, he gave me a whimsical smile and crossed the room. He stoked the fire a bit and added another log. Then he went quietly up the stairs. I could hear him putting on his jacket and boots, and I heard the door open and close, as he went out into the snow.

these are the times that try men's souls

It was Saturday morning, the one morning that I could sleep late. So it was nine o'clock before I came down into the kitchen to partake of whatever Audrey had whipped up for breakfast.

At my place at the table was the folded up newspaper and as I picked it up, she asked, "Did you get a good night's sleep?"

"Certainly," I replied, and I gave her one of those 'slept like a baby' lines.

"Good," she said, "You're going to need it?"

"What do you mean?" I asked. "What is he up to now?"

"He is searching for his soul," she replied. "He's been up since six o'clock. He's down in the family room with the usual stack of books around him."

"His what?" I exclaimed more than asked.

"His soul," she replied, "he's not sure he has one. Are you sure you have one?"

"Of course I have one," I shot back, quite frustrated that she would ask me such a ridiculous question so early in the morning. And I quickly corrected my thought, so 'late' in the morning.

And as I thought of the little man downstairs in the family room I mumbled to myself, "This should be an easy one for a change. I will handle this one in a single swoop." And, once I had finished all of the edibles, I poured myself a second cup of coffee and with an unprecedented air of confidence I headed down the stairs. Yes, to Audrey and all the others this would seem to be an insurmountable challenge. But to me it was just another day on the job.

And there he was, just as Audrey had described him hunched over with his dark hair and dark eyes with at least a dozen books scattered on the table around him. There were a couple by Albert Einstein who I had come to know was his patron saint. One on existentialism, one on Buddhism, another on how the brain works, and still another on how medicine works. And there was one that had nothing to do with the others, an industrial magazine of some sort, "The Inner Workings of the Modern Chemical Plant." And I don't recall any of the subjects of the others. Just that they were there. Stacked up along side one another. A scene that I had become accustomed to for most of my fatherly life.

I wondered what the rules of the local library were that allowed a kid to take out so many books at a single time. That had enabled this little fellow of eleven to have already read more books than an average man reads in eleven lifetimes.

The room was cold, and I walked over to the fireplace and stoked the fire and added a couple of logs. He, obviously, was so engulfed in his reading that he hadn't noticed the cold. In fact, he hadn't even noticed me as when I walked over to where he was, he looked up with a sudden start.

I thought I wouldn't give him a chance. "It might give him the edge," I thought, and from my past experiences with him I knew I couldn't afford to give him the edge. So I led with the answer,

"You believe in Jesus. Don't you?"

"Sure, sometimes it's a struggle. But, in that I am a Christian, yes," he answered.

"Then that is all you need," I proclaimed,

"You asked me if I believed in Jesus," he replied, "That doesn't give me any answers. What I need are the facts, not beliefs. If I am going to plan my life, I have to have the facts. I must know. I must know within a shadow of a doubt that I have a soul. I just can't guess at it. Maybe other people are satisfied at guessing at it. But, to me, it is far too important. I must know."

"You must know?" I exclaimed, "And just how do you intend to find out?"

"I'm not absolutely sure yet," he answered, "For starters, at least I know where it is. At least, I think I know where it is."

"You know where it is?" I asked somewhat surprised.

"Sure, right here," pointing to his temple, "Our ability to know right from wrong is our direct link to God. Our soul is a part of God. So if one has a soul, it must be here," and he, again, pointed to his temple.

"How do you know that it is not here?" I asked, pointing to my heart.

"Because, what is here," he pointed to his temple, "controls what is here," he pointed to his heart. And he said this with great conviction.

He undoubtedly had gotten himself ready for my onslaught. Like a spider in his lair he now had me in his web and it was too late for me to go back. I could only wait for the inevitable. But I decided to try anyway. "So if you know where it is. You know you have a soul. You know right from wrong." And I thought to myself, "why in all of my life I had never thought of it in this way. Perhaps it was because I never thought it was important enough to think about."

"I said I 'think' I know where it is," he corrected me, "but, I want to know more than just that. I want to be certain that I have a soul. Plus, I want to know where the mind leaves off and where the soul begins, that *part of me which is a part of Him.*"

"What do you mean that *part of you which is a part of Him?*" I asked.

"My soul. My soul, like all souls, is immortal. Only God could be immortal. As one knows, all living life as we know it on the planet eventually dies. So, if my soul is immortal, then it must be a part of God. A part of Him." he replied.

"More specifically," he added. "I want to know where the 'function' of the mind leaves off and the 'function' of the soul begins."

"You're attempting the impossible," I answered, "It can't be done. You're wasting your time."

"Pull up a chair," he directed, and he added with an air of solid instruction, pausing after each phrase, "I will tell you of the body... and of the mind... and of the soul."

And as I sat down he pulled forward the industrial magazine, the one that I had wondered how it had ever gotten into the stack to begin with. He opened it to its center page spread. And there was a picture of a large chemical plant. It reminded me of the giant sprawling Dupont plant that I would pass in Wilmington whenever I would take the train to New York.

And setting it aside for the moment he began, "One of the great problems with the common man today is that he never wants to stop at first base. Somehow he goes past it and tries to score. In this case, one is talking of the function of the body, and of the function of the mind, and, yes, the very function of the soul. Most people go through life without even bothering to learn how the body works. And almost none of them have any idea how the mind works, let alone how the soul works.

"We live in a world of specialization," he went on, "We assume that except for that specialized function for which we, ourselves, are specifically responsible, that everything else is the responsibility of some other specialist. It is none of our business. In this case, the function of the body is the responsibility of the doctor, and the function of the mind is the responsibility of the psychiatrist or the psychologist, and the function of the soul is the responsibility of the preacher. It is none of our business.

"Common sense tells one that there can only be one God for there could have been only one beginning. So one would ask, why the great tycoons, the great businessmen, the great politicians, all the great men and women through the ages, the most prominent men and women through the years, have mostly died believing in the very same religion that they were born into? Why the Kennedys have all died as Catholics? Why the Rockefellers have all died as Protestants? Why all the sultans of

Arabia have all died as Muslims? Why all the princes of India have all died as Hindus? Why all the emperors of China have all died as Taoist?

"And the answer is quite obvious. Because they all felt that it was none of their business. It just wasn't that important. It was the business of the specialist. It was the business of the preacher. It was the business of the particular scripture they were born into. It was none of their business.

"But I have decided to make it my business. To know my destiny, to know my body, to know my mind and, most important of all, to know my soul."

He paused for a few minutes as if collecting his thoughts about what he was about to say. Or, perhaps, to give greater emphasis to what he had just said. And then he started again. Started toward me who struggled desperately in his web.

"You told me that because I believed in Jesus I must know I have a soul. That to believe in Jesus is the beginning and the end of it all. But you are wrong, terribly wrong," And he reached into the stack of books and pulled out one that I hadn't noticed before. One that had nothing at all to do with the subject we were caught up in, *Confessions of the Criminal Mind*.

"As you know, my friend Danny is a *born again Christian*. His parents tell him that when he gets to be a teenager he must, on his own volition, accept *Christ*. Accept as fact that *Christ* came to earth to rid the world of *Original Sin*, and died for the sins of mankind. And then, and only then, will he go to heaven.

"So I asked Danny, 'What happens if something happens to you now? What if someone was to blow up the school and kill us all? What happens to us then?'

"And he told me that we would all go to heaven. He said that Jesus said, '*Blessed are the little children for theirs is the Kingdom of Heaven.*' And he told me that Jesus said this not once, but several times, in the *New Testament*. So I checked him out, and he is right. Jesus said it several times. And it is exactly what Christ said, and there is absolutely no doubt about it. According to Christ's very explicit testimony we would all go to heaven.

"And we all know that a fundamental message of Christianity is '*that many are called, but few are chosen*'. Few means 'few'. Normally one thinks of three out of a hundred. But it can be more. Perhaps, as much as ten out of a hundred. One in ten. If one goes to twenty, then one is definitely talking about 'some', not 'few'. So, let's go with that, one in ten.

"So the criminal who blows up the school guarantees that all the children go to heaven. All the children, not three in a hundred, not one in twenty, not even one in ten, but all the children. Yes, perhaps, sacrificing himself, like *Christ* on the cross, he sacrifices himself for the sake of others. These children, that if they were to attain adulthood, would have a scant chance at eternal happiness."

"Why was he doing this to me?" I thought, "Why does he make me suffer so? Why doesn't he get it over fast, instead of so heartlessly playing with me in his web?"

"And this kind of thing happens," he went on. "Here," and he flipped through a few pages of the book, this book on *Confessions of the Criminal Mind*, and read, "'*Their mother and I were to be divorced. I knew that she was not a churchgoer and that they would cease to go to church, that in the end they would be destined for eternal damnation. So I killed them, all five of them. And now I am at peace with myself. For I now know they are in heaven.*'*"

*reprinted from the public record of the confession of John List, 1980

"According to Christian doctrine," the little man went on, "this was a good man. A holy man. One who was so virtuous, that he sacrificed not only his life on this earth, but possibly his eternal life. So great was his love for his children that he would do this."

"This is not the way it's supposed to work," I thought to myself. Once again he had me cornered. I knew it was only a matter of time. And just a hair beyond his grasp, I struggled uselessly.

And, knowing that he had me where he wanted me, he let up a bit, "We 'think' we know that when the man blows up the school that all the children have gone to heaven. But, on the other hand, we are outraged by the horrific action because we 'don't' know that the children have gone to heaven," he exclaimed, "We only 'think' we know. And that's not good enough for us. So we try him in court and send him to death row. And we send the preacher into death row to talk to him, to save him so to speak. And he has a long time to sort things out, this man we call a criminal. And he, too, goes to heaven, to live happily ever after with the children, these children who he had murdered in cold blood.

"So when we finally put him in the electric chair and pull the lever, all the mothers and fathers of the children who had been killed feel vengeance in their hearts. This, despite the fact that the preacher assures them that their children are in heaven. But, in reality, they haven't gotten their revenge at all. For according to their beliefs, their most sacred beliefs, they have sent him to heaven, to paradise for all eternity. They have rewarded him so to speak. They have rewarded him for having killed their children. Yet, they 'think' they have had their revenge because they don't really believe.

"**This is the real world**," he exclaimed, as if he was holding every card in the deck, "**When all is said and done, we don't really believe. And we don't really believe, because we only 'think' we know.**"

"And this is seen even more clearly in the Christian belief in miracles. One might ask, 'Why, of all the religions of the world only the Christian believes in miracles?' And the answer is in the bucks, men's greed. It is a part of the deal. Not only does one get an afterlife for paying the preacher, one also gets a bonus in this life. If the Christian really believed in Christ then there would be no point to miracles. For if one is to define a miracle it is *'a supernatural happening that reverses the will of God.'* When one prays for a cure for terminal cancer, for example, one is praying for preference over all other people who are suffering from the disease, that God would favor some of his children over others. And it makes no sense that a good Christian should plead for his life if he 'knows' that he is about to join Christ for all time? And the reason he pleads for his life is because he only 'thinks' he knows. **The Christian does not really believe in his God and this is a matter of fact and he proves it as fact in his actions."**

My mind was exhausted. "Perhaps," I thought, "that it was finally time to bring in one of those experts, one of those specialists, one of those psychologists to help this little fellow of mine who had strayed off the beaten track. But, no, for if I did that I would be making his point. That I didn't think it was my business. That it was the business of the specialist that handles this sort of thing." So, I decided to stay in the ring myself.

And he continued, "So, although this man, this man *John List*, did something that, according to the *Bible*, was good, was virtuous. That he had saved his children from damnation. And his act could not have been more virtuous, for another part of the *Bible* says *'thou shalt not kill.'* That to kill another person one would risk ones soul. So this man John List was so virtuous that he was willing to forfeit not only his life but possibly his eternity for those he loved. Yet, we, a Christian society, every single one of us, condemned him, because we knew he had done something wrong. How do you suppose we knew this?" he asked.

I just sat there. I didn't know what to say. The man had obviously made the ultimate sacrifice of having giving up not only his life, but possibly his very soul for those he loved. Even *Christ* did not love us enough to risk His eternity. So I decided to wait for more.

And he had more, "Because of this," he answered without hesitation, pointing to his temple and lowering his voice almost in reverence, "*this part of every single one of us, which is a part of Him.* That part of us which has always, throughout the history of mankind, enabled us to do what is right, that has consistently, through the years, overridden what is written in the book. Any book," he again pointed to his temple, "This which overrides what is written when what is written is wrong. To override what is said when what is said is wrong. Wrong for him. Wrong for her. Wrong for humanity."

I began to shudder on the edge of his web.

"This man," and he held up this book of *Confessions of the Criminal Mind*, "really believed. And we know that there is great danger when one really believes. When one confuses *belief* with *reality*. One must never forget that religion is only a guide to ones life. It is at the very best a guess at the truth. One must never let oneself get carried away with it. It is only *belief*. It is not the truth. It is not *reality*. The great danger is when one begins to think that it is *reality*. Begins to believe that it is the truth.

"So what all this means is that just because I 'believe' in Christ does not necessarily mean that there is a soul. For belief can never lead one to the truth. The truth can only come from knowledge. It has nothing to do with belief. So to 'think' I know is not good enough for me. For I must know beyond any shadow of a doubt." And he spelled out the first four letters of each word, "<u>T H E O</u> LOGY is <u>T H E O</u> RY. Theology, that which were refer to as the study of religion, is in reality the study of various ancient theories on how we all came about. It is the study of various ancient guesses on how we all came about."

Lucien Gregoire

these are the times that try men's minds

And he went on, "So, I had to skip a couple of squares here and touch on the soul. But to really understand the function of the soul one must first understand the function of the mind. One must first understand how the mind functions? Just what determines how one thinks?"

Finally, I thought that I had a chance to score at least a few points. I would give him the answer he is looking for. And I replied, "The brain does all the thinking for you. It controls the nervous system that runs throughout the body and controls all of the body's senses, its movements and what have you. That's it in a nutshell. I'm surprised, with all the books you've read, that you don't know that."

"Wrong," he replied, "the brain does not determine how one thinks. It is something else that does our thinking for us."

And he paused and looked up at me as to give me a chance to correct myself. But, knowing that I was right, I thought I would let him go ahead and paint himself into a corner.

And he pulled forward the picture of the huge chemical plant. The one that reminded me of that one in Wilmington that I would pass each time that I took the train to New York. A number of large tanks, and miles and miles of piping and tubing running here, and there, and everywhere.

"This is a picture of the human brain," he said quite decisively, "Most people think the brain is what does our thinking for us. But they are wrong. Very wrong." He said it as if he were a world authority on the subject.

I had never before thought that there could be anything wrong with reading so many books. For it is common knowledge that it is the brain that determines how one thinks. And I said to him, in as kind a way as I could muster, "Johnny, perhaps, you should lay off the books for awhile. Perhaps, you've been reading too many books."

"Conversely," he shot back, "perhaps, someone else has not been reading enough books."

And without hesitating, "The brain does not determine how one thinks. The brain is simply a housing of what does our thinking for us. And like this great chemical plant it has its think tanks and its extensions, its piping and tubing, which reach the most remote parts of the body. This thing we call 'the nervous system'."

Then he reached for a rather large book. A picture book. It was entitled 'The Human Brain'. And he opened the book to what was a diagram of the human brain and placed it right next to the picture of the chemical plant.

Almost immediately, I noticed what he was getting at. There was great similarity between the two pictures. The chemical plant had two rows of four giant tanks each running parallel to each other. The brain, correspondingly, was split down the middle into two sections and each section was divided into four subsections.

And he started his presentation, "The brain is divided down the middle into two halves, technically known as 'hemispheres'. Aside from controlling the motions of the opposite side of the body, the overall function of a hemisphere, the right from the left, is quite different.

"In a right handed person," he went on, "the left side of the brain sees the whole. It is this part of the brain that will enable one to harmonize the entire range of a great orchestra into a single whole, a single performance. Or, for that matter, view the overall wonder of a great oil painting. The other side, the right hemisphere, is the analytical side. It deals with the parts. It enables one to single out the tone of a single violin, and enjoy it as an individual contribution to the whole, or, in this case, to the symphony. Or, for that matter, recognize the individual colors and shapes in a painting. When the person is left handed, just the reverse is true."

"Each hemisphere is divided into four parts, or, technically, what are called, 'lobes'. The frontal lobes, these two up front," and he pointed to the 'forehead' of the brain, "are responsible for controlling movement and instinct and emotions. The ones at the back of the head, technically the optical lobes, control vision. And between them, along the lower sides, run the temporal lobes, which control memory and knowledge. And just above them, to the center point of the head, run the parietal lobes, which have the critical role of evaluating, sorting out, integrating and compiling information that flows to them through the five senses, vision, hearing, smell, taste and touch. So that when one peels a banana, it will look like a banana, it will feel like a banana, it will smell like a banana and, it will taste like a banana, and, yes, sound like a banana." As he went along he continued to point to each of the parts of the brain that corresponded to what he was talking about.

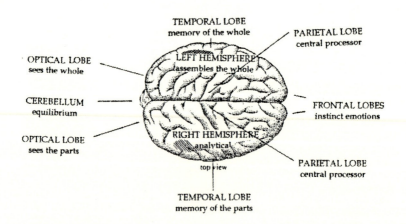

"So the parietal lobes, these two here in the center at the top of the brain, can be likened to 'INTEL', the central processing unit of a computer. Actually twin processors. Here lies the intelligence of the individual. And the relative speed and accuracy at which the parietal lobes can gather, store, retrieve, analyze, compile and evaluate information is measured in ones intelligence quotient (IQ). And this is what determines aptitude as well. After ones fifth birthday, that time at which the brain is fully grown, saving a catastrophic happening, ones intelligence will never change. This is why it is said that an individual's max IQ is reached at that age.

"Ones intelligence is usually specialized. Einstein who is at the very top of the scientific ladder could never paint a single stroke on canvas. Yet, Rembrandt, who is at the very top of the artistic ladder, could never solve the simplest mathematical formula. This is why determining a child's aptitude is so important for had Einstein and Rembrandt chosen each other's fields we would not have the *Theory of Relativity* or, for that matter, the *Night Watch* today. And there are some exceptions in which intelligence is not specialized and one sees this quite clearly in Leonardo DaVinci, who was a towering giant in both fields.

"And, of course, independent of the two hemispheres is the cerebellum. Located here in the lower rear base of the brain, it controls the body's posture and its equilibrium," he pointed to a tank that was set at the base of the two rear tanks in the chemical plant and then to the base at the rear of the picture of the brain.

And then, passing his hand over all of the 'tanks' of the brain, he said, "These are the think tanks of the human person. But just how do they do our thinking for us?" he seemed to ask himself more than having directed the question at me.

"Let's take the element of sight. How does it tell us what color is what color, what form is what form, what composition is what composition?" And he pulled forward another book, *Albert Einstein's Theory of Relatively*. A picture of his *patron saint* in his long white hair dominated the cover.

"One looks at a picture, a great work of art," he continued, "Unlike what one might believe, the chain of events does not begin with the eye, nor with the brain. It begins with the painting. What happens in this immensely complex chain of events, is that the painting emits various particles of energy of light. Some are in blues and reds and yellows and browns, and others are in various tones and shapes of blues and reds and yellows and browns. And it is these particles that strike our eye, not the other way around. Just think," he added, "if there was nothing there, one would see nothing.

"So here, once again, our very good friend Einstein is involved. We are talking here of just another aspect of his great theory," he pointed out, "And these impulses of energy are transmitted from the object to the optic nerve and then to the optical lobes which are located, as I said, in the rear of the hemispheres of the brain. And one of these lobes records the individual colors and tones, and the corresponding lobe, on the other side, orchestrates them all together for us." And he pointed to the two rear tanks in the chemical mill and then to the two rear lobes of the brain.

Knowing that he was probably taxing all of my mind power he paused for a moment as to let me catch up with him. But it was becoming clear to me that he was indeed painting himself further and further into a corner, for he was about to confirm that it is the brain that controls the way one thinks. "Soon," I thought, "I will have him on the edge of his web."

But I was about to lose another one. "How do you suppose these particles of color, these particles of energy, reach the optical lobes that are located at the back of the head?" he asked. This time giving me a look of apprehension as if by chance I might come up with the correct answer, which of course would be devastating to him.

But I was not to disappoint him for I replied in triumph, "The optic nerve does it. It's a function of the optic nerve. You just said it yourself," and I kind of hoped that I had not hurt him too deeply. But I was soon to find out that I had not hurt him at all.

A God for Lions

"That's not what I said," he countered, "I said that the impulses are transferred through the optic nerve to the rear of the brain. Now, what actually does the job? What actually determines how we think?" he asked again, more certain this time that I would come up with the answer.

His statement could not have been more confusing so I decided not to say anything.

"The chemical balance of the brain," he exclaimed, "This is why we all think differently. The brain together with its nervous system is simply a housing, just like this chemical plant here." And he looked down at the picture of the chemical plant. "It is the chemicals that are within it that do the job. Just like the chemical plant, without the chemicals which run through its endless array of piping and tubing, could never do anything at all.

"The colors, and forms, and composition of the painting are transmitted through a complex series of chemical reactions. This is how we see. This is how we smell. This is how we feel. This is how we hear. This is how we taste. This is how we think.

"Now, what do you suppose is a chemical reaction?" he asked.

"I guess," I hesitated, "it's when you put two different types of chemicals together and they interact with each other?"

"Well, not bad," he replied, giving me a satisfying look of compassion. "Specifically, it is when one puts two different 'particles of energy' together. We use the word 'chemical' simply as a physical manifestation of the word 'energy'. Chemistry is, in reality, the study of the interaction of different forms of energy. And my reference for saying this is Albert Einstein," and he said it with such conviction as if he were talking of Jesus Christ, Himself. And he paused, once again, for a long time as to allow time for what he had just told me to sink in.

"So once we collect the individual particles of energy in one of the optical lobes, the parietal lobes, the central processing unit of the brain, interacts with both optical lobes, so that we can see its whole. And once we can make out its details and its whole, the parietal lobes take the resulting composition of energy and deposit it here in the temporal lobes," and he pointed to the temporal lobes in the diagram of the brain, "and this is what we call memory. So that we can remember what we saw. So the job is done, and the only question is, 'how long will it remain there?' 'How long will we remember it?'

"If the capacities of the temporal lobes were infinite, then we would remember everything. But, as you know, we remember relatively very little. And the reason we remember very little is that our temporal lobes are greatly limited in *bytes*. A man of sixty, is likely to remember the names of two or three children he went to grade school with and he is even less likely, without the aid of a photograph, to remember what they looked like. Even, in the very short range, memory is quite limited. Hence, we make a list when we go to the store. So one retains in memory only an infinitesimal fraction of what one has been exposed to during life. And the reason for this is generally the very limited size and capacity of the temporal lobes. The very limited capacity of that part of the brain which retains memory.

"The smallest computers have considerably more memory capacity than does the human brain. And because of its very limited capacity we are constantly subconsciously purging our memory lobes in order to make space for newer and more interesting information.

"And," asking himself more than asking me, "in this purging process, just what determines what we remember and what we tend to forget?"

And he answered himself, "Time and relative importance are two of these factors. It is those most important things that occur in the last few years of life, or better, yet, the last few days of life, that one is most likely to end up with. And the second major factor is what we want to retain. What we want to take with us. A man who loses his mate at a very early age will carry the memory of her with him all of his life. And, all through life he will often magnify the image, the fondest of her memory. Whereas, others who he wants to forget, he puts into his past, and tends to forget.

"And there are some things that he wishes he could forget and can never forget. For example, the times bad things happened. And these, too, he will carry with him to the end.

"And keep in mind that there are two very different types of information stored here in the temporal lobes. There are our 'memories' which I have just talked of, and then there is our 'knowledge' which is the more important of the two. As one can live without memories, but one will not get very far without knowledge. For if one does not know that the stove is hot one will burn oneself time and again and if one does not know that one cannot fly one would not hesitate to leap from a cliff to get from here to there. A man's knowledge is actually the cumulation of the memory of his fellowman, other men, both of today, and yesterday, which has found its way into his temporal lobes. It is what, throughout all of his life, has enabled man to live beyond the apes in the forest."

just what are we trying to save?

"So we have touched on the soul, and on the mind. Now when one comes to the end of ones days, and one prays to his God for his salvation, just what is he trying to save? Is one trying to save ones soul, something he has never known and doesn't understand, or is one trying to save ones rear end?" He stopped to allow me time to etch the alternatives in my mind before he took them away from me.

"And we will find when we come to the end of this day, that he is not trying save either one of these. For when he finally lays on his deathbed, he will realize what he really is. If he is old and gray and wrinkled and frail, he will have a body that he really wouldn't want to keep. And, if he is young, he will know that his body, one day, would have grown old and gray and wrinkled and frail, a body, which in the long run, doesn't count at all. But, he will be something far greater than a simple body that has met its date in time. For he will be a collection of memories, some wonderful ones, some horrible ones, and some recent ones, and, of course, what he knows.

"That of all the people of the world, of all the people who ever were, of all the people who ever will be, only he would possess this particular combination of memories and knowledge. No one else comes close. So, yes, this is definitely something that he would want to save. And we will make a note of this less we forget it later." He pulled forward a notepad and wrote in bold letters,

WHAT WE ARE TRYING TO SAVE

- KNOWLEDGE AND MEMORIES - TEMPORAL LOBES

"So is this what we seek in immortality? Is this is what we are trying to save? To make last forever? This complex formation of energy which is stored in the temporal lobes? That makes up the person?"

"It sort of looks like that," I answered his question.

"Not entirely," he corrected me. "That which is here in the temporal lobes," he pointed to the diagram, "will change from time to time. As a matter of fact when we are born there is nothing there. The word 'temporal' means exactly what it says, 'temporary'. If one were to say that what is stored in the temporal lobes defines a person then a person would be a different person every day of his life. If a man were to die at sixty he would be saving an entirely different man than if he had died at thirty. So in addition to ones memories and knowledge there must be something else that one would want to save. Something else that is also a part of the 'individual'?"

I decided to let him answer his own question.

"And we will get to that something else very soon. But, first we must lay some groundwork. Let us, from a practical point of view, look at how this works.

"This is going to be a real tough one, so perhaps you'd better get another cup of coffee, better make this one black," he advised. And without saying so much as a word, I got up and climbed quickly up the steps to the kitchen and returned a minute later with cup in hand.

Jekyll and Hyde

I had not yet sat down when he started, "It is the chemical balance of the brain, the energy balance of the brain, that the psychiatrist is often faced with. And, what's more, he knows it. The problem is that few others know it. Even you didn't know it."

And I thought to myself that what he had told me was quite interesting. I never really knew how the brain functioned.

And he continued, "Schizophrenia is the most prevalent form of mental instability one can be born with. And there are an endless number of different forms of the illness. And how do you suppose the psychiatrist treats such a disorder?" he asked.

"He talks to them. He tries to figure out what they are all about. He tries to understand their thinking and tries to correct it." I replied.

"Wrong," he corrected me again, "The psychiatrist knows, in this case, that he is dealing with a chemical imbalance of the brain. His solution is to correct the chemical imbalance, to correct the balance of energy in order to correct the way one thinks. He knows that the only way he can correct a chemical imbalance is with other chemicals. A chemical imbalance is a physical condition and a physical condition cannot be corrected with therapy. Schizophrenia is something that one is born with, it cannot be acquired. Therefore it can only be treated with chemicals, medicine.

"So the psychiatrist gives a relatively sedative individual an exhilarating drug to try to achieve a balance of some sort, halfway in between. Or in the case of a person with an exhilarating personality he prescribes a sedative drug, again to bring the chemicals in the brain and the nervous system into some kind of reasonable balance."

Then turning toward me, he added, "What you are talking about is what the psychiatrist used to do a hundred years ago. Administer therapy. And he did that because, at that time, he was totally unaware of the chemical balance of the brain. And where were all the schizophrenics then?" he asked.

"In mental institutions," I acknowledged.

"Yes," he agreed, "and that was because the psychiatrist, at that time, thought that he was dealing with a mental illness whereas, in fact, he was dealing with a physical illness, a chemical imbalance of the brain. A physical imbalance which manifests itself in abnormal mental behavior."

And he asked again, "And where are the schizophrenics now?"

"For the most part, leading normal lives," I responded.

"Yes, as long as they take their medication, it will temporarily control their condition and they can continue to lead normal lives. For the doctor now has the antidote that will change *Mr. Hyde* back into *Dr. Jekyll*. But *Dr. Jekyll* must keep taking his medicine or he will revert back to being *Mr. Hyde* overnight. He will begin again to think that when he has done something wrong that he has done something right.

"Schizophrenia, in that it most often involves itself with ones ability to know right from wrong, deals with the chemicals contained in the frontal lobes of the brain, these two up front," he pointed to the two tanks that were first in line and then to the forehead of the brain. "These tanks that the biologist calls the 'frontal lobes' are the reservoir that contains everything that is unique about us at the time of birth. And what we have here can never change. This is why schizophrenia is not curable, it is only controllable. If the good doctor *Jekyll* fails to take his medicine he will revert back to the evil *Mr. Hyde* overnight.

"So here in the frontal lobes is our ability to know right from wrong," he pointed to the frontal lobes. "Yet there are other things up front here in the frontal lobes that define us as a person and they are also things that will not change for the rest of our lives?"

Other than the ability to know right from wrong, I couldn't think of any so I remained silent. After all, that's all that I thought was there.

Instead of giving me the answer he decided to help me, "Okay," he said, "just what is the ability to know right from wrong?"

But I was unable to come up with anything so he gave me the answer, "It is an instinct, a basic instinct. So what are some other instincts?"

And I, unable to come up with some others, he gave me some others, "'Survival' is probably number one. Then there is 'compassion'. And, of course, there is the instinct that tells us who we are. Is one a boy? Is one a girl? It is this instinct that enables the girl toddler to reach for the doll and the boy toddler to reach for the truck. And then there is the instinct that makes one laugh and makes one cry. And the ability to fall in love is here too. It is an instinct that determines who we will fall in love with. This is why we can't otherwise control who we fall in love with. This is why most of us can only fall in love with one of the opposite sex. And it is also why some of us can only fall in love with a member of the same sex, homosexuals. The phenomenon of *falling in love* is a manifestation of the instinct of compassion.

"Just think," he offered, "there have been cases in which sets of twins have been studied. Although a six year old is not usually aware of his or her sexual orientation, it is possible through clinical analysis to determine if a six year old is a heterosexual or a homosexual or for that matter a transsexual. Twins that have never been separated, not even in the bathroom, who have shared an identical environment since birth, even wear identical clothes, one is determined to be a heterosexual, and the other is determine to be a homosexual. How is this possible? And the psychiatrist knows why it is possible. For he knows that sexual orientation is a basic instinct. And this is probably most clearly seen in studies of adult Siamese twins, one of which is a heterosexual and the other of which is a homosexual. Actually, studies have shown that the rate of homosexuality among both identical twins and Siamese twins is consistent with that of the general population, about one in fifteen. Two people who have shared an identical environment all of their lives, that have heard and seen the same things day after day.

"One might ask why the preacher can't understand this? Why he does not agree with the psychiatric community on the subject of homosexuality? And the reason is that he has an entirely different definition as to what 'homosexuality' is."

"A different definition?" I repeated his word in a question.

"Yes, quite a different definition," he replied, "The preacher defines 'homosexuality' as *who one has sex with.*' Just think," he clarified his position, "the preacher would have no objection to two men living together in a long term loving relationship as long as sex was not a factor. He would have no objection at all. It is the fact that when two men live together in a long term loving relationship that it most likely involves sex that bothers the preacher, not the fact that they are in love with each other. The preacher is concerned with 'lust', not with 'love'.

"On the other hand the psychiatrist defines 'homosexuality' as '*who one has the ability to fall in love with.*' His concern is 'love', not 'lust'. And the reason he does not consider 'lust' in his definition is because he knows that 'lust' is a product of the temporal lobes and not of the frontal lobes," and he pulled forward the diagram of the brain and pointed to the temporal lobes, "Unlike love or compassion, lust is not something that one is born with, it is an acquired trait. It is a form of knowledge that is stored here in the temporal lobes." And he pointed to the lobes that were located directly above the ears.

And conversely, *'who one can fall in love with'*, the greatest manifestation of the instinct of compassion," is here, and he pointed to the frontal lobes in the diagram, "and like everything else that is contained in the frontal lobes it is something that one is born with and will eventually die with.

"There are some heterosexual men who follow a homosexual lifestyle. And the practice is not limited to prisons. It happens in everyday life. But a heterosexual man who practices this kind of thing can never fall in love with his partner. The driving force is 'lust' and not 'love'. The preacher thinks of these men as homosexuals because his definition is limited to *'who one has sex with.'* Whereas in reality they are heterosexuals.

"When the psychiatrist speaks of homosexuals he speaks solely of those who can *fall in love* only with one of their own sex. His barometer is 'love' - a product of the frontal lobes - which cannot be changed by therapy. He does not include those who are driven by 'lust' - a product of the temporal lobes - which can be changed by therapy. For example, a straight child if molested might follow a gay lifestyle but the condition can be changed by therapy. Yet, a gay male child all of his life will only be able to *fall in love* with one of his own sex."

He paused for a long time. He searched my expression to make sure that I had gotten his point, that I had understood the complexity of the problem, and that I had fully understood his explanation. And it was not until I had given him the 'nod' that he went on, "So yes, our basic instincts are also 'us'. Probably not as uniquely 'us' as are our memories and knowledge, as most of us share similar instincts. Most of us are heterosexuals, most of us know right from wrong, most of us have a similar level of compassion, most of us have a strong instinct of survival, and all of us laugh and cry about the same things. Yet, we all posses different degrees of these instincts, so if we want to define the 'individual' as he is at the time of death, yes, we would have to include them," he pulled forward the pad and made the addition,

WHAT WE ARE TRYING TO SAVE

- KNOWLEDGE AND MEMORIES - TEMPORAL LOBES - TEMPORARY

- INSTINCTS - FRONTAL LOBES - PERMANENT

Again, FRONTAL means PERMANENT and cannot be changed. TEMPORAL means TEMPORARY and will change from time to time. At the time of birth very deep in these frontal lobes there is a reservoir of basic chemicals, or energy, that controls the basic instincts and emotions of the human body. As we have said this includes the instinct to survive, the instinct of compassion, the instinct to procreate, the instinct to cry, the instinct to laugh, and the deepest instinct of all, that which allows us to fall in love, why we are able to *fall in love* only with members of the opposite sex."

"An instinct makes us laugh and cry?" I questioned his reasoning.

"Of course," he answered, "We don't teach babies how to cry and how to laugh. They already know these things at birth. And all babies will cry about the same things and all babies will laugh at the same things."

And I began to realize what he meant when he had said that what is in the frontal lobes cannot be changed. That it cannot be changed by therapy. It would be like trying to condition someone to laugh whenever something sad happened and to cry when something funny happens.

"I know what you are thinking," he interrupted my thinking, "but it is not that fixed in concrete. After all, as I just mentioned in the case of the schizophrenic, a person who does not know the difference between right and wrong, we have had some success in at least correcting the condition on a temporary basis. And it is likely that if there was a point to it that would justify putting millions of dollars into research we could develop a drug that would successfully reverse the laugh-cry instinct. So that when something sad happens the person would laugh, and when something funny happens he would cry."

And I offered, "If that is true, then it might be possible to develop a drug that would change a homosexual into a heterosexual?"

"Yes, as in the case of other instincts, the instinct to know right from wrong, the instinct to laugh and cry, if one wanted to put enough money into it, it is likely that one could come up with a drug that would change a homosexual into a heterosexual. But if he didn't keep taking his medicine he would revert back to the person he was. Science can only control the condition, it can never be permanently changed. At least as far as we know today.

"So a man of eighty, barring any catastrophic damage to the brain, will die as the very same person he was at the age of five. If he is a homosexual he will die a homosexual and if he is a schizophrenic he will die a schizophrenic. And on his deathbed he will still cry over sad things and laugh at funny things. His basic instincts will never change.

"And the only modification to the person he was at five, will be some knowledge and some memories that he has picked up along the way which as we know are temporary in nature. So this is 'him'," he pointed to the center of his forehead with the forefingers of both hands and ran them back over the ears, "It is what more than anything else that is unique about a person, that makes him an individual. It is what one wants to save. Ones body, as we have said, if not old and wrinkled at death would eventually grow old and return to dust, certainly nothing that one would want to save."

And pointing to the top of his head he added, "And yet we must also consider what is in the parietal lobes. For relative intelligence is also a part of what we are, a part of what we are trying to save. Yes, we all have it, but we have it to varying degrees. So let's add that one to the list,

WHAT WE ARE TRYING TO SAVE

- KNOWLEDGE AND MEMORIES - TEMPORAL LOBES - TEMPORARY

- INSTINCTS - FRONTAL LOBES - PERMANENT

- INTELLIGENCE – PARIETAL LOBES – PERMANENT

"So this is what we are at the time of death. It is all that we are trying to save. If these things cannot survive beyond death then we, as we have been in this life, are mortal. We will cease to exist at death." He reached over and pulled the picture of the brain in front of him and added the following functions, those things that we are tying to save,

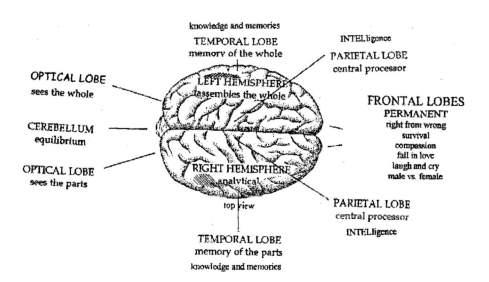

Lucien Gregoire

the computer versus the brain

"The computers of today, as I have just said, have immensely more memory capacity than do the temporal lobes of the human brain," and he again pointed to the two lobes which ran just above the ears along the sides of the brain. "And some sophisticated computers can even duplicate the function of the optical lobes," and he pointed to the two lobes in the rear of the brain. In fact, computers can perform all five senses of man and at immensely greater speeds and ranges. For example, if properly designed and programmed, a computer can detect the drop of a pin or record the detailed image of a painting a hundred miles away. And, as we know, a computer can send a message around the world in the blink of an eye.

"And, of course, the simplest computers are much faster and much smarter than are the parietal lobes here at the top, the human central processing units," and he pointed to the top of the brain. "The very slowest of computers can think faster and more accurately than the most brilliant of men. To put it bluntly they are much more 'INTEL'ligent than men. And this can best be demonstrated by comparing the ability of the human brain to perform a mathematical calculation versus the ability of a computer to perform the same calculation. We know that calculations that a man of genius intelligence takes a month to perform, can be accomplished by a simple PC in a matter of a few seconds."

He continued to speak very slowly as to give the slowest child in the class ample time to fully understand that which he was saying, "But when one talks about the frontal lobes, these two here," and he pointed, again, to the forehead of the brain, "no computer can perform any of their functions, namely instincts and emotions.

"Computers will always have this limitation. That they will always be limited to perform the functions of only the parietal, temporal and optical lobes, and perhaps all the other functions of the human body except those of the frontal lobes.

"And we know that what is in the frontal lobes cannot be changed permanently. And the psychiatrist knows that any condition that has its cause here," he pointed to his forehead, "cannot be treated with therapy. It can only be treated with chemicals, medicine.

"Yet, there are some mental problems that can be treated with therapy. What do you suppose those are?"

And, again, he had to answer his own question, "Problems that one acquires, those that one picks up along the way. Things that are deposited in the temporal lobes that confuse the basic instincts that are in the frontal lobes.

"For example, there are some forms of schizophrenia which render the afflicted person dangerous to others. That can cause them to be harmful to others or to themselves. One might call the condition 'homicidal insanity'. But, nevertheless, this is an insanity, a chemical imbalance, one is born with. And one that can, to a great extent, be controlled by chemicals, medicine.

"Yet, on the other hand, one can acquire the same identical traits, the traits of a homicidal maniac. John List was not born a killer. He was in no way a schizophrenic. But, yet, he had no regrets at all of having murdered his children. Just like the schizophrenic, he had done something wrong and thought that he had done something right. In fact, he felt that there was something wonderful about it. For his scriptures had convinced him that there was something wonderful about his gruesome deed. And this was because his preacher had convinced him that his scripture was a matter of fact.

"And his problem, having resulted from conditioning, can only be treated by conditioning. His condition cannot be corrected by the application of chemicals. No amount of medicine can change the way he thinks. His 'illness' will only react to therapy. Whereas, a schizophrenic, who is a homicidal maniac, suffers from a chemical imbalance of the brain, and has a condition that can only be treated with chemicals, it will not react to therapy.

"The result of both problems is identical. The individual does something wrong and thinks he has done something right. To solve a problem, one must attack the 'cause' of the problem, not the 'result' of the problem,

- If the cause of the problem is 'chemicals' it can only be corrected with 'chemicals'

- If the cause of the problem is 'conditioning' then it can only be corrected by 'reconditioning' or 'therapy'"

And, once again, he paused for a long time as to allow me to catch up with him. And then, as if to assure himself that I had understood all that he had said, he repeated, "Again, one must attack the 'cause' of the problem, not the 'result' of the problem. John List's problem resulted from weakness, not evil. He was an easy believer. He believed the preacher, and he believed him unconditionally. And this was his undoing.

"And therapy is not necessarily always applied by the psychologist, the 'expert' in this case, so to speak. Sometimes the condition can be corrected by other conditioning that becomes an incidental part of a person's life. Sometimes things one hears in the classroom, on television, or just in everyday conversation can change the way one thinks. Can mold the child of bigoted parents into a better member of society.

"Let's use the gays and blacks as an example. Bigoted parents cause their children to grow up with prejudices of these people who appear to be different. And these are prejudices that have been passed on from family to family for centuries ever since Moses first spelled out the difference between black and white, and straight and gay, and man and women almost four thousand years ago. But, if one grows up in the right schools, or reads and learns about these things, the truth about these things, the facts, then they are more likely to drop this basic thinking of prejudice, which will make them better members of society.

"So education is the answer to much of this problem called 'bigotry'. For example, in the case of the gays if one knew the scientific definition of a gay, *'one who can only fall in love with ones own sex'*, one would be far less likely to believe the bigot preacher's definition, *'who one has sex with'*.

"To the informed person the preacher recognizes only the physical union of a penis and a vagina. He ignores the sacred mental union of the parties – the perfect balance of energy between two people that we had concluded - that day we talked of the *Birds and the Bees* - can only be made by God. This perfect balance of energy – *falling in love* - that today we know as a matter of fact can exist both between people of opposite sexes and also between people of the same sex.

"All preachers recognize the union of a man and woman who are sterile or aging who like homosexuals, although they can parent them, have no chance of bearing children. If the preacher were truly God's representative, then he would recognize this sacred balance of mental energy that we know can only be made by God – the state of *falling in love* - whenever it might exist between any of God's children.

"Until the gay revolution of the seventies homosexuality was the leading cause of suicides among children and teens in the United States and it remains so in many Bible states today. The preacher capitalizes on the ignorance of parents of these children. Again, lack of education is the cause of the problem."

the importance of dreams

"And, aside from all this of which we have been speaking, there is the unique ability of the mind to function while unconscious. While in a state of sleep. Its ability to function in the subconscious, dreams and, sometimes, nightmares. In fact, dreams form the very substance of Christianity. It is our tendency to believe in dreams, particularly dreams of others, that makes us Christians."

"That makes no sense at all!" I stopped him, "We don't believe in dreams. Particularly someone else's dreams."

He smiled, again, a kind of delightful smile, as when one senses victory. As one comes up over the rise and sees the enemy tattered and torn and struggling across the field carrying a white flag, "Much of the most important testimony in the *Bible* is the retelling of dreams. Including the single most important testimony of all," and he repeated it as if I had missed it the first time, "the most important testimony in all of the *Bible*. That *Christ* was the *Son of God*. And he stood up and went over to the bookcase and returned with his copy of the *New Testament*. And sitting down, he turned to the very first page and began to read, *'Now the birth of Jesus Christ was on the rise: When His mother Mary was espoused to Joseph, before they came together, she was found to be with child. Then Joseph, her husband, being a just man, and not willing to make her public example, was minded to put away her privily. But while he thought in these things, behold the angel of the Lord appeared to him in a dream, saying: Joseph, thou son of David, fear not to take unto thee Mary thy wife: for that which is conceived in her is of the Holy Ghost. And she shall bring forth a son, and thou shall call his name JESUS: for he shall save his people from their sins.'*

A God for Lions

"This is Christianity in a nutshell," raising his voice as to emphasize the point. As if he had not raised his voice, I would have missed the point. "One cannot be a Christian and not believe in Joseph's dream. Believe literally in his dream. For Joseph's dream is the very foundation of Christianity. The very essence of everything we believe in. It amazes me that highly intelligent people when reading the *Bible*, cannot distinguish that which is important from that which is not. This is the pivotal point of *belief* for the Christian. If Joseph's dream was true, then Christ is the Son of God and it makes good sense to turn the page. But, if Joseph's dream was just a pipe dream, or just a story, then Christ was a bastard, literally a bastard, and it would make no sense whatsoever to read the rest of the book.

"And as we have already discussed one must not only believe in Joseph's dream but one must believe that Matthew who tells us of his dream in the *New Testament* got his information on good account. For as we know the *New Testament* tells us quite explicitly that Matthew had not yet been born when Joseph had his '*dream*'.

"Yes, the skeptic will claim that Joseph may have in fact had such a dream, but that it was driven by his own subconscious will, his own hope that Mary, his beloved, had not cheated on him. But the Christian must believe that the angel of the Lord actually did appear to Joseph in the dream. And, the skeptic will ask, why didn't the angel just appear to Joseph directly? Why was the dream necessary in the first place? Why was this, the most important testimony in all of the *Bible*, simply a dream? And why the angel, when all of the other fundamental testimony of the *Bible* involved *God the Father, Himself,* appearing in His own person to Abraham and to Moses and the other prophets? Three hundred apparitions in all. Why did *God the Father* feel that this most important testimony in all of the *Bible* could be carried out by an emissary? An emissary with wings who appeared to an unconscious man? A story that would be related to the Christian world by a man who had not witnessed the event, as he had not yet been born?

"Yes," he continued lowering his voice, "today, we don't believe in dreams, our own dreams or those of others. But, in those days it was commonplace to believe in dreams, both ones own dreams and those of others.

"Even in Mohammed's day, some six hundred years after Christ, people still believed in dreams. Islamism, like Christianity, is based on *belief* in someone else's dream. And, in the case of Islamism, the dream was Mohammed's dream. In his dream '*the Angel Gabriel came and placed him upon Borak, a winged horse with a woman's face and a peacock tail. Borak transported Mohammed to Jerusalem where he met Abraham, Moses and Jesus.*' So yes, today, we no longer believe in dreams, except those dreams of others which occurred many, many years ago."

Then he startled me with his next statement. "Yes, you have been thinking all along that these things are very interesting, but not necessary to live ones life. That is except for the specialist that handles these sorts of things. For I have been reading your mind. And you are wrong. These are basic facts of life, which determine the individual, himself or herself, and furthermore, society, itself.

"Yes," he concluded, "most things in life are best left to the specialist. The 'expert' in these things. But there are a few things that it is dangerous to leave to the specialist, or the so-called 'expert'. Two of these are the body and the mind, their development and maintenance. It is not just the business of the doctor and the psychiatrist. It is everyone's business. Here we should depend not on what we believe but on what we, ourselves, know. And the other is the soul. It is not just the business of the preacher. It is everyone's business. Here, too, we should depend not only on what we believe, but on what we, ourselves, know."

the immortality of the mind

"So, what have we learned today?" he asked himself. And he answered himself, "Well, I suppose, we are much closer to where the mind leaves off... and the soul begins. Not quite there, but definitely much closer.

"One thing is certain. The soul, if it exists at all, is not linked to the body. It would have to be linked to the mind. For one knows that it would depend on the mind for its identity.

"And one knows now that the mind, itself, is physical. That it is a physical composition of chemicals. Chemicals that give us consciousness and control the way we think. And when at death the chemicals disintegrate our consciousness ends. We become unconscious. So we know, as a matter of fact, that the mind and the soul are not one and the same. For one is physical, while the other is spiritual. For one is based on chemicals and the other is based on nothing at all.

"So all that we have discussed now narrows to two very different questions,

- Can the consciousness, the contents of the parietal, frontal and temporal lobes, be transferred to 'another mind' at death? The fundamental hope of the eastern world.

- Can the consciousness, the contents of the parietal, frontal and temporal lobes, be transferred to the 'soul' at death? The fundamental hope of the western world.

"So let us take them in order. Can the consciousness, the contents of the parietal, frontal and temporal lobes, be transferred to another mind at death?"

Lucien Gregoire

the case for reincarnation

"I told you that I had read your mind. And I knew I was right in my statement as you flushed. How can one person read the mind of another? How can a thought move from the peripherals of the temporal lobes of one person to the peripherals of the temporal lobes of another person without the use of any of the five senses?

"And we know this happens every day. When one is in a room and a certain discussion is at hand and one of the participants knows something that he or she does not want to be brought up, he or she will try to think of anything else in order to suppress the thought for fear that someone might pick it up." And he asked, "How is this possible? How does a thought get from one mind to another without the use of the senses?"

And he answered himself in the very same breath, "In the very same way that the reds, blues, greens and yellows move from the painting to the optic nerve. In the very same way that one hears distant thunder.

"And this phenomenon of mind reading exists to an extent in all individuals. Yes, some are better senders and others are better receivers. But, nevertheless, unlike fortune telling and reading the future and the seances in which one speaks with the dead, the ability of ones mind to read the thoughts of another mind is a proven fact. Or better yet, the ability of the mind to be able to send a thought from ones temporal lobes, through ones parietal lobes or central processor to the parietal lobes of another person which deposits it in his or her temporal lobes is a proven fact." He had now picked up speed and began to take on the air of a steamroller coming down the road toward me.

"Let's take the world renown psychic on television who claims to get messages from the departed loved one of the person he is addressing. He is able to describe with uncanny accuracy the names, descriptions and often actual incidents that occurred during the deceased life. He is, in fact, not receiving the messages from the departed, but is getting them from the person who he is addressing who may or may not be thinking of the deceased. The psychic happens to be a strong receiver or gatherer of thoughts that have been deposited in the temporal lobes of other people. Storage vaults of memories of other people.

"And, if he is an exceptionally strong receiver, he is able to gather up these thoughts, these particles of memory energy, from the temporal lobes of the people he is talking to, without even the people themselves bringing them to the surface of their temporal lobes. That is, without even the people themselves, thinking about them."

And I knew he was right for earlier that week I had sat in a conference room trying desperately to hold back a thought for fear that someone would pick it up. And then I thought, "My God, could he have read my mind?" But what he had to say next floored me.

"And there are some others," he concluded, "those that are strong senders of thoughts. That day, when I sold my bike, it is I who sent you to the desk to get the extra money for Mrs. Jackson. It was also I who left you with the thought of the *Widow's mite.*

"And remember the day that I fell in love with Jeannie? When we had talked of the energy transfer between people? That it is both physical and mental? That there exists both energy givers and energy takers? And that the transfer of that energy can be profoundly felt by both the giver and the receiver? And, again, that the transfer of that energy need not involve the use of the senses?"

And having made his point he resumed his position as if he were addressing a symposium of Nobel laureates, "But what is most important here is that a thought, the composition of knowledge and memory, can live independent of the chemicals that gave birth to it. That the composition of knowledge and memory can exist independent of its source. That the composition of knowledge and memory can be transferred without the use of the five senses. And these are important facts. For it is crucial to our understanding of the question at hand, 'Can the consciousness, the contents of the parietal, frontal and temporal lobes, be transferred to 'another mind' at death? The fundamental hope of the eastern world.'

"So the question is, 'When at death the chemicals of the brain disintegrate, could the resulting energy, the thoughts and memories, still be there and can they be transferred to another mind, to another chemical base?'

"And we already know that they can live independent of their source. So what we have to concentrate on is can they possibly be transferred to another mind at death? And the best way to see this is to look at what happens to another form of energy when the source that gave birth to it disintegrates.

"We know as a matter of fact that the energy produced by oil and coal can survive their demise. The coal and oil are gone but the resulting energy, the electricity, is still there. And, more importantly, we know something else. We know as a matter of absolute fact that electricity can be trasferred to another chemical base, another 'mind', once the chemical base, the coal and oil, that gave birth to it has disintegrated.

"And we know this to be an absolute fact because the great prophet, Edward Volta, proved it to be a fact. When, in harnessing energy, electricity, for the very first time, he successfully stored it completely independent of its source.

"That Volta was able to transfer electricity after the demise of its chemical base, coal and oil, to another chemical base in a thing called a battery is the only scientific fact that we have that suggests that the intelligence, instincts, memories and knowledge that are contained in ones parietal, frontal and temporal lobes can be transferred to the corresponding lobes of another person at death. That could suggest that when ones chemical base dissolves at death, that ones intelligence, instincts, memories and knowledge THAT WHICH WE ARE TRYING TO SAVE could possibly be transferred to another chemical base, to another mind, after death.

"We must draw a line of course, between that which is in the parietal and frontal lobes versus that which is in the temporal lobes. For as we have said we know as a matter of fact that our thought processes, our knowledge and memories, can be transferred to another person without the use of any of the five senses. We do not know as a matter of fact whether this could also be true of our intelligence and instincts. All we know concerning our intelligence and instincts is that the chemical base of another person's parietal and frontal lobes could sustain them. Whether or not they can be transferred is just a guess.

"As we have said, our composition of intelligence, instincts, knowledge and memory are very much like electricity. Both are the product of various kinds of chemicals, energy reactions, in the case of electricity, the chemical reactions of coal and oil, and, in the case of intelligence, instinct, knowledge and memory, the chemical reactions of the brain. As I have just said, both thinking processes and electricity are invisible. They are both the results of chemical reactions. The scientific difference between them as we know it today is that we know that electricity can be transferred to and be maintained by another chemical source other than that which gave birth to it whereas we don't know if knowledge, memory and instincts can be transferred at death to another person. But, to a certain extent, science tells us that it is reasonable to believe so.

Lucien Gregoire

a third millenium frankenstein

"Of course, for reincarnation to be a reality it must involve immediate transfer of these things that we call intelligence, memory, knowledge and instincts to another host, to another brain. And this is because there exists no 'battery' for their temporary storage, as is the case with electricity."

"But let us say that science were to develop such a 'battery' together with the technology needed to transfer the contents of the parietal, frontal and temporal lobes to it. It would seem that since all energy, both mental and physical, has the same energy base then it would seem that this would be possible.

"If that were to happen, that such a 'battery' were developed, then the case for reincarnation would change dramatically. Particularly, if one were to combine it with other advancements of modern science.

"Take cloning for example. When a man is aging and wants to do it all over again he goes to the clinic. The medical team transfers the contents of his brain to the 'battery'. A battery that contains the same chemical base as does the temporal lobes of his brain. And at the same time let's say they have made a clone of him. So not only would his mind survive but so also his body. The medical team then transfers what is stored in the battery to the brain of the clone much like one jumps a car battery with another battery. And the individual gets to do it all over again.

The clone would already contain the same chemical base in its parietal and frontal lobes, that with which one is born with, as had its donor. That a clone would have the same basic instincts as had its donor because a chemical base is physical and not mental. So one would be dealing only with a transfer of what is in the temporal lobes, the possible transfer of which as we have said before is already known to be a matter of fact.

"And even without such a 'battery' it may someday become possible for science to transfer the chemicals themselves that are contained in the temporal lobes to a clone before death. Perhaps later in life when one is looking to roll back a few years. If such a thing were done, the intelligence, memories, knowledge and instincts would obviously go along of the ride.

"One should keep in mind that in both cases there would be some variation in the 'InteL'igence that lies in the parietal lobes as one knows that much of this development takes place after birth in the early years of life. So the subject would survive as the same person he died as with some variation in intelligence.

"Of these two options, the latter possibility, direct transfer versus use of a battery, is a much stronger one. As there are few in the scientific community today who would doubt that this is a realistic possibility for the future. Certainly a much stronger proposal concerning what science knows today versus those theories once posed by Galileo and Volta in their day. After all, we already know as a matter of fact that what is in ones temporal lobes can be transferred to another mind without the use of the five senses.

"And if this sort of thing were to happen then all of the Jews, and all of the Christians, and all of the Muslims would forget all about what Moses had to say. They would all become Buddhists overnight.

"This does not mean that reincarnation could not be taking place as we speak. As we have discussed and as we shall see in what is yet to come there is considerable circumstantial evidence that it does take place. Just that it would make it more controllable. And, of course, it would lock up the prize for Buddha."

across the miles,

"From what one knows of reincarnation today the host, the receiving person, could be anywhere in the world. In fact, all of the evidence that we have that supports the possibility of reincarnation suggests that the host, the receiving brain, is rarely in proximity to the deceased. And we see this very vividly demonstrated every single day. A single thought, a single beam of energy, sent around the earth in a split second of time with no physical vehicle involved at all. Call it radio transmission, or satellite communication, or the Internet, or what have you. This was the contribution of another great prophet of the Creator, Alexander Telsa who theorized that not only could energy live beyond its physical source, but that it could be transferred anywhere through space in the blink of an eye, completely independent of any physical vehicle. Who proved his theory in his first successful wireless transmission, radio.

"Like Einstein who had so explicitly told us where we had come from, that man is not a single entity by himself but a composition of trillions of bits of energy all going about their work in unison with each other, and Darwin who had told us how we had come from there to here, Edward Volta and Alexander Telsa now tell us how we are going to get from here to there, the hereafter.

"So can this collection of energy of intelligence and of memories and of knowledge be successfully transferred to another mind at death?' This collection of energy which makes each one of us different from each other, which more than anything else defines us as individuals. That which we said is WHAT WE ARE TRYING TO SAVE. For the Buddhist and the Hindu, the only question is, will it be successfully transferred to a successor mind? And we now know that the answer to this question is a possible 'YES'. And we will come back to this possibility later."

the case for saving ones 'soul'

"And now how about those in the west, 'Can this collection of energy, of intelligence and memories and of knowledge and of instincts, be successfully transferred to the soul at death?" This collection of energy which makes each one of us different from another, which more than anything else defines us as individuals. That which we said is WHAT WE ARE TRYING TO SAVE. For the Christian, the Jew and the Muslim, the only question is, will it be successfully transferred to the soul? And we know the answer to this question is 'NO'.

"And one can best understand this by defining the difference between the 'spirit' or the 'mind' and the 'soul'. And believe me there is a difference between them although when most people talk of the 'soul' they assume that they are talking of the 'spirit' or of the 'mind' and nothing could be further from the truth. So let's define them so that we understand what we are talking about.

"The 'spirit' is what we have been talking about, WHAT WE ARE TRYING TO SAVE. The spirit is ones mind without ones body. It is what we have defined as 'us'. So the 'spirit' is synonymous with the 'mind'. It is what those in the east want to save.

"Except for the Muslims, who like those in the east are trying to save their spirits, those in the west on the other hand are not trying to save their minds, their sprits, they are trying to save their souls. Both the preacher and the scripture will tell one that one is trying to save ones 'soul', something else, something that we don't understand. Otherwise the preacher in his sermons and his scripture would use the word 'mind' or 'spirit'.

"So how does one know that there is such a thing as a soul? And the only place the westerner can go for his salvation is to his scripture. And the existence of the soul depends entirely on the fact that heaven is an entirely different creation than is earth. That it has an entirely different energy base, one that we do not understand. And as I said the only place one can go for the answer is scripture. And scripture tells us quite conclusively that the heaven of the Christian, the Muslim and the Jew has the exact same energy base as does the universe we live in. Scripture tells us quite explicitly that when the great prophet Einstein spoke of *relativity* he was speaking not only of earth but of heaven as well. That all matter, heaven and earth, is made up of moving parts, known as 'energy'.

"And we know this because the *Bible* and the *Koran* and the *Vedas* and every other major scripture of the world tell us that there was only one creation. That *God the Father* created both heaven and earth as a single creation simultaneously in the very same action. And he pulled the *Old Testament* in front of him and read from its very first page, '*And God created the firmament, by separating the waters, that were there, to the heavens above, and to the sea below. And God divided the waters which were under Heaven from the waters that were above Heaven. And made the firmament. And He called the firmament Heaven. Then God said, Let the waters under the Heaven be gathered together in one place, and let the dry land appear; and it was so. And, God called the dry land earth; and the gathering together of the waters He called the sea. And He saw that it was good.'"

He paused again, and taking a deep breath, "It is a Biblical fact that there is no soul. There is nothing there that we don't understand. For God created heaven and earth by splitting a single atom. That all that is heaven and all that is earth have the same parent. That is, they share a common energy base. And we know this to be a fact because the *Bible* and every major scripture of the world tells us it is a fact.

"If the *Bible* is right and heaven and earth share the same energy base then from a scientific point of view there could be no such thing as the 'soul'. We know that chemicals and the different forms of energy they give life to are necessary to sustain thought processes whether they are of either the frontal or temporal lobes. So we know as a matter of scientific fact that the soul if it exists at all is an unconscious being of some sort. As if it were conscious we could see its chemicals. So we know that it cannot think in the way in which the mind thinks. Otherwise the mind and the soul would be synonymous with each other. And there is no preacher that would agree to that scenario.

"And this tells us quite conclusively that if one is dependent upon ones soul for salvation, that who one has been in this life, WHAT WE ARE TRYING TO SAVE, ceases to exist at the time of death. That the Christian, in trying to save his 'soul', instead of his 'sprit', is mortal.

"And, of course, one has the dictionary definition, that the soul is synonymous with compassion and emotions. The dictionary draws this conclusion in that compassion is normally felt as if coming from the heart. But one knows that it, in fact, comes from the frontal lobes of the brain. The heart cannot think, as a matter of fact it cannot even move without the brain. And if it is compassion that we are trying to save, one knows that compassion is not all of WHAT WE ARE TRYING TO SAVE. And one also knows that there is a wide range of compassion among people. There are very few who would have the homeliest girl on ones arm at the dance and there are even fewer who would save the baby rat from the cold. And we have many still with us today like those who ran the concentration camps who sent over a million children to the gas chambers without so much as a thought. So the dictionary doesn't give one a very good guess at what this thing one calls a 'soul' is.

"And if one resorts to the streets or asks those that are coming down the steps of the church, 'What are you trying to save?' They will answer, each and every one of them, 'My soul.' 'And what is a soul?' And they would answer, each and every one of them, 'A soul is something that we don't understand?' And then it would be our turn again, 'You are trying to save something that you don't understand?' Well," he stopped himself, "let's not go down that road. It would be too mind-boggling.

"But, nevertheless, let's give it chance. Let's assume that the story of creation is wrong. After all, Galileo proved that there wasn't much that was right about it. Let's assume that God did create heaven with a different energy base than that of earth. If one were to make such an assumption one would still have to determine if there is really such a thing as a 'soul.' Or, is it just simply a guess? Or, is it something that crept into the scriptures over the years?" And he stopped for a time before I realized that he had directed the question at me.

And as I had not answered he followed up with a more specific question. This time speaking more precisely and much more slowly, "If the soul does indeed exist, how much do you think it knows? Is it possible that it knows nothing? That it can never know anything? That it is without intelligence? That it is without, what we know as, the parietal, frontal and temporal lobes?

"We know our minds possess a very specific collection of memories and knowledge that is unique to each of us. That no one else knows what we as individuals know or remember. It is our minds, not our souls, which make us individuals. Now, what do you think our souls know?"

For a moment I remained speechless. After all I had no idea what our souls knew. But I decided to take a stab at it anyway, "I suppose our souls would know all things." I answered. "Yes", I repeated, "souls by their very nature would know all things. In that they are immortal they are of divinity of some sort. So chances are, like God, they would know all things. They certainly would not know nothing at all. For if they knew nothing at all they would not be our souls."

"Yes," he responded, "you are most likely correct. A soul, by its very definition, if it exists, would know all things. Would remember all things. And, if that were true, then it would have no individuality for all souls would know all things. They would all be the same. And this means, conclusively, that man as an individual is without a soul. We have been fooling ourselves.

"For immortality to have any real meaning it must involve the individual, not the mass. And it is what we know, much more so than our bodies, that makes each one of us individuals. It is that we all know different things that make us separate beings.

"So if one is to believe in the immortality of ones being, one must put aside the premise of the soul. For the soul cannot represent the individual. It can only represent the mass. For other than our bodies which we know are mortal, it is what we know, our intelligence, our memory and to a certain extent our instincts that defines who we are. As a matter of fact, it is the only thing after death of the body that could define us as individuals. It is the possible preservation of the product of our 'minds' not our souls that is our only chance at immortality."

He stopped for some time as if the curtain had fallen on act two and he were waiting for it to rise again. And, then, he went on. "So much for the 'mind' and for the 'soul'. And now how about the 'body'? How about this thing called resurrection?"

"Resurrection of the body?" I asked.

"Yes, resurrection," he said, "perhaps it is time for another cup of coffee, "bring me down a coke," he ordered as he disappeared into the bathroom. And I scampered up the stairs.

Lucien Gregoire

the case for saving ones 'body'

When I returned he was waiting for me and, once again, he didn't give me the chance to sit down before he started up, "As a matter of fact all western religions peddle resurrection of the body. And, on the other hand, no eastern religion believes in resurrection of the body. All eastern religions believe only in the salvation of the 'spirit' or the 'mind' after death. Why is this so?"

"Why is this so?" I questioned his question.

"Yes, why is it so? Why this strange coincidence that every single western religion speaks of resurrection of the body and not a single eastern religion mentions it?"

"Well, you already told me that there are two Gods, God the Father of the western world and the God Brahma of the eastern world." I offered.

"That's a part of it," he agreed, "but more specifically the answer lies in the ancient hieroglyphics. The timing of Moses was fourteen centuries before Christ and seventeen centuries after the Egyptians had first come up with the idea that the body would rise again. Actually if one must give credit the prize goes to the Pharaoh Naumer in 3100BC, the first man to claim that his body would rise again after death. And one can see this quite clearly in the thousands of Egyptian tombs that have been uncovered to date that predate the time of Moses. For each one contains implements of human life. In a typical tomb one will find bowls and water jugs and tables and chairs and tablets and chariots and stores of grain and even portable toilets. For the Egyptians were convinced that they would rise again. Yes, in very early times only Pharaoh was believed to rise again. But by the time Moses came along all Egyptians believed that their bodies would rise again. For after all, like the Hebrews and Christians and Muslims that would come after them, Egyptian scripture, the hieroglyphics, speaks of a *Day of Judgment*. '*That on the Day of Judgment, Anubis, protector of mummies, would place the heart of each of the deceased on a scale and weigh it against a feather. Those whose hearts balanced perfectly with the feather were given up to Osiris, God of Resurrection, and entered into eternal life. Whereas, those who were rejected were devoured by Ammit, monster of fire and the dead.*'

"And these early hieroglyphics have other significance too. For it is the first time anywhere in the world that anyone recognized the existence of hell. And the 'fiery hell' the ancient hieroglyphics speak of is identical to that which both Christianity and Islamism later built into their textbooks.

"And this is another major difference between all eastern and western religions. No eastern religion whether it be Hinduism or Buddhism or Shintoism or what have you recognizes the existence of hell. In the east the objective is to make it into the next life. In the case of the Hindu this means Nirvana or heaven. In the Buddhist world it means to make it back into this life. The penalty for not leading a good and contributory life in both the case of the Hindu and the Buddhist is possible loss of existence, one will possibly cease to exist.

"So it is only natural that the Christians and the Muslims who believed in the God of Moses thought that like the Egyptians before them their bodies too would rise after death. That for them too there would one day be a *Day of Judgement,* that if they were good they would go to heaven and if they were bad they would go to hell. That when the western prophets claimed that they had gotten this message of 'hell' from God the Father, they in fact had gotten it from the Egyptians who had come before them. They hadn't spoken to God at all. And if this is true it would mean that there is no such thing as hell. I might point out that the hieratics I just quoted are dated 1853BC, four hundred years before Moses was born. The archive itself is in the British National Museum today.

Lucien Gregoire

"As we have said before, it is quite obvious from Christ's testimony that He was entirely unaware of the Indians and the Chinese who were living in the East at His time. And the history books tell us this too, that the East did not meet up with the West until after Christ's time. So those in China and India were unaware of the Egyptian beliefs of hell and that the body could rise again when they were going about forming their own religions many centuries before Christ. So they based their religions on survival of the spirit only. After all, it was quite obvious to them as it was to those in the west before Naumer's time that the body would never rise again.

"And this is consistent with all primitive societies, those that survived into the twentieth century unscathed. Like certain Aborigine tribes in Australia and South America, and certain tribes in deepest Africa and those Eskimos who lived in the frozen lands of the north. Never having heard of the Egyptians they all believed that the sprit escapes the body at death. Common sense told them that their bodies would never rise again. And although they had never encountered each other's cultures they all believed independently of each other that these spirits, the minds of the dead, could be of some harm to them. And they took measures to protect themselves from the spirits of the dead.

"And this goes back to the Neanderthal Man two hundred thousand years ago. For although not much is known of their beliefs we know that they buried their dead. And we know that they only buried their male dead. Had hygiene been their motive then they would have also buried their female dead. And this tells us why they buried only their male dead. That they had some fear of the spirits of the male dead and that females being smaller and weaker could not hurt them. And this is confirmed in that the bigger the body, the deeper it was buried. Smaller bodies being buried just beneath the surface and larger ones being buried progressively deeper up to a depth of as much as ten feet.

"In that all human beings throughout history, even those in these primitive societies, have buried their dead, is fitting testimony that the practice started with the Neanderthals and was passed on to the Cro-Magnons and then onto modern day man.

"And it is for this reason that all these primitive societies, the Eskimos, the Aborigine Indians and the African natives, have been so receptive to Christianity and Islamism, as these western religions bring something new into their world of the hereafter, that their bodies, themselves, will live forever. Eastern religions, on the other hand, have made no significant inroads into Africa, Latin America or Australia as these natives have always 'known' that the sprit will live forever. To them the eastern religions brought them nothing new.

"And we know from the *Book of Revelations* that no matter how far a body has disintegrated it will be resurrected for this judgment. That '*even the sea will give up its dead.*' Even those who perished in the Titanic will be resurrected, even *Jack Dawson* will rise again. That in the meantime, until the day of judgment, which the believer continues to hope will be at the end of the current millennium, all those who die, will find that their spirits will be suspended in time until they are reunited with their bodies on the *Day of Judgment*. Except '*those who are to be unsaved, in which case, their spirits will be cast at the time of death into a state of conscious punishment called Hades.*' A place of temporary punishment. That on the day of Judgment, their spirits, too, will be rejoined to their bodies and at that time they will be cast, both body and sprit, into '*the eternal lake of fire.*'

"And the Muslims, too, who do not follow the way of their scripture, shall find themselves in the very same hell as do the Christians. This great lake of fire." And he pulled the *Koran* in front of him. "'*Even for the evil doers is a wretched home - Hell - wherein they shall be burned in the Great Fire, forever.*'"

Lucien Gregoire

the case for saving ones 'spirit'

"But, nevertheless, let's consider that. Let's say that our bodies will be resurrected after death, that the *New Testament* and the *Koran* and the Egyptians were right. The question is, in what form would one come back? And the answer is most likely, how would one want to come back? As the embryo, the unborn fetus, as the newborn infant, the handicapped person, or the ugly person, or the aging, frail, white harried, wrinkled up person one died as? Or would one want to come back as Tom Cruise or Elizabeth Taylor? And the answer is quite clear. Few of us would choose to come back as the person he or she died as. We would all prefer to come back as the epitome of what we perceive a physical human being to be.

"Sadly for the Christians this will not be. For there is no provision in the *New Testament* for anyone to rise again in any form other than one died in.

"And just what will Christ look like?" he asked himself, "Well, chances are in His case He will resume the same body that He had when He carried out His ministry. And no one actually knows exactly what He looked like. Keep in mind that no one knows that such a man ever existed, one only believes that He at one time walked the face of the earth. And there is the fact that no one made any drawings of etchings of Him while He was alive. Which considering the miracles He is alleged to have performed is unbelievable in itself, as hundreds of etchings of other men of his time survive today.

"The closest renditions of what He most probably looked like can be found in the few early Byzantine icons which have survived which were painted not long after his death. And these portray Him as a rather weak, olive skinned, relatively unattractive man. As you might know, Emperor Leo, in the eighth century, ordered all these icons destroyed and a hundred years later the church commissioned that new likenesses of Christ be painted which has forever changed the public's perception of Christ's image. It was Charles Manson's remarkable resemblance to the few early icons which survived which enabled him to convince his followers of his possible divinity.

"So according to the Book of Revelations we will all come back in the form that we died in. There we will all be, the embryos, the unborn fetuses, the newborn infants, the lame, the deaf, the blind, some suffering from AIDS, leprosy, cancer and other afflictions, some ugly, others the aging, frail, white harried, wrinkled up people they died as? There we will be surrounding Christ on his great white throne, tens of millions of us, our 'minds' totally captivated by Him.

"And that we come back as we were in this life physically is important, as there would be no other way to tell us apart. For remember we will take only our souls and not our minds or spirits into this place. Mentally, if there is any mentality, we will all be the same. So who we are, what we are today, our memory and our thought processes, will not survive in the Christian heaven. For it is the Christian dream to be there for Christ alone. Our minds, if we have any at all, will be totally focused in adoration of Christ ruling from His great white throne.

"But for the Muslim the picture will be much different. For his scripture, the *Koran*, does provide that those who will be saved will all come back as the epitome of what one perceives a physical human being to be. That in the Muslim heaven all of God the Father's, Allah's children will be equal. Something that He did not consider when He placed us here the first time.

"This, as you might know, was the greatest problem Albert Einstein had in accepting the existence of God. He just *'could not accept that God would play dice with humanity.'* That it was this doubt in the existence of a Creator which inspired his work that resulted in his *Theory of Relativity* in which he proved the existence of a Creator.

"So in the Muslim heaven Einstein's prayer will be answered in the resurrection. '*That the child born blind would not remain in darkness. That the child born a deaf mute would not remain in silence. That the deformed would be formed.*' That the ugly duckling would, too, have her chance to dance at the ball. So, yes, they will all be the same. They will all be perfect. And, only one thing will make them individuals. Only one thing will make each one of them different from one another."

"Only one thing?" I asked.

"Yes," he answered, "that which they 'know'. How they 'think'. Which has its foundation in our 'memory' and our 'thought processes'. That which we talked of earlier. That energy that at the time of death rests there on the peripherals of the brain. That which, even today, far more so than our bodies, makes us different individuals. Which defines 'me' from 'you', 'him' from 'her', 'us' from 'them'. For Mohammed, unlike his Christian counterparts, did not accept the *Old Testament*'s theory that there was a 'soul'. He believed that the 'spirit', that the mind', would survive after death. So he gives one a much better salvation, one in which one survives with a perfect body and ones own mind forever.

"And when this resurrection thing happens, the Egyptians and Muslims will still have one more advantage over Christianity." he added.

"And," I questioned, "what's that?"

"Sex," he replied, "sex."

"For unlike its counterparts in the east and the Egyptians, Christianity views sex as sinful and shameful. That there is no room for sex in the Christian heaven. For there is no room for sin in the Christian heaven. We will all be without sex, asexual. That is, we will rise in a state of total castration. Eunuchs so to speak!"

I thought it was embarrassment that I felt at the time. But, today, as I think back, I know it was fear, unparalleled fear.

"So strong was the Father's condemnation of the horrific act of sex, that He chose to bring His Son into the world free of it, that His would be a stainless conception. That all other conceptions were dirty, filthy so to speak. And the Catholic Church has taken this one step further in extending this concept of purity to Mary, the Mother of *Christ*. *The Immaculate Conception,* meaning free of sin.

"The act of fornication is the most damned sin in all of the *Bible*. In all, thirty eight condemnations of it. I know because I have counted them all, each and every one of them. And, in three specific cases, Christ separates Himself, forever, from the fornicator. '*The fornicator, among all men, shall not enter the Kingdom of Heaven.*' One would have to be an imbecile not to get the message. Or to make believe that it somehow pertains to someone else. Yet, most Christians ignore it. And, they ignore it because the preacher steers clear of it in his teachings for he knows that it would not be good for business. As a matter of fact, it would bring an end to his business.

"Yes," he added, "as I told you once before, there will be no penises and vaginas in the Christian heaven. Remember," he said, smiling and pointing to his temple, "The preacher told me so!

"Besides," he added, "there will be no need for love making. There would be no pregnancies in this land the *Book of Revelations* calls the *New Jerusalem,* the new heaven. For the newborn would have no chance at being *born again*. For he or she would already be in heaven. Remember, '*unless one be born again one cannot enter the Kingdom of Heaven.*' So that which, today, we perceive as life's greatest joy, its greatest dream, the hope to grow up and fall in love and have children, will not be.

"That on the *Day of Judgment,* the final bell would have rung. That procreation of the human race will no longer be a factor.

"In fact, there will be no highs, no lows, no ups, no downs, no pleasure, no pain, no illness, no cuts and bruises, no sadness, no joy, no good times, no bad times. How will we ever know when we are happy, if we don't know what it is to be sad?

"Richard Nixon's farewell address will be lost in oblivion. '*Only when one has walked in the shadows of the deepest valley, can one realize how magnificent it is to be at the pinnacle of the tallest mountain.*'

"Just the same thing, day after day. For in its resurrection, the human body would be immortal, blood and guts going off into eternity on an even plane? Is this to be our reward? Is this what one calls paradise?

"There would be no football, no baseball, no tennis, no golf. No winning, no losing. No television, no movies, no entertainment at all. For our destiny, our eternity, would consist of a single thing. Perpetual adoration of the Magi. All of us clustered about Him, in adoration of Him for all time.

"And, then, of course, there would be one more thing." he added.

"What's that?" I questioned.

"Every once and a while we would have to go to the bathroom. For we will be human you know. And, every once in a while, *Christ*, Himself, would have to excuse Himself, from his audience, and leave the great white throne and go to the bathroom. Because, according to the *Book of Revelations*, according to the *Bible*, He too would resume His humanity."

"But, Johnny, you're reading it wrong." I corrected him. "We won't have to go to the bathroom in heaven." And I quoted to him directly from memory from the *Book of Revelations*, "'*for there will be no thirst or hunger there.*'"

And somewhat startled, he replied, "Not to have to go to the bathroom? Human beings that don't have to go to the bathroom?" he questioned. "No mouthwatering porterhouse steak with the baked potato and sour cream and chives? No cheese omelet with sausage and hash browns? No crepe suzettes with the wild berry sauce? No chips and dips? No Ben and Jerry's ice cream sundae with the chocolate sauce and whipped cream and the cherry on top?

"The next thing you will be telling me is that we won't have to go to the barber to get our hair cut. That Mom won't have to go to the beauty parlor to make herself beautiful for the adoration. That we won't even have to clip our nails. Or scrub our feet. Or clean our ears. Or brush our teeth.

"But aside from all that, perhaps the thing that bothers me the most about this *Book of Revelations*," he continued, "is that '*there will be no sea.*' For the new earth, what we call heaven, will be just solid earth, actually solid gold. You and I won't be able to go fishing together. Or even go hiking to search for the cascading waterfall at the trail's end. And our many friends in the sea will not be. There will be no seasons of winter, of spring, of summer or fall. There will be no thunder and lightning on a midsummer's night. No pitter-patter of the rain on the window pane. There will be no snow and no longer will I be able to beat you down the slopes. There will be no thirst quenching soda pop for me, or a beer for you. For I stand corrected. You are right, '*there will be no thirst or hunger there.*'

"Yes, according to the *Bible* our bodies will rise again, but not as we know them today. But much closer to how Hollywood portrays them in *The Night of the Living Dead*. As a matter of fact the producers of that film used the *Biblical* description of those who are saved in the *Book of Revelations* to characterize their *living dead*. Our only anguish will be that we will not be able to hug one another as all our love will be reserved for Him. And, perhaps, the knowledge that many of our friends and loved ones didn't make it. Our only hope would be that we will be unable to hear their screaming down below in the great pit of fire. For our entire existence, '*for all of eternity, will be before the throne of Christ, to serve Him day and night in His temple of gold.*'

"*God the Father's* instruction, which he set forth so many times in the *Old Testament* including in His Tenth Commandment, will finally be realized. That slavery be a way of life. Or that, more precisely, it will be a way of eternity. For the successful Christian will remain in slavery for all eternity. At least that is the very explicit message of the *Bible*, '*To serve his Master for all eternity.*'

"And just who are those who won't make it? Who will be screaming down below? Well, we know almost for certain, unless, of course, one believes that it is not necessary '*to be born again to be saved*,' that it is not necessary '*to be baptized to be saved*,' that it is not necessary '*to believe in Christ to be saved*,' that Anne Frank and the other six million Jews that were murdered in the Holocaust will be there. We know that all of the descendants of Hamm, who were cursed to be born to be promiscuous or homosexuals, will be there. We know that almost all the Chinese will be there because Christ did not provide for them as He did not know that they were there. We know that all those before Christ's time will be there for they had been born before the coming of the Savior. We know that most people who die suddenly in the prime of life, the ages twenty to fifty, will be there. And we know this because they are the most likely to have been caught with their pants down, so to speak. In fact, anyone who dies very suddenly is more likely to be there. Simply because it is those who die suddenly who are more likely to die in an unrepentant state. Yes, they will all be there, down below. Screaming their lungs off.

"And just who will be there next to *Christ's* side in His *City of Gold?* We know, almost for certain, that Adolph Hitler will be there. We know that he was a Christian to the end. And we also know that he had loads of time in the bunker to plan his impending death and make amends for his sins. We know that for him to defy his most inner beliefs and go to his death in an unrepentant state would defy all logic. And we know, for a fact,

A God for Lions

that he was thinking of his time after death. That he was planning that time after death, when according to Christian scripture, he would rule at *Christ's* side."

"How do you now that to be a fact?" I stopped him.

"We know it is a fact because he married his mistress, which was required of him by his scripture, by his religion. He knew that if he were not to marry his mistress that he would be living in a state of sin at the time of his death and would not die in the state of grace. That this was required of him, if he were to rule at Christ's side for all eternity as promised him in the *Book of Revelations*. There was no other logical reason for him to have married Eva Brawn. There was no other logical reason for him to have the ritual performed. After all, he would be dead, they would both be dead.

"And one also knows that Hitler's place will be high. For it was he, as we have previously discussed, who had led the great war which aim was to give the Aryan race sole rule of the world. To fulfill the dream of *God the Father* when he spoke to Moses, *'that it was the children of his brother Aaron, the Aryan race, which would alone, in the end, rule at my side forever. Those who breed contempt for my rule shall be annihilated and destroyed.'* The Christian dream. The fascist dream.

"That Hitler failed in his quest to destroy the Jews will probably not count. That he tried, that he tried to make come true this very important dream of *God the Father* in the *Old Testament* will count much toward his place at *Christ's* side."

And he concluded, "So, yes, Hitler is most likely up there waiting for us now. Perhaps, he is working directly for St. Peter, separating those of the Aryan race from the others as his henchmen once did when the rail cars would come into to the concentration camps. 'This one to the camp.' 'That one to the ovens.'" He stopped for just a second or so to make sure that I had gotten the picture firmly in my mind. Of Hitler standing there at the hallowed gates directing a few this way while casting most to the fires below. And then he added, "Of course during the adoration, Hitler would take his place at Christ's side.

"And who else would be there in heaven? There would be most people who do not die suddenly in the prime of life as aging people become very conscious of impending death, that they will most certainly keep their repentance up to date. And, of course, they are far less likely to be caught with their pants down. And the children, how about the children? Just where will they be? As we've just discussed, we don't really believe that they will be there. We don't really trust the *New Testament*. We don't really trust the word of Jesus. We don't really believe that the *New Testament* is truly the word of God or inspired by God as some skeptics prefer to say. That *Christ* actually said, '*blessed are the little children for theirs is the Kingdom of Heaven.*'

"But, if they are there, we know that they will all be there. And, if they are not there, we know that they will all not be there. For they would have died at a time short of their ability to be *born again*. Short of their ability to accept *Christ* on their own. But, as the case of *John List* proved quite conclusively, we don't really believe that they will be there. Because we only 'think' we know.

"But, nevertheless, it will be a strange world. This world that the *Book of Revelations* calls the *New Jerusalem*. Do you think, do you really think, that this is what our Father wants of us? To fall down before Him and adore Him? That this is His dream? A selfish dream?

"Or do you think, perhaps, He would want us to be out playing with our friends, going to the football games, and taking the girl of our dreams to the junior prom, and growing up and falling in love, and having children? To become independent of Him? Unselfishly giving us up. A chance to be on our own. A chance to be individuals?

"Yes, this would be a great sacrifice on His part, far greater than was His charade of having died on the cross. But, nevertheless, it would be one that would lock up our love for Him, and our adoration of Him, forever."

He let me think a while as to allow me time to soak up all that he had said or, perhaps, to anticipate what he was getting at. Then, once again, he went on.

"What all this tells us is that the human body is not a very viable vehicle for eternal life. For if the resurrected body were truly human, it would have its ups and downs, it would continue to grow old, and eventually die. And die again, and again, and again. Then rise again, and again, and again.

"Keep in mind that the human body is not an entity by itself. It is a composition of billions of Einstein's little friends going about their work. Each one a separate entity, a separate being, as we can see under the microscopes of today. That if, in fact, our bodies would rise again, it would mean that all of these microcosmic creatures would also be saved. Will also live on forever. And for them this would be quite a reward. As in this life many of them live for only a few hours, some for only a few minutes.

"Nevertheless, Hollywood does come remarkably close as to what we will be in our resurrection in its *Night of the Living Dead*. An unbelievably accurate description of what the *Bible* says we will be upon resurrection. Our minds focused in a trance like state focused on Christ with Adolph Hitler at His side for all eternity. That, in fact, all of our minds will be the same. And this is, undoubtedly, the most important point. That since all of our minds will be the same, our current minds, those that identify us as individuals, today, will not survive beyond death according to Christian doctrine.

"And this is, for the Christian, the most important point of all. That, according to the *Bible*, our minds, as we know them today, are not immortal. Only our bodies, with some biological modifications, like the sexual modifications we spoke of, and that we won't have to eat or drink or go the bathroom, will survive beyond the grave.

"For the Christian 'mind' in the hereafter will be totally focused on adoration of Christ for all time. That it will have no need to remember either the good or bad things of this life. That there will be no need for it to respond to alternatives and make appropriate decisions. As there will be no alternatives.

"And this means quite conclusively that the Christian, unlike the practitioner of all other faiths, accepts his mortality, that when he dies, he will kiss his 'rear-end' goodbye forever. And this is exactly what his preacher has promised him. That when he dies he says 'goodbye' to those who he has known in this life forever. For if a Christian were to ask his preacher, 'What is this thing called 'a soul' that I am trying to save?' The preacher, every Christian preacher will say, **'It is that thing within us that drives our adoration of God, that trance-like mesmerized feeling that one experiences at the moment one is *born again.* That wonderful feeling that one feels when one accepts Christ is all that we as Christians will carry forward into the next life. That we will be there in adoration of Christ alone for all time.'**

"So we know as a matter of Biblical fact that the Christian upon death returns to become a part of the same scientific energy flow that created him upon birth, precisely Einstein's conclusion a century ago. *'That all matter is made up of moving parts called energy and that these moving parts are constantly changing from one form of energy into another."* That the Christian definition of *'God'* is that **God is the infinite energy flow from which it all had its beginning and to which it will all eventually return.**

"That the Christian in trying to save his 'soul' instead of his 'mind' is mortal. That he will cease to be what he has been in this life for all time. And what's more he 'knows' this, the reason why he prays for miracles!"

the case for saving ones 'mind'

"On the other side of the world the Buddhist returns to a body that is biologically the same sexual body as he or she had in this life. Only the features will vary. And the Buddhist mind will survive essentially as it has been in this life, with a continuation of the abilities of decision making, creativity, invention and accomplishment that it had in this life. Its ability to think freely and make appropriate decisions. And the Buddhist if he succeeds in his salvation will remain one step ahead of both the Christian and the Muslim."

"What's that?" I asked.

"In that he will not know all things he will have a future," he replied, "he will still be able to experience this thing we call 'change' and ..."

I cut him off, "and what?"

"He will still be able to dream and ..."

And I cut him off again, "And what?"

"He will still be able to take a chance and have on his arm the homeliest girl at the dance!"

As I had once told him of how he had come about, he looked first to the right, and then to the left, and I looked first to the right, and then to the left, and then again to the right, ... and I decided that it was as good a time as ever to get another cup of coffee.

the reality of reincarnation,

When I returned as before he didn't give me a chance to sit down before he started up again, "So we have found that although there are millions of religions, millions of beliefs, there are only two prizes offered in the great arena of theology, the promise of Heaven on the one hand, or the promise of reincarnation on the other. The promise of saving ones 'soul' on the one hand, or the promise of saving ones 'mind' on the other. Except, perhaps, for sheer survival of the spirit in the current environment as was once believed by primitive societies, there are no other real options. Just two to choose from.

"If one discounts *belief* and looks for concrete proof of which theory is right in the case of the body rising again there is none, absolutely none. Yes, there is *belief*, overwhelming *belief*, but no proof, no possibility at all. It is quite incredible that we as Christians laugh at the Egyptian' belief that their bodies would rise again, while our own New Testament tells us quite explicitly that our bodies will too rise again, the basic message of the resurrection of Christ, what we believe in.

"But regardless of what the *Bible* says or Hollywood might want us to believe in its renditions of the *Bible* and ancient Egypt, it remains strictly *belief*, a reaching for the straw, simply a guess driven by hopeless despair. But, on the other hand, in the case of the spirit, the mental processes leaving a dead body and finding their way into a new body, there is considerable evidence.

"There is the remarkable chain of coincidence, in the search for successive Dalai Lamas, for example, that a successor is often found. The current Dalai Lama was found to be born in a remote part of eastern Tibet. And his potential successor, a seven year old Canadian boy, who was found to be speaking in the ancient language of the Tibetan Buddha. Just one of many signs that the reincarnated spirit of Buddha or that of one of his immediate followers has been found. And one would ask how would this composition of energy get halfway around the world from Tibet to Canada. And the answer is clear. The very same way a beam of energy circumnavigates the globe in a split second in satellite communication.

"And this phenomenon does not limit itself to those at the top. As there are many of us, ordinary people, who can remember the details of life in another country, of which we have never been to or even read or heard about. Of things that have happened long before we were born.

"And, very often, one meets someone for the very first time, and thinks that he has known him or her all of his or her life. And for some of these, who one has never met before in this life, one immediately has bad vibes about, and others very good vibes about. And one usually finds out that ones vibes were right.

"And then there is the practiced Buddhist, himself, as he reaches into his past life through meditation. To the onlooker, one would think that he is searching into the future. But, in reality, he is searching into his past. Searching for the strength that those who have gone before him have passed on to him. And, we know at least that he must be having some level of success at this. Less he would cease to meditate.

"And then we have those things we spoke of earlier. The fact that a thought can be transferred from one mind to another without the use of the five senses. The example of the world renown psychic reading the minds of his subjects with uncanny accuracy. And the fact that the mental transfer of energy can be decidedly felt by both the giver and the taker as we discussed that day when we talked of the birds and the bees.

"Yet, perhaps, the most remarkable evidence we have that reincarnation may, in fact, be a reality is found in gender identity. In the transgender population or what is more commonly referred to as the transsexual population.

"Genetics and nutrition are overwhelmingly the major determinants of what we end up being both physically and mentally. How a woman's mind can end up in a man's body, or how a man's mind can end up in a woman's body, cannot be explained by either one of these sources scientifically. In fact, the only possible explanation for this phenomenon seems to be reincarnation.

"We know that this is a condition that exists at birth. For it manifests itself in early infancy. That from the very start the impaired little boy will reach for the doll and from the very start the impaired little girl will reach for the truck. And, of course, the condition persists into adulthood, that the young 'man' desires to wear dresses, and the young 'girl' desires to wear trousers.

"And how is it possible that the normal little girl knows that she should reach for the doll and the normal little boy knows that he should reach for the truck, unless, of course, one has been a little girl or a little boy before?

"And then there is, as we have already discussed, the amazing phenomenon, that one is able to transfer ones own thoughts to another without the use of the senses. And this kind of thing happens every day entirely without the aid of a chemical reaction.

"And just how does this happen?" he asked himself. And he answered his own question, "As we have already said, exactly the same way that a beam of energy finds its way by way of a remote control device across the room to change the channel.

"And there are, of course, dreams and sometimes nightmares. In our dreams appear many of those that we have known in this life, and, yet, many others appear from time to time with images and personality traits every bit as vivid as those we have known in this life. Could these be visitors from our past? And in our nightmares we often suffer a variety of trauma and near death experiences from someone or something in pursuit of us, to swords, to bullets, to falling from great heights, to even being buried alive, that we seem to lie in a frozen state of some kind unable to get up. Could these be reenactments of how we actually met our ends in past lives?

"And then one has aptitude, that which rides on the back of intelligence in the parietal lobes. Just how does it come about?

How is it possible that an Einstein and a Rembrandt who rose to the top of their two respective fields could never get past grade school in each other's field? How is it possible that Mozart at the age of six totally eclipsed everything that was about him in the world of music?

"Physically at birth we are a composition of only two things, our parent's genes and nourishment, genetics and nutrition. Hundreds of population and clinical studies have proved that intelligence and aptitude have nothing to do with genes. For example, a genius is very often born to an idiot and vice versa and most of the world's greatest artists have been born into families with no history of art at all. So one would be left with the only other alternative. That something we eat makes some of us into nuclear scientists and others into poet laureates. Certainly, not a very reasonable conclusion. And this leaves us with only one other possibility. The 'genius' in each one of us has been there before.

"So in all there exists a mountain of evidence in support of the possibility of reincarnation. We have the scientific fact that a thought can be transferred from one mind to another without the use of the five senses. And we have the fact that a little boy knows that he a little boy and little girl knows that she is a little girl, and that occasionally a little boy is born into a little girl's body and occasionally a little girl is born into a little boy's body. And then we have all the other things that we have talked of. All the way down to aptitude, that a child often possesses skill in a particular calling that normally one would take a lifetime, or many lifetimes, to achieve.

"And then we have the fact that all newborn infants laugh and cry about the same things. And there are our other instincts that we are born with, that most of us can only fall in love with one of the opposite sex and that most of us know right from wrong. Could it be that those few of us who can only fall in love with one of their own sex developed their orientation in a past life? Could it be that those schizophrenics who don't know right from wrong were rogues in a past life? Since studies have proved that none of these things have anything to do with genes, is it reasonable to believe that they are the products of something we eat? Or is it more reasonable to believe that these things are carryovers from past lives? And if the latter were true it would mean that not only would the thoughts that are in our temporal lobes, and the intelligence and aptitude that is in our parietal lobes, but the instincts that are in our frontal lobes, would be carried over into successive lives. And this would mean that all of WHAT WE ARE TRYING TO SAVE will survive in the process of reincarnation.

"Not enough, in all, for us to say with absolute certainty that reincarnation is actually taking place, but certainly enough to enable us to consider with a fair degree of confidence that this is in reality the case. Otherwise one would have to believe that it is something we eat that causes these things to be. For there are no other alternatives. Whereas there are no facts, no facts at all, in either heaven or earth in support of the possibility that the body can rise again. And more importantly, that both scripture and science agree that there is no such thing as the human soul. The existence of the soul, of something that we don't understand, is simply not possible. It is simply a fantasy. It is simply a dream. A pipe dream. Because it could not possibly exist without God's fundamental unit of creation, this thing that the great one in the long white hair called, 'energy'."

He stopped for a moment or two to allow me time to realize the full impact of his summation. Then he exclaimed, "So we messed up. We messed up," he repeated himself.

"We messed up?" I questioned.

"Yes," he replied, "we messed up. We should have included aptitude among those things that WE ARE TRYING TO SAVE. For it is unique to each of us, even more so than is intelligence which is simply a matter of degree. For it is most likely the cumulation of knowledge that we have acquired in past lives. That it has been with us from the very beginning of our days and it most likely will be with us until the end of time."

"And then we have Christ," he said it with a hint of finality.

"Christ?" I questioned his reasoning.

"Whereas it is reasonable to believe that the evangelists plagiarized the teachings of Buddha in writing the gospels it is certainly as reasonable to believe that Christ actually lived. That He was in fact the reincarnated sprit of Buddha. If one takes the time to read both the *Tripitaka* - the teachings of Buddha and the Gospels - the teachings of Christ one will find as I did that they are carbon copies of each other.

He quickly pulled the *Tripitaka* before him, "'*When all is done there are only two measurements of life. Oneself and others. The first will lead to treasures in this book of fools. In this book of this life. The other will lead to treasures in the true book. The vast book of eternity.*'

And then he reached for the *New Testament*, "'*Lay not up for yourselves treasures upon earth, where moth and rust doth corrupt. But lay up for yourselves treasures in heaven, where neither moth nor rust doth corrupt. For where your treasure is, will be your heart also...*'

"The similarities between the two scriptures are so vast and exact that it is reasonable to believe that the thinkings that once rested on the peripherals of Buddha's mind may have indeed found their way to rest for a time on the peripherals of Christ's mind. And this could explain why Christ so blatantly contradicts many of the teachings of His Father. Why one knows today that Jesus could not have been the same God who ordered the brutal murder of the Canaanites. Why Ghandi so often said, '*I love Christ, but I hate Christians!*'"

the sure bet

And I broke the silence that followed with, "Incidentally, I was going to ask you, what are you doing with a book about Buddhism?" I said it in almost the same tone that, several years before, I had told him that his private parts were dirty.

"If it happens," he replied, "that, in the end, I am unable to find my soul, then, of course, I must find another form of guidance. Christianity would become meaningless to me. Buddhism would be a possible choice. Not in its recent, more popular, more intricate northern variety, the Mahayana, with its endless parables of paradise, its embarrassing puppets dedicated to the pornography of worship, naked maidens squirming up the sides of the giant phallus. In its overemphasis on meditation and the culture of ones mind. In its promise of salvation in a future body. No, the possibility lies in the more distant Hinayana, the less popular ancient instruction that dictates that man is without a soul, that his deeds will, themselves, create his sprit, his soul, which will live on in his fellowman. That emphasizes contribution rather than simple meditation or belief. That death is what the Christian fears above all else, this type of Buddhist welcomes. For he is certain that what he has done here, in this life, will live on forever. As a matter of fact, he is the only practitioner of any kind of scripture who is certain of his destiny.

"As we just discussed, the Christian does not enjoy this level of certainty. Otherwise, one would blow up the schools and not risk that the children not go to heaven. For, as we 'know', if they reach adulthood, at the very most, only one in ten will be saved. For the Christian is not certain that the children will, indeed, go to heaven. He does not really believe that the children will go to heaven. He does not really believe what his scripture is telling him. He does not really believe in his God. And, this, again, as we have just proved, is not just something I am saying. It is a fact. And, we know it is a fact because the *Bible* tells us that it is a fact and the Christian confirms it as fact in his actions.

"The United States is the only nation in the free world that imposes a death penalty. And it is no secret that it is the *Christian right* that forces this rule among its populace. And the fact that it does so is living proof that the Christian doesn't really believe in the hereafter. As it would make no sense whatsoever to give the criminal ample time to repent, and then send him to heaven. For the Christian 'knows' that the criminal is not going to heaven. As a matter of fact he 'knows' that he is not going anywhere.

"For the Christian, this is the *proof of the pudding*. For, the Christian, in truth, weighs the value of the present life far above the possibility of an afterlife, regardless of what his scriptures tell him. His is only a guess at an afterlife. And, as we just discussed, a guess at a highly restricted afterlife. And, as we have just said, it is a guess driven by hopelessness and despair. For the Christian knows that his chance at an afterlife is a much longer shot than is his winning the lottery."

And he paused and repeated it, this time speaking more slowly and decisively as if it were the most important conclusion of his entire dissertation, "The Christian, in truth, weighs the value of the present life far above the possibility of an afterlife. The reason he prays for miracles. His is only a hope of an afterlife. He does not really believe that it is there. This thing he calls 'heaven'. Otherwise, he would blow up the schools and guarantee that all the children go to heaven. Otherwise, the Christian would not lament so at the good fortune of those who have been called to the *Great House* before him. One would not put the man who blows up the school in the electric chair but instead would have parades and celebrations for him in recognition of his great courage for having risked his soul to save the children.

"But, this type of Buddhist, the Hinayana," he went on, "knows that it is the cumulation of his current life that will become the very substance of his afterlife. He is certain of his afterlife. For he is building it every single day that he lives. One 'believes', while the other 'knows'. The Christian 'believes', while the Hinayana 'knows'."

And I interrupted him, "You mean that if this type of Buddhist makes a great contribution to society then we will remember him?"

"It has nothing to do with remembering someone. It is much more than that," he replied. "Let's take Lincoln, for example. Before Lincoln's time half of the people in the United States believed in slavery. They thought that it was good. Because it was God the Father's instruction of the *Old Testament* they thought there was something holy about it. But, today, no one thinks that slavery is good. We all know that it is bad. Lincoln has obtained immortality in that today he is part of the way all of us think. As we have just said, a man is defined by how he thinks. Much more so than by his body which will return to dust. As we have just been discussing it is how we think that we want to live on forever. And Lincoln has become a part of the way all of us will think for all time. So his consciousness, the way he thought, the energy, the product of his mind, WHAT ONE WANTS TO SAVE, will live on forever.

"For Lincoln is much more today than the simple soul that his Christian *Bible* promised him. For today he is a God, a part of the Creator," and he pointed to his temple," a part of that *God who tells us what is right or wrong!*

"And then we have Mother Teresa on the other side of the world. Yes, as a Christian, if there is any truth to the *Bible*, she will live on forever. But, we all know that is a very long shot. It is the example she set that guarantees that she will live on forever. For by her example she has encouraged millions, perhaps, billions of others to lead lives of helping others. She has become a part of the way they think, a part of each of them. Much more so than did any pope who pranced around in luxurious robes of silk and satin and drank from jeweled chalices and prayed before golden crucifixes. Or any evangelist who carried on his relentless persecution of blacks or gays.

"That Lincoln and Mother Teresa live on in this thing we call 'divinity' today proves Hinayana scripture, that the Creator's job was done upon creation and that the rest of the job is up to man. That men and women who make the world a better place to live in will live on forever. That they become *a part of Him that is a part of each one of us,*" and he pointed to his temple, "And that those who fail to contribute to a better world or work to the detriment of society will cease to exist.

"Hitler in his day was a much more powerful person than was either Lincoln or Mother Teresa. Yet, today he has ceased to exist. That is, the way he thought, WHAT ONE WANTS TO SAVE, has ceased to exist, as very few of us think the way that Hitler thought. So, yes, we remember him, but that is all.

"So this kind of Buddhist, the Hinayana, unlike the modern more popular type of Buddhist who must seek out an individual body to host his spirit, will find his way into many bodies, many hosts, many minds. And will go on forever. And unlike the Christian, who can only believe, he knows that he will go on forever. And this is not a matter of theory or theology, as I just explained in the case of Lincoln and Mother Teresa, it is a matter of absolute fact!

"So much for the *sure bet,* the ancient Buddhist known as the Hinayana. Yet, there remains considerable chance that the modern day Buddhist, the Mahayana will too live on forever. Unlike the Hinayana not a *sure bet,* but yet, as we have proved, a realistic possibility. Whereas the Christian fears the evolution of science, the Buddhist welcomes it. Science, as you know, has risen as a great adversary of Christianity. The stronger and stronger science grows, the weaker and weaker Christian doctrine becomes. Whereas, this type of Buddhism, actually all of Buddhism, welcomes science as a great friend. As more and more scientific information becomes available, the stronger and stronger seems to become the validity of this type of reasoning. As, in ancient times, the Buddhist, like the Christian, did not know how the mind works. Whereas, today, both know. And the more and more that we learn about the human mind, more and more does the balance of religious credibility tilt toward the east. As the scientific facts that we have today seem to tell us that the end product of the mind, its instincts and its knowledge and its memory, can survive beyond the passing of both the body and the brain.

"Whereas the comfort level of the Buddhist concerning his chance at salvation has been rising, the comfort level of the Christian concerning his chance of salvation has been declining, and it has been declining at a rapid rate. Galileo, archeology, and now more recently genetics have been taking their toll."

"Genetics?" I questioned.

"Yes, genetics. As you know, science has now proved beyond a shadow of a doubt through repeated DNA applications that the Cro-Magnon man is the direct ancestor of modern man. This tells us as absolute fact that Moses was talking through his hat when he told the story of Adam and Eve and Original Sin. Keep in mind that Christ claimed to be the Son of God who came to earth to rid the world of Original Sin, that Christ claimed to have come to earth to save it from Original Sin as was once foretold in a fairytale. For me, this is the final nail in the cros… ." he stopped himself, "the coffin. It is why I am searching for alternatives.

"The Christian preacher does not require contribution in this life. How one leads ones life, and ones accomplishments, don't count. For the Christian preacher provides for the Christian the 'loophole' of repentance. As we have just said, one of the great contradictions in life is that Christian countries require harsh penalties including capital punishment for transgressions by their fellowmen. Being the HYPOCRITE that he is, the Christian falls on his knees each night and lies to his God. *"...and forgive us or sins as we forgive those who trespass against us..."* Yet, these very same Christians that enact these harsh laws expect that in their own case they will not have to suffer for their transgressions. That the great one above will welcome them into paradise no matter how evil has been their life on earth.

"That they believe that there exists a different justice system in heaven than they themselves enforce here on earth? That if one gets away with it on earth the coast is clear to eternity? The preacher sends a very firm message to the serial rapist and murderer and pedophile that he can go with his wickedness as long as he doesn't get caught and as long as when he lays on his deathbed he repents.

"What kind of fools are we Christians that pay the preacher a few bucks for what is very obviously a counterfeit ticket to heaven? Believe me," he looked up at me with his dark eyes now more serious than ever, "if one is a Christian there is no substitute for what Christ demands. One must give up ones bike, or perish forever!

"Moreover, the philosophy of the Christian preacher does not permit the mind to think. It is a philosophy based entirely on belief. All one need do is believe in *Christ* and one will be saved. All one need do is forego ones God given ability to think, to *reason*, and simply have faith. And, of course, drop ones pence in the box."

He was now very much on a roll. There was no stopping him, not a chance.

"The Christian way is one of desire, of floundering after sex, wealth, fame and what have you. For its basic teachings stress the evil of these things and makes them tempting. And this establishes the wanting, the craving, the desire.

"Let's take sex, for example. The story of Adam and Eve, in fact, the overwhelming message in the *Bible*, paints sex to be sinful and shameful. It is the fig leaf that creates the wanting, the craving, the desire. The overemphasis of sex in the Christian world. And what is the result?" he asked himself, "In the Christian world, the act, itself, is, most often, driven by lust.

"And wealth, let's consider wealth, too. In a Christian society, contribution is incidental to the drive for wealth. The commune is limited to the individual. It does not even extend to the family. 'This is mine and that is yours' is the lifeblood of every matrimony. Even prenuptial agreements have been creeping in. We define from the very start what is 'mine' and what is 'yours'. This so called union made in heaven?

"And the preacher tells his followers that they are 'sinful by nature' so as to give them an excuse, permission one might call it, to pursue these things. And, perhaps, most important of all, Christianity is a faith based on bigotry, one of a chosen few. And those Christians who don't think so, have never bothered to read the scriptures. For the very act that ignited Christianity, the invasion of the Promised Land, the very foundation of Christianity, was precisely that, a horrific act of prejudice and bigotry and murder. Also, that it was Moses who first spelled out the difference between man and woman, and white and black, and normal and handicapped, and straight and gay four thousand years ago. It was Moses who was the founder of ethnic cleansing and slavery in the western world. And the problem is that Christians for the most part leave the job entirely up to the specialist. Leave their thinking, their reasoning, entirely up to the 'expert' in the field, the preacher. The man he is paying for his salvation.

"The Buddhist way, on the other hand, is entirely centered on how one leads one life. It very much requires the mind to think. Contribution to mankind is its sole 'commandment'. For the strength of ones accomplishments form the fibers of ones immortality. And, it is very much a philosophy restricted to love.

"For example, Buddhism has no preference among men. There is no caste system among men or women, or blacks and whites, or straights and gays. Like the Shinto in Japan, the theoretical foundation of the Buddhist is respect for the fundamental human rights of others regardless of how different one is. And, I might add that, of all the world's major religions, these are the only two that respect the equality of all men and women, even today. It is why this Christian nation of the United States of America that bills itself as the *land of freedom* does not have an *equal rights amendment* in its constitution today. It is why the preamble of the Declaration of Independence is intentionally kept out of the Constitution,

> *'We hold these Truths to be self evident, that all Men and Women are created equal, that they are endowed by their creator with certain inalienable rights, that among these are Life, Liberty and the Pursuit of Happiness.'*

That, in America, it is the bigoted preacher who keeps these words out of its constitution. For it is he who decides who should be free and who should not be free."

"Wait a minute," I stopped him, "What do you mean bigoted preacher? Preachers are not bigots. They are only preaching what their scripture tells them."

He looked at me as a teacher looks at a student when he realizes that he has a hopeless learning disability, "That's not true at all. There is very little in his scripture that supports his position in most discriminatory matters. It is solely a matter of prejudice, not scripture. I can't possibly read the whole *Bible* for you, you will have to do that yourself. But maybe I can give you an example or two. Let's take the gays for example. Just what does the *Bible* have to say about them?"

He took on a tone of authority as if he already knew that there was no way he was ever going to lose this one. "There is one explicit condemnation of homosexuality in all of the *Old Testament*, It comes in *Leviticus* in the *Old Testament*, '*Thou shalt not lie with mankind as with womankind. It is an abomination.*" Note that it does not call for the death penalty or exclusion from heaven. And then there are a half dozen others that are vague as to their meaning.

"There are two condemnations by Paul of those males who are unfortunate in having been born 'effeminate' in modern versions of the New Testament, which have been taken out context from that which appears in the 4th century text that is held by the British National Museum. These come in Paul's letters to the Corinthians and the Romans.

"One is the same passage you mentioned earlier that the preacher claims is Christ's condemnation of the gays. Whereas it is quite explicit that it came from Paul and not from Christ. The preacher not only takes it out of context but he lies to his congregation in order to make his point. In all of Christ's testimony not once did He ever condemn the gays. Keep in mind that Christ, Himself, was not straight. He was asexual, one born without the ability to fall in love with either sex." He paused for a moment as if reaching for a thought, "And besides it makes no sense at all that Paul condemned the 'effeminates'."

"No sense at all?" I questioned.

"Yes, no sense at all," he replied, "as he would have left out the girls."

"So what do we have? We have one explicit condemnation that does not call for the death penalty and does not bar one from entering the *Kingdom of Heaven*. And less than a half dozen other mentions in the *Bible* which requires that one read between the lines to try to figure out what they have to say. And what do we have on the other side?"

"What other side?" I queried.

"Heterosexuality. What does the *Bible* have to say about heterosexual sex? And the answer is that there are eighty eight condemnations of fornication and other heterosexual activities in the *Bible*. And every one of them is explicit. Seven of which are made by Christ Himself in the New Testament. Twenty three others bar one from the *Kingdom of Heaven* for all time. And still twenty seven others require the death penalty.

"Bigoted preacher? Is that what you questioned. I have given you the answer. For the preacher's motive has nothing at all to do with his scripture, for if it did he would be condemning heterosexuals, not homosexuals. No, his thinking is driven solely by prejudice, what the bigot preacher who had come before him has passed on to him. What the preacher who had come before him had conditioned his mind to think.

As General Patton so profoundly stated at Milan at the gravesite of a gay *Congressional Medal of Honor* winner,

'It is the soldier who shed his blood on the field of battle and not the preacher who cowers in his pulpit who should determine who should or should not be free.'

"And although the *Bible's* position concerning Negroes and women and slavery is somewhat stronger than it is concerning the gays, if we had the time I could prove that in their case too the preacher is coming from a position of bigotry. And in that the overwhelming majority of preachers preach these kinds of prejudices, I am on firm ground when I refer to them as bigots. For that is exactly what they are, men and women whose good conscience has been unable to overcome the prejudices that other bigots have built into their minds over the years.

"Yes," he nailed the lid on the coffin, "if there were no preachers then bigotry would come to an end. If there were no preachers the word 'hate' would no longer be in our vocabulary. No longer would we hate others that seem to be different. We would put aside our differences forever, and for the very first time we would make Buddha's and Christ's commandment a way of life, *'Love Thy Neighbor as Thyself.'* We would make Patton's dream come true.

'It is our differences that have made us into the great nation of one that we are. And the day will come when men and women of good conscience will no longer heed the words of those preachers who choose to use them to divide us. And when that day comes all children will be born into a world of equal opportunity. Only then will America and the world be truly free!'

"How easily one forgets," he closed, "that it was the preacher who conditioned the minds of our southern neighbors to think that the subordination and persecution of blacks was a holy thing to do. And when Abraham Lincoln and Lyndon Johnson took it away from him, he turned his hate toward gays."

"Okay, you probably have me there," I agreed, "But concerning your thinking that an *equal rights amendment* be built into the Constitution is way off base. Just think," I told him, "if we did that women and the handicapped would have all sorts of rights, it would cause all sorts of problems." But realizing that I was not on firm ground concerning women and the handicapped I decided to weaken his position concerning the gays instead, "And *'pursuit of happiness'* would give the gays pursuit of happiness. It would give them the right to live among us in long term loving relationships."

And like a lion in his den he was ready for me, "Yes, just what the bigoted preacher fears the most. Why not let them too have this thing we call, *'pursuit of happiness.'* After all they fought for it like everybody else. Why not recognize their unions? As it is, exiling them from society forces many of them to lead lonely, often decadent lives. And maybe it is God's will, that in all His wisdom He gave us the gays as a solution to one of the world's greatest problems. And instead we treat it as another problem."

A God for Lions

"You must be joking," I stopped him, "how can one problem solve another problem? That makes no sense at all."

"In the United States we kill over a million unborn children every year. And the reason we kill most of them is that they would be born to young girls who are unable to afford them and that the Christian republicans with their welfare-reform bill refuse to pay for them. And elsewhere in the world many more of these 'murders' take place every day. It seems to me that if we recognized gay unions the gay population could provide the economic and loving support for these children which would allow them to be born.

"Orphanage statistics tell us that in states that do permit gays to adopt children that they take many children who are less than attractive and otherwise handicapped. This is one reason these states permit the practice, as these children would otherwise remain forever in orphanages as straight people usually shop for a child very much as one goes into a pet shop in search of the cutest puppy.

"And one other thing. The numbers also tell us that gays are much more likely to cross racial lines in adoptions. And this is important as most of these children if allowed to be born would be black, and the population is predominately white."

And I stopped him again, "But these people would never stay together. They would split up. It would put the children at risk of growing up with only one parent."

"You must be kidding me," he responded, "there are almost as many divorces every year as we have marriages. And the only significant study that has been done so far of control groups of gays and straights that adopted children over long periods of time found that on the average that the gays stayed together longer. The study concluded that the reason for this was that people of the same sex are more likely to share similar interests, that they make better companions of each other. What you say makes no sense. Do you think that it is better never to have been born than to have only one parent?"

I knew then that I should have never gone down that path. It would have been better to have attacked the women in this thing. I shut up like a clam. I just sat there hoping that he would change the subject on his own.

But he didn't, "So the gays, rather than being a problem, are actually the answer to one of the world's great problems, as they, being unable to bear children, are the only population in the world that is significant enough to supply loving and economic support for children who otherwise can never be born.

"So they have something we need and we have something that they want. So let's make a deal with them. Let's give them what they want. Recognition and equality. A small price to pay for the lives of tens of millions of children each year. Are we so steeped in these things called 'bigotry' and 'hate' that we are unwilling to trade them in for the lives of these children? Are our minds so warped by the preacher, that we would prefer to have the blood of these children on our hands?"

"So he wins another one," I thought to myself. He paused again as to allow me time to summarize in my mind this latest diversion he had taken. He returned to the subject at hand.

"But let us return to the Buddhists and Shintos. In recognizing all people to be equal, both Buddha and the Shintos of Japan had to defy God Brahma's commandment as set forth in the ancient *Vedas*. In the very same way that Lincoln and Susan B. Anthony and their followers defied God the Father's commandments in the ancient *Bible*."

I gave him a questionable look as if I didn't understand what he was talking about. So he gave me an answer.

"The tenth commandment," he said, "'*Thou shall not take from thy neighbor his property including his house and his wife and his slaves and his ox and his ass*,' If you want some more I could go on forever on that one. We should heed the words of John Paul

I, the pope who was murdered in the Vatican by those who did not believe in what he had to say, *"Never be afraid to stand up for what is right whether your adversary be your parent, your teacher, your peer, your politician, your preacher, your constitution, or even your God."*

And that I gave him a look of defeat, he returned immediately to the discussion at hand,

"And this points to the most basic similarity and difference between eastern and western theology. Like His counterpart in the west, the God Brahma too created a caste system society, five levels of society ranging from the peasants at the bottom to the rulers and the philosophers at the top. And His rule was that one would remain at the level one was born into in this life, but for leading a contributory life one could move up the caste system in the next life. Unlike His counterpart God the Father in the west, the God Brahma's caste system was not based on sex, race or creed. This is the reason people in the east don't grow up with the prejudices that we do, prejudices as we have said are perpetuated by the preacher in the west. One who was Mongoloid, a Caucasoid, an Aborigine, a man or woman, straight or gay could be born into the highest level.

"On the other hand here in the west, God the Father based His caste system on sex, race and creed. And He even went so far as to draw a line between normal people and handicapped people and between heterosexuals and homosexuals. But, unlike His counterpart in the east, He did not decree that all levels of His society were to live in harmony with each other. Rather, He requires that all those who do not fit the specs of the white Aryan male and all those who do not believe in Him are to be either subordinated, persecuted, enslaved and in some cases even annihilated, the reason why Hitler murdered the Jews and homosexuals in the concentration camps. The same reason why the preachers try to keep the women and gays in their place even today.

"But let us speak more specifically of the Buddhist. The entire effort of the Buddhist is concentrated on accomplishment of deed in life, of contribution to ones fellowman. Although he recognizes the Creator, belief in a Redeemer, is not a factor, as the Buddhist link to the Creator is direct. He wastes no time falling on his knees in adoration of the Magi. It is his thinking that the Creator's job, the Magi's job, was completed upon creation, and that the rest of the job is up to man, that the rest of the job is up to himself. That he, himself, is an extension of the Creator. Precisely Christ's claim in the New Testament. And as I just said in the case of the Hinayana Lincoln and Mother Teresa are today a part of the Creator Himself, for they tell us right from wrong.

"Unlike the Christian, the Buddhist way is decidedly free of desire. It teaches that all of God's gifts are good. So there is no wanting, no craving, no desire. These things become less material.

"Again, lets take sex, for example. In the Buddhist world, sex is recognized as being good and beautiful. There is no fig leaf. It is just something that is a part of life, a part of nature. It is simply there. There is no wanting, no craving, no unbounded desire. There is no overemphasis of the role of sex in life. And, the result?" he again answered himself, "the act, itself, is most often driven by love!

"Whereas the Christian defines morality, in what is acceptable or unacceptable in sex, the Buddhist defines morality, in what is right and wrong humanely. It is his overemphasis in sex that makes the Christian preacher think this way. That 'morality' is somehow synonymous with 'sex'. So overly conscious is he as to what others might do with their sexual bodies that he thinks this way. If one has to have a synonym for 'morality' it would be 'compassion'. It has nothing, nothing at all, to do with 'sex'."

Description of the Heavens

"And wealth? Wealth in the Buddhist society is incidental to contribution. Just the reverse of what it is in the Christian society. The drive in the land of Buddha is toward contribution, not wealth. Contribution to the common good. Not contribution to oneself. Not accumulation of wealth. In the Buddhist world, the commune has no boundaries in the individual, in ones family, or even for that matter, in ones society. For all of mankind is oneself. There is no such thing as 'this is mine' and 'that is yours.'

"For achievement of vast wealth is the end objective of the Christian endeavor. For it is the Christian way to search for the pot of gold at the end of the rainbow. It is why the Christian culture thrives in a capitalistic society. As a matter of fact, it is this Christian goal, itself, that creates a capitalistic society. For it is the promise of the *New Jerusalem,* where all those who are to be saved will spend their paradise." And pulling the *New Testament* directly in front of him, he quoted the explicit description of the Christian heaven from the *Book of Revelations*,

"*'That the great city is made of pure gold, as pure as glass. That the streets of the city are paved of pure gold, again, like transparent glass. That the very foundations of the houses are of jasper, of sapphire, of chalcedony, of emerald, of diamond, of ruby, of beryl, of amber, of amethyst. The stones, all together, making for magnificent rays. The twelve gates to the city, themselves, to this New Jerusalem, are huge single pearls... there is no sea, no forest, no mountains, no valleys, no waterfalls. Not even pigeons or puppies to dirty the golden streets.'* Simply a great golden urbanization *'without a sun, a moon or stars, without day or night, without a yesterday or a tomorrow.'* A perfect world of extraordinary wealth. And as I have said, *'one without a sea'.* This is the Christian goal. And, this is precisely what his scripture gives him. A city without aquariums, zoos or parks, for there will be no sea, nor animal, nor plant life there. A city which houses are without kitchens or bathrooms, for as you have pointed out, *'there will be no thirst or hunger there!"*

"And then there is the Taoist heaven," he offered.

"The Taoist heaven?" I questioned.

"Yes," he answered, "The Chinese. For in my dream I have had the good fortune to have visited those places which, as we all know, lie beyond the wall for the Chinese. And for each of them, I have found that the Father provides that they will live beyond the wall as they have chosen to live on this side of the wall.

"First, I was granted the privilege of seeing Hell. As I peered in through the gates, I saw an immense room with many long tables. On these were so many bowls of cooked rice and gourmet delicacies as one could imagine. Properly spiced, aromatic, inviting.

"The diners were all seated there, filled with hunger, two at each bowl, one facing the other. And then what?

"To carry the food to their mouths they had - in oriental fashion - two chopsticks affixed to their hands, but so long that no matter how great their efforts, not a single grain of delicacy could reach their mouths. Although starving, they could not take of these things.

"And, then, I was able to peer into Heaven. And, here again, I saw a great room with the same tables, same gourmet delicacies, same long chopsticks. But here the people were happy, smiling and quite satisfied. Why?

"Because each, having picked up the food with the chopsticks, raised it to the mouth of the companion that sat opposite, and all was right.

"So we must learn here, as we make our way toward the great wall, how to use the chopsticks, else we will not know how to use them when we are on the other side of the wall.

"And this is precisely Christ's overwhelming message in the New Testament. The very reason why I sold my bike!

"Yet, the Buddhist reward is much different. It offers a heaven of fresh air, of living plants, of towering trees, of crystal lakes, of running rivers, of sparkling brooks, of snow peaked mountains, of green valleys and cascading waterfalls. Of dogs and of cats and of our many friends in the forest. It is a land of marigolds and violets and tinker bells and buttercups and bees and butterflies which go from here to there. It is a land of reds, of oranges, of greens, of blues, of yellows, and of purples. Of apples, of apricots, of limes, of blueberries, of peaches and of plums. Of the sun, of the moon, of the stars, and of the sea. Where the creatures live in waters as deep, as high does the eagle soar. Not a perfect world. But, at least one where one can look forward to growing up, and taking the girl of ones dreams to the junior prom, of falling in love, and having children. Of hugging children. Of loving children. And, of watching ones child grow up, and take his girl of his dreams to the junior prom, and of falling in love, and having children. Yes, a land of ups and downs. One which gives one the opportunity to walk in the shadows of the deepest valleys and, yet, climb the tallest mountains. This is the Buddhist goal. And, this is precisely what his scripture gives him.

"And, very important, too, is the lack of reunion in the Christian heaven with ones loved ones with whom one has shared this life. The *Bible*, in total composition, one of the largest books ever written, makes no mention in either its *New Testament* or its *Old Testament* of this possibility. It makes no mention at all that we will have any interaction with others who we have known here on earth. In fact, there are several references in the *Bible* that explicitly say just the opposite. For example, in *Jeremiah*, '*Thou shalt not take thee a wife, neither shalt thou have siblings or sons or daughters in this place.*'

In fact, the *Bible*, in general, stresses that, in the hereafter, '*all of ones love and all of ones concentration will be for Christ alone.*' That in his or her eternity the successful Christian will be as if he or she is the bride or bridegroom of Christ as foretold in the *Book of Isaiah*. '*for he shalt clothe me in the garments of salvation, he hath covered me with the robe of righteousness, as a bridegroom decketh himself with ornaments, and as a bride adorneth herself with jewels.*' And, as confirmed in the *Book of Revelations*, '*that he who shall be saved will be as the bride of Christ*'. That all of his or her eternity will be solely for Him. That the marriage ceremony will feature Adolph Hitler as the best man. So when the Christian says his last goodbye to those that he leaves behind, one can be fairly certain that it has, indeed, been his last goodbye. Not only to his loved ones but to himself, as he has known himself to be in this life. That is, of course, if one puts any credence in the *Bible* at all.

"In the Buddhist hereafter, however, reuniting with ones loved ones is still a possibility. In fact, it seems probable. And there is some evidence of this. The great mystery of why two people are so uniquely attracted to each other. How they are able to *fall in love*. This unique phenomenon that the energy balance between them could be so perfectly even between them. Could they have possibly shared a life before?" And, very often, as we have said before, one meets someone for the very first time, and thinks that he has known him or her all of his life. And some of these, who one has never met before in this life, one immediately has bad vibes about, and others very good vibes about. And one usually finds out that ones vibes were right.

"Still, that we will be reunited with our loved ones in the future life provided by the Buddhist world remains just a chance. Whereas, for the Christian, reunion is just not in the cards. Just not in his scripture. It is not a part of the Christian game. For in the Christian heaven '*all of ones love will be solely for Christ alone!*'

"Yes, the Christian and Buddhist 'heavens' are two entirely different worlds. Two entirely different prizes. One of wealth and security and sameness. The other of love and hope and variation. One, of certainty. One, of chance. One dependent entirely on what one believes. The other dependent entirely on what one does. One dependent entirely on forgoing the exercise of ones mind. And the other dependent entirely on exercising ones mind.

"And there is yet another prize. The Muslim prize." and pulling the *Koran* in front of him he read, '*for the good Muslims in the hereafter shall return to the Garden of Eden, whose portals shall stand up to them. Therein reclining, they shall there call for many a fruit and drink.*' And, as is mentioned in this very same part of the *Koran*, the Muslim, like the Buddhist and the Hindu, will still enjoy the great gift of sex in the afterlife, '*And with them shall be virgins of their own age, with modest retiring glances. This is what ye were promised at the day of reckoning. Yes! This is our provision: it shall never fail. And youths shall go round them beautiful as imbedded pearls. And fruits in abundance will we give them, and flesh (sex) as they shall desire.*'

"It is this reference to sex in the Muslim heaven in the *Koran* that the Christian preacher and the Jewish rabbi use to disclaim Mohammed as a prophet. 'It is quite obvious,' say the preacher and the rabbi, 'that God would not permit such evilness in His house.'

"And it is also this promise of sex with the virgin of ones dreams that causes so many young men of the Muslim faith to become suicide bombers. For they think what they have been unable to get in this life, will be theirs for certain in the next life.

"And unlike the *Bible*, Muslim scripture specifically promises that those who live good lives will be reunited with their loved ones in the hereafter. '*And to those who have believed, those offspring who have followed them in the faith, we will again unite them with their offspring. And enter ye and your wives into Paradise. Dishes and bowls of gold shall go round unto them: there they shall enjoy whatever their souls desire, and whatever their eyes delight in; and therein ye shall abide forever.*'

"And, one might ask why, if they both believe in the God of Abraham, the Muslim can be rejoined with his loved ones in paradise, and, yet, the Christian cannot. And, the answer is very simple. In the case of the Muslim, we are all God's children, so He welcomes us back into His house as a family. That he requires that in His house we must all love one another. It is Christianity that requires *that in the hereafter all of ones love must be for Christ alone.* Therefore, in Christianity, there is no point to have ones loved ones in this life accompany him or her. For one will have Christ, all of ones love will be for Christ alone. As the scripture says, *'that he who shall be saved will be as the bride of Christ.'*"

He stopped for a moment or two as if to assure himself that he hadn't left anything out and concluded, "So we have covered them all, the Christians, the Muslims, the Indians and the Chinese. We now know where they are going. And then, of course, there are the Jews."

"Yes, the Jews," I repeated, "Where do they go?"

"They go to Philadelphia," he laughed, "and, if it's a nice day, they go to the park!"

And I laughed with him before he went on. "Actually," he explained, "the Jews have nothing in their scripture that promises a heaven as they have nothing equivalent to the *New Testament* or the *Koran*. Their faith is heavily concentrated in the Five Books of Moses. As a result Judaism is not so much a guidance into the next life as it is a guidance in this life. So the Rabbi doesn't preach heaven or hell, yet he leaves the possibility open to his customer.

'And suddenly the image of the carousel popped into my mind. And as on that wintry December night so many years ago, I could still see its lights, and I could still hear its music, and I could still see its stampede of lions, and tigers, and pigs, and horses, and sheep. But now because of what little Johnny had put before me, I no longer wondered what was their destination? Wondered

A God for Lions

where they were going? Wondered what was their dream? And he was quick to interrupt my thought.

"Nevertheless, it seems to me that in this great carousel of life that one would first decide on which prize one wants. The Christian *City of Gold*, where one will forever be free of the great scourge of sex. This monster which dwells within us which would have been cast below into the great lake of eternal fire. That ones first act when entering through the golden gates, will be to check ones penis or vagina at the door, so to speak. That St. Peter, himself, perhaps with some help from his personal assistant, Lorena Bobbitt, will cast them into the great lake of fire below. Free, forever, of the horror of bearing and rearing children and watching them grow up and go off by themselves. One will truly, at last, be free.

"Or, perhaps, one might prefer the Buddhist version of heaven. The mountains and valleys and forests and waterfalls and the sea. Still to be burdened with the great 'scourge' of sex. This 'monster' which dwells within us. Which will never let us be. Still besieged by the 'horror' of having to bear and rear children and watch them grow up and go their separate ways. Still to be human as we have known it to be human in this life. A world in which little boys and little girls are, indeed, just that, little boys and little girls, and not just something in between. This, which the Buddhist sees as eternal happiness, the Christian sees as eternal suffering. This, which the Creator has given, the Buddhist is quite content with, the Christian is not satisfied with. The Christian craves for more. The Christian goes for the gold!

"And, then there is something in between, the Muslim heaven. For those in the middle who can't make up their minds.

"One of the great misinterpretations of faith is that the typical Christian completely ignores what is explicit in his scripture concerning his hereafter, but rather believes in the hereafter as is described by Mohammed in his *Koran*. And his preacher does nothing to correct this misjudgement. For it would not be good for business.

"Yet, one knows that the Christian can never reach the Muslim heaven for he is following the wrong rules. For realization of the Muslim heaven has nothing to do with keeping ones repentance up to date. Rather it depends entirely upon daily prayer and the weight of good versus evil done in ones lifetime.

"So it would make all the sense in the world to first decide on what one wants in the afterlife. And then follow the path that leads to it. The Buddhist way, *great exercise of the mind and great contribution to mankind*, will never lead to the Christian *city of gold*. Conversely, it will lead one directly away from it. Whereas, the Christian way, *mere belief, and drive for material wealth*, will never lead to the Buddhist version of paradise. Conversely, it will lead one directly away from it.

"One is surely a fool to play a game, the most important game one can play in life, this *game of faith*, and not consider its prize. And, yes, perhaps, it is possible that the *Universal Creator* will award the winners of each game the very prize they have sought. That, perhaps, it makes no difference what one believes, as long as one believes. As long as one foregoes ones ability to *reason* and simply believes. It makes no difference whether or not one believes in Jesus Christ, or Mohammed, or Buddha, or Brahma, or Joseph Smith, or ones next door neighbor, or what have you. As long as one believes.

"But, nevertheless, the bottom line remains. Would one want to do it all over again, and again, and again? Or go for the gold? That's the difference between the *School of the East* and the *School of the West*. That's it in a nutshell.

"It seems to me that one would be a complete moron, not be in control of ones faculties, to play a game and not consider its prize." And he paused for what seemed several minutes to let his statement sink in. And, then he went on.

A God for Lions

"Yet, unlike the Christian who must rely simply on '*belief*' for his salvation, on the words of others, who must go through the 'middle man', through the preacher, this type of Buddhist, the Hinayana, 'knows'. He is the only one who knows. And he knows, because his link is direct to his Creator. Who has created him, he himself, as his own Redeemer. He, himself, is the provider of the afterlife. He 'knows' that, at the very least, how he thinks, will live on in his fellowman forever. He, alone, 'knows' that how he thinks, WHAT ONE IS TRYING TO SAVE, will live on forever. He alone knows that he is, indeed, immortal.

"And, what's more, he alone knows exactly what his afterlife will be like. Because he has been there before.

"The Christian, on the other hand, as we have just proven, beyond a shadow of a doubt, only 'thinks' he knows. And, he only 'thinks' he knows, because he is dependent upon the word of an emissary, and the word of others. He believes other men of motive who tell him so. The preachers who he pays to tell him so. Those who it is their livelihood to tell him so. So he only 'thinks' that his being will live on in eternity forever. Or should I say 'hopes' that his being will live on forever.

He paused for a few minutes as if his mind was concentrated on what would be the composition of his finale. Of how this little man would sum up in a single phrase all that he had said. As for myself, I was still trying to put together all that he had just said, and trying to catch my own breath, when he suddenly interrupted my thoughts and finished up. And, this time he spoke very steadily, very slowly, as if to make every single word count. He paused very briefly after each phrase, as if to give the Creator above time to etch them in heaven for all eternity. The room fell respectively quiet. Even the logs in the fireplace ceased crackling as they waited anxiously for what he was about to say.

Lucien Gregoire

finale,

"If I were not a Christian, that is, I knew I had no soul, I would want to free myself from desire, which is the mainstay of a Christian society. I would want to live a life of great contribution because, if I had no soul, I would know that the only way that I will live on forever is in my fellowman. In his ambitions, in his hopes, in his struggles, in the realization of his dreams.

"That, when all is said and done, and I come to the end of the day, when the last sigh has been spent, and all the dials return to zero, when this machine has finally read its last book and drawn its last conclusion, and done its last deed, that I would know in my mind and in my heart that I would go on forever. Like Lincoln, like Edison, for that matter, like Einstein, himself. That I would have made my mark and know that it will never be erased by time. That I will remain there in my fellowman for all the days to the end of the earth!"

And he finally stopped. He stared straight ahead transfixed in total apprehension, as does a great actor who stands on the grand stage at the conclusion of an epic performance, as if awaiting applause.

And it came. It came in the form of a smile, my smile, my reassuring smile. I didn't say anything, not a thing. For nothing I could have said could begin to either add or detract from what this little man had put before me. So getting up, I said nothing, and headed for the stairs.

"I wonder," I thought to myself, "I wonder," I repeated to myself as I started up the stairs. And raising my thoughts to a mumble, "Soul? Soul? I wonder if, I wonder if, I have a soul?" and I repeated it several times, "I wonder? I wonder? I wonder? Perhaps, I, too, don't have a soul?" And as I staggered into the kitchen with a stare such as Hollywood builds into its '*living dead*', Audrey greeted me with her playful all knowing smile, and asked, "Well, did he find his soul? Or did you lose yours?"

afterthoughts

And later that afternoon I thought back a few years to that time in Holland. Of that time when the young girl in Utrecht had told me of the story of General Patton in the Italian cemetery. Of his farewell to the young gay soldier who had so courageously given his life for freedom, and with still another kind of courage had spoken his cause to make it real.

"After this war is won. After the final volleys are fired, after the smoke clears and the tears begin, America must fight a new kind of war. And that war will be fired by a new kind of courage.

Yes, this war will win for America and all mankind this thing called 'freedom'. But that war, the war within, will someday win for America the great prize of 'equality' for all men and women, something that this war cannot do. For freedom without equality is not what it pretends to be. The diamond would be made of paste.

It is our differences that have made us into the great nation of one that we are. And the day will come when men and women of good conscience will no longer heed the words of those politicians and preachers who choose to use them to divide us."

And then I thought of what Johnny had just told me. Of Pope John Paul I when he had paid homage to Lincoln for having defied the only written word of his God, the Ten Commandments, in having freed the Negroes, *"Never be afraid to stand up for what is right whether your adversary be your parent, your teacher, your peer, your politician, your preacher, your constitution, or even your God."*

And I picked up the book that Johnny had been reading, this book MURDER IN THE VATICAN, and read, "When asked by an eight year old boy, 'How is it possible for Christians to be on the *far right* if Jesus is on the *far left?'* the pope responded, 'They are not very far apart, for only two things separate Christians from

Christ, **greed and prejudice**. If we can get them to give up just those two things they too could live their lives in *Imitation of Christ*.'"

And finally I thought of the guide who had taken me up into the attic in Amsterdam. And, once again, did he hand me a book with a picture of a small girl smiling with dimples on its cover. And, once again, I heard him tell me in a quiet and reverent voice almost as if not to wake her, "This is what she was," and, then moving to the center of the room, he added still more silently, "This is where she lived," and taking me to a window he added, "This is what she saw," and taking me to a chair that sat in a corner, "This is where she spoke of things that used to be," and taking me to a small table set against a wall, "This is where she wrote of things that were," and taking me into a tiny room off to one side he said, his voice now edged in solemnity, "This is where she thought of things that had never been and dreamed of things that were to be," and finally, taking me back to the doorway of the room, "But the things she dreamed of were not to be," he whispered almost hopelessly, "for this is where she was no more!"

And I saw him point once again to a black and white photograph of a factory with its chimneys smoking. A factory that could be any factory, except for a single thing, a swastika flag flying from its mast!

And I opened the small book he had given me, *The Diary of Anne Frank*, and read,

"*I still believe that people are really good at heart ... when I look up to the heavens, I think that it will all come right, and that peace and tranquility will return again.*"

And I wondered if there would ever come a day that what she dreamed of, those things that she had hoped would come to be, would come to be, for her, and for me, and for all humanity.

A God for Lions

six months after this episode

'Johnny' and his mother, 'Audrey', were killed in a commercial airline disaster

he was eleven years old

To those who made this book possible. To Audrey, to Johnny, to the little girl in the attic, to Patton, to the two girls in Utrecht, to Hans, to Pope John Paul I, to Einstein, and mostly to those who we left behind in the cemetery near Milan.

And, yes, one more. To that youth, who you are about meet, who now so very long ago, came in from the street, and left his tears in my shop.

Lucien Gregoire

author's commentary

General George S. Patton, made the address quoted on March 29, 1944 in a small cemetery southeast of Milan, Italy at the gravesite of a *Medal of Honor* winner who had admitted to his homosexuality while he lay dying in a military hospital. The young soldier's action drew an official reprimand from Eisenhower and he was ordered buried in a village cemetery that contained the graves of several American black soldiers. Normally holders of the nation's highest military award were buried in the great military cemeteries of Europe or returned to the United States for interment at Arlington.

As stated herein, it is believe that between twenty and thirty *Medals of Honor* are held by homosexual men who fought in the Second World War and by many others in Korea and Vietnam. Although twenty seven African American men were recommended for the nation's highest honor during the world war, General Eisenhower successfully blocked them all. Several of these recommendations had been made by General Patton. In 1997, seven of these medals were awarded, six of them posthumously, to African American men.

During the world war the United States military segregated blacks in separate battalions, something that Patton did not approve of. It was the American evangelist who used his influence with American generals to cause this separation in the very same way he uses his influence today to restrict gays in the military. But he was not the only culprit.

At the time, except for a few Jews who lived in Rome, Italy was entirely Catholic and as a result the populace was controlled by the Vatican. The Roman Catholic Church, like other Christian churches of the time, fostered fascism, which as one knows is the law of Moses which preaches prejudice against women, blacks, gays and others who are different. As a result blacks were not allowed in Italy at all. They were not even allowed to pass through Italy on a train. The objective, of course, was to maintain the purity of the Aryan race as to make come true God the Father's dream in the *Old Testament* in which the sons of the sons of the sons of Aaron are to rule at His side forever. This was the very same reason why segregation was the mainstay of the Christian preacher in the United States at the time.

Prior to the war the pope entered into formal alliances with both Mussolini and Hitler in the interests of promoting fascism. And these alliances are in black in white for all to see today in the documents commonly referred to as the German and Italian concordants. Keep in mind that in the thirties that 'Christianity' was synonymous with 'Fascism'. The word 'fascism' like the word 'communism' at that time did not have the connotation that it has today. And it is for this reason that communism was the great enemy of Christianity as it sat together with Buddha, Tao and Christ on the other side of the political arena. And one can see this clearly in that Christianity continues to preach fascism, its war against women, gays and some others, those things that society, men and women of good conscience, have not yet taken from it.

Patton was unaware that blacks were not permitted in Italy as he stormed his way across North Africa toward Sicily. Patton frequently used black soldiers for high risk reconnaissance missions behind enemy lines as they could blend in easily as natives. By the time he reached Tunis on the North African coast, the casualty rate was more than thirty percent among his black soldiers whereas it was only fifteen percent among the balance of his forces.

As he planned his advance on Palermo, a chaplain told him that blacks were not allowed in Italy and suggested that he leave the black battalions behind less he offend the pope. At first Patton thought it to be a joke, but then he realized that the man who wore the cross was serious. The next week when the black troops marched in triumph into Palermo there was a white army chaplain among their ranks. When Eisenhower learned that Patton had broken his rule on segregation he reprimanded the general. Of course, if one were to count up the number of reprimands that Eisenhower bestowed on Patton, they would far exceed the great general's commendations.

Field Marshall Montgomery was once asked by a reporter why he and Patton had so much trouble with Eisenhower? Alluding to the fact that many of Eisenhower's decisions were politically motivated, the general replied, "I guess it is because we have different objectives." "Different objectives?" questioned the reporter. "Yes," replied Montgomery, "for us the objective is Berlin." "And Ike?" asked the reporter. "For him," replied the general, "it is the White House."

The story of Patton in the Italian cemetery is taken from the author's biography on John Paul I, MURDER IN THE VATICAN. The young girl's 'uncle' was actually the uncle of one of the real life characters in that book. It is told out of context. Patton had in fact assigned a colonel to head up the honor guard. When he learned that the officer had delegated the task to a corporal, Patton called for his car and arrived as the ceremony was ending and it was then that he made his (*italicized*) remarks. On March 29, 1974, thirty years after the incident, the young soldier was awarded the *Medaglia d'Oro al Valore Militare*, Italy's highest military award, at the cemetery with twenty one of the twenty seven children he had rescued looking on. He remains today the only American to hold the highest military award of both an allied and axis power.

Although some have been embellished all of the stories in this book are true. Some of them like the story of Sam the baby rat, and the girl at the prom, and the little girl in the attic, and of Hans the waiter in Utrecht are told precisely as they had occurred. Johnny's dialogue has been materially expanded on the basis of research by the author.

A God for Lions

Not Quite, Yet, a Man

the four sections of an orchestra,

the string section

the wind section

the brass section

the percussion section

at war's end,

Many years ago I had returned from the front and for the last time I changed from my military gear into my civilian uniform, an old shirt and blue jeans. I got on a phone, and then I got on a plane, and then I got on a train, and then I got on a bus, and then I got in a car, and I finally walked the rest of the way to the crest of the pond.

As I walked along its edge, the mystery of nature was all around me. Everything was green. Even the water reflected all that it could see. The dew had just lifted and a haze remained suspended over the pond as if intending never to go away. Dark clouds loomed off in the distance as to foretell what was about to come. And, all was silent. Not even the whisper of a breeze could be heard.

Then the hum of a bee going about his work on a nearby rose bush broke the stillness. And then the song of a bird, a whippoorwill, in a nearby tree, made its entrance. And, from right in front of me, came the trumpeting of frogs. And off in the distance was heard the first rumbling of thunder. And finally came a flash of lightning. Each one speaking in its own tune, as if the great maestro, above, was sleeping.

And I came to the spot where Audrey and I had once walked and talked of things that were yet to come. I knew her then, and I have never forgotten my last goodbye. As she lay there the pallor of her lips seemed to eclipse the mystery of her smile. She was in death every bit as much as she had been in life. I had not known that a human face and form if not translated into art by a great painter or sculptor could be so beautiful. Mere mortal flesh, bones and hair, I reminded myself trying to dispel the wonder one feels in witnessing perfection.

And I thought back to that time, when I had reached over and touched her hand, so as to confirm to myself that this was indeed, forever, goodbye. And, I remember that one of those things one calls tears climbed up out of my heart and crept out of the crevice of my eye and started toward its lid. And realizing this, I glanced around the room, looking first to the right, and then to the left, and again to the right, and finally to the left, once more. All the time fearing that someone might notice and expose me, destroy me so to speak. For I was now a man and men don't cry. So I held it there and I have carried it there ever since.

On the other side of the pond was a small cottage that most would call, perhaps, a shack, An old friend of mine lived there alone kind of pacing his time until he too would go to join my Audrey.

I proceeded out away from the water onto the dirt road that circled the pond and as I came up to the front of the cottage an overflowing trashcan greeted me. There atop the debris was an old violin, decorated with a fresh sprinkling of rain spots. And with it, a bow.

I took them with me toward the door and the door opened and the old man stood there, "I'm so rich," he laughed, "I threw away my old *Stradivarius.*" And taking the violin he held it up in such a way that the light shone into the small opening atop the instrument. And I looked into the violin and sure enough, there, much to my surprise, a label read, '*Stradivarius, 1904*'. He told me there were thousands of these copies made around the turn of the century and that, in actuality, they were worthless. But he let me take the violin with me and I made him promise not to tell anyone that I was picking trash.

two years later,

I had moved to Chicago and a couple of years later I received a short note in the mail. It was from one of his neighbors that the old man had died. And I went to the corner of the room where the violin lay. Picking it up, I took the overstuffed chair that sat by the fireplace, and thought of the old man. I thought *of all the good times, the bad times and the changing times,* and once again the tear started to move toward the edge of the lid. And, once again, I cautiously looked around the room, first to the right, and then to the left, and again to the right, and finally to the left, once more. As if a ghost might be watching. And, once again, I forced it back.

The next day, thinking to have the violin repaired and intending to place it on my wall in memory of my old friend, I took it to a musical instrument shop. The man behind the counter looked at it and without bothering to even give me the courtesy of checking the label he told me, "It will cost you four or five hundred dollars to restore this thing and if you make this investment you'll be able to sell it for about fifty dollars to anyone who knows anything at all about violins."

Then noticing the stringless bow, he picked it up, and stretched it out from the level of his eye, as if he were zeroing in on a doe. He said, "You might have something here?" He waived it a couple of times through the air, first to the right, and then to the left, and again to the right, and finally to the left, once more. Then he took a tiny screwdriver from his pocket and removed the ivory casing that enclosed one end and read the carved name of the maker.

He thought a moment and then asked me, "Five hundred?" Not knowing what he meant, I hesitated. He then said, "A thousand?" I asked, "What do you mean a thousand?" He said, "Okay, I'll give you two thousand in cash." And I thought of the old man and gathering up the bow and the violin, I headed toward the door. And he called out after me, "Five thousand - ten...?" And, following me out onto the street, he yelled, "Twenty thousand dollars!"

I hurried away down the street, all the time, glancing first to the right, and then to the left, and again to the right, and finally to the left, once more. And, reaching my house, I nervously fumbled for my keys and with my hand shaking uncontrollably I unlocked the front gate and hastened up the walkway and up the steps to the front door. Entering the house, I went directly to the closet where I kept my tools and hardware. Then I moved quickly into the great room and up over the fireplace I hung the violin together with its bow. All the time, glancing first to the right, and then to the left, and again to the right, and finally to the left, once more. All the time struggling desperately to hold the tear that hovered precariously on the edge of the cliff.

several years later,

Through the years I had prospered. However, there occurred a sudden downturn in markets in which I had invested heavily and I fell on bad times. I moved back to Baltimore, hoping to start all over again. I opened a small shop not far from the *Peabody Conservatory of Music.* I took a small room nearby.

In a desperate attempt to pay off what was to me almost insurmountable debt I was selling off most of what I had. One day I sold my computer to one of the advanced students at the school and the next day one of the instructors of the great institution came into my shop and said, "I understand that you have a small computer desk for sale?"

We proceeded out of the shop and down the street to the old rooming house in which I had taken a room. Midway down the street I suddenly stopped and stooping down I picked up a dime. And he said to me, "Lucky dime, huh?" And I lied, "Yes," as I put it in my pocket together with the other eight 'lucky' dimes that I had collected earlier that week.

Once upon a time,
I came upon a dime,
with the other eight,
there were nine.

As we climbed the creaking steps, he made the proverbial remark, "These things could sure use some oil." On reaching the landing we proceeded down the long narrow hallway which seemed to have the same dark paint on its walls that it had when the building was built some seventy or some odd years ago. We passed by the open door to the less than sanitary bath that I shared with the six or seven other people who lived on the floor.

As we entered the room, thinking that this could be a halfway house of some sort he said, "Do you have to pay to live here?" "Not very much," I replied as I led him to the desk and started to give him the sales pitch.

But my words fell on deaf ears, for there next to the desk was the violin with its bow poking itself out of the top of one of the packing crates. Like the man in the shop in Chicago, he ignored the violin and picked up the bow in his hand in such a manner as if he were handling God's scepter itself.

He put it to his eye and stretched it out toward the light, this time as if he was going for a great stag. Like the man in Chicago, he then waived it through the air, first to the right, and then to the left, and again to the right, and then finally to the left, once more. And he paused and exclaimed, "Wow!"

And I offered a screwdriver, and he refused. And I said, "Don't you want to know who made it? When it was made?" And he answered, "I already know. I knew when I first saw it."

And then he pondered as if thinking very deeply. And I looked at the place I had reserved for it on the wall and I thought again of the old man and of Audrey. And I knew that someday when I would go to join them that the violin and its bow would remain behind, perhaps forever, on the wall.

And clearing his throat he interrupted me saying, "Would you consider...?"

And I cut him off, "Perhaps, perhaps," I said, "there is a needy student. One that could use the bow?"

A God for Lions

And the instructor looked around him. The bare floor poked its way, here and there, through the worn linoleum that spread itself across the room. The only visible thing that might work was the bare light bulb that hung from its chain in the center of the room and an old hot plate in one corner. A ragged army cot occupied the other. And between them perched on the windowsill sat a roach who seemed to be cleaning his whiskers. And just outside were a carton of milk and a half-bottle of orange juice trying to keep cold.

Then he looked at me as one looks at someone who is about to jump off of a high building.

And I continued, "Let's say that you replace the strings and you polish it up a bit and you carefully search out a student who is in great need, let's say, one who without the bow could not go on?"

He looked up at me and I noticed a tear creeping toward his eyelid. He looked around the room to reassure himself that no one had seen him. He looked first to his right, and then to his left, and again to his right, and finally to his left, once more. Then he glanced back at me as to assure himself that I, too, hadn't noticed.

And I, so as to save him from exposure, to preserve his manhood so to speak, led him quickly to the door with bow in hand. And I quickly closed it behind him.

The packing crate with the violin still in it remained on the floor. Feeling that I had separated two friends forever, I looked first to the right, and then to the left, and again to the right, and finally to the left, once more. And I carefully rolled the tear from the edge of the lid back into the corner of my eye.

a few months later,

In the months that followed, busy with my new shop, I had forgotten about the incident.

Then one day an Asian college aged youth came into my shop. He carried with him a small case together with all the beauty and aspiration one usually associates with youth. His black hair splashed down evenly from its center part stopping just short of his ears. And the wonderment and enlightenment of his dark eyes did much to obscure the mysterious gloom that was behind them.

Stopping at the counter, he looked across at me and forcing a slight smile, asked, "You are Lucien?" I nodded, and he told me, "My name is Paul Tseng. I have your bow!"

He then proceeded to tell me about his trip from the horror of Tiananmen Square to the United States. Together, with his twin brother Len, he had come to reap that promised by the lady *who lifts her lamp beside the golden door*. "We had everything going for us," he said, "then two years ago my brother was diagnosed with AIDS and the medical bills have chewed up everything we had and, perhaps, everything I will ever have.

"Hal gave me the bow in memory of my brother the day we buried him. I've not been too well since or I would have come in sooner."

As he went on, the tear started moving once again from the corner of my eye to the very edge of my eyelid. And, once again, I looked first to the right, and then to the left, and again to the right, and finally to the left, once more. As to be certain that no one was watching. And then back at the boy, as to be certain that he, too, had not noticed.

And reaching down into his case he pulled forward the bow and said with great emotion, his voice vibrating with every word, "With this, which you have given me, I will make such music," and raising his almost solemn voice and glancing upwards toward the ceiling, he added in unparalleled conviction, "that it will be heard in the heavens above." Then lowering his voice and looking deep into my eyes, "Thank you, thank you, from the very bottom of my heart," and with two great tears rushing away from the corners of his eyes, he turned and reaching the door, *not quite, yet, a man,* they broke out onto his cheeks and fell to the floor. And, he said, "I will never, never forget you." And he was gone.

And I paused and thought, "Yes, it's still there, still on the edge of the cliff," and I, checked, once again, first to the right, and then to the left, and again to the right, and finally to the left, once more. And I carefully rolled the tear back into the corner of my eye.

a few years later,

With my new business, I had regained my ground and had purchased a nineteenth century house in Baltimore's coveted Federal Hill district. The house fronted on a cobble stone street and its rear decks overlooked the city's great harbor.

One day a letter, in kind of a greeting card envelope, arrived. It was postmarked 'New York City' and had been forwarded from my old address. Sitting at my desk that I had strategically located next to the library fireplace, I took the letter opener and sliced the letter open. Out fell a partially dried up rose and a newspaper clipping, 'Young Artist Stuns Carnegie Hall'.

Carefully laying the letter on the desk in front of me I read,

Dear Lucien:

Forgive me for addressing you by your first name. Although I have known many much longer, I know no one better.

Last night I stood at the pinnacle of life. I have saved here, for you, a part of the roses and ovation. For they, indeed, belong to you, at least mostly, to you.

Yes, it was my hand that scratched out the simple concerto that was meant for the lone violin that I held. But, it was your gift that translated my meager work into the great symphony that was heard in the grand hall last night. Yes, the bow, itself, is only a simple composite of wood, ivory, string, and what have you. But what sets it apart from all the others, is what you have unselfishly added to it. That you have chosen to weigh compassion above material gain and, perhaps, even your very survival has made you forever a part of it.

And, believe me, for as long as I live, perhaps, long after you are gone, and, perhaps even long after I am gone, whenever the hand touches the bow, it will move across the strings of a thousand violins, it will bring up the howling of the wind, it will call forward the power of the brass, and it will roll the drums, and it will orchestrate all these things to the final crash of the cymbals. And the bees will hum, and the whippoorwills *will sing, and the trumpets will blare, and the thunder will roar, and the lightning will strike deep into the hearts of all those who are privileged to listen.*

We together, you, I and this composite of wood, ivory and string, will gather up the tears from all their hearts and move them up to the corners of the eyes and we will drain them dry. And, in their place, we will forever leave something else. The very same thing you left in my heart that day when I left my tears in your shop.

And we will do this, Lucien, not for ourselves, but for him, and for her, and for all humanity.

Paul

And as I looked up from the letter I thought of Paul and of his brother and of the old man of the pond, and little Johnny, and of my beloved Audrey. And one of those things one calls tears came up out of my heart and started from the crevice of my eye and moved toward the lid. And I looked first to the right, and then to the left, and again to the right, and finally to the left, once more. And, yes, it was still there. And I would carry it there all the remaining days of my life.

many years later, the Great House,

"When the wolves came," He said, "you bravely stood your ground and risked your life for your neighbor's cub. Now come into my room, here to my side."

I was led into a great theater, as many people as could hold all the stadiums of the world, and as I glanced around I saw that there were still some seats available. And, in the lodge were both Mom and Pop, and just below them was Jack my old high school chum. And just above them, in the balcony, were Grandma and Grandpa and some others from my past, scattered here and there, throughout the great audience. I was ushered all the way down to the front row and there He was, and with Him was my emissary the instructor from the conservatory, and Paul's brother Len, the old man of the pond, and yes, my dear, dearest Audrey. And I took my seat just to His left, which was just to her right.

Then the curtains that protected the great stage that was set before us began to part. And the lights of the great theater began to dim and the drone of all those present grew silent.

And as I looked up I thought I recognized the darkened stage that lay before us. It was, indeed, the great stage of the great symphony hall in Vienna. The very same stage, that at one time had witnessed the miracles of Beethoven, Mozart, Handel and others. It was enveloped in a slight haze, so it was difficult for me to see where it joined the theater.

I sensed that we were about to witness something, someone who we had left behind?

And, suddenly, there in the light of a single spot, stood Paul. And in his hands were a violin and the bow.

And Paul moved the violin up to the crevice of his neck and raised the bow and once more I heard the hum of the bees, and the song of the whippoorwill, and the blare of the trumpets, and the roll of the drums. And, looking over at the one who sat beside me, I noticed that He suddenly looked first to His right, and then to His left, and again to His right, and finally to His left, once more. And, with the crashing crescendo of the cymbals, I saw them come up out of His heart, and I watched them run from the corners of His eyes to the edge of His lids, and splash down onto His cheeks.

And behind me I heard the roar of the crowd, and I looked up at Paul, as he took his bow to the cascade of the roses. And I looked back at He, who sat beside me, with tears still streaming down his cheeks, and I thought, "*Not Quiet, Yet, a Man!*"

Lucien Gregoire

Two Pieces of Gold

Then He rose and went up to the stage. He gave Paul a great big hug and placed in his folded arm a dozen of the most beautiful roses I have ever seen. And Paul came toward me, and reaching down, handed them to me. And holding out his hand as to beckon the audience behind me I, once more, heard the roar of the crowd. And then returning to the center of the stage the Father whispered something into his ear. And Paul turning and taking the violin back up to the crevice of his neck raised the bow once more, and began walking away into the endless depth of the great stage. And with the sound growing fainter with each step was heard the hum of the bees, the song of the whippoorwill, the blare of the trumpets, and the roll of the drums.

And as the great curtains closed to the final clap of the cymbals, was heard a faint whimper, no a cry, then another cry. Yes, a baby's cry and then another and another and another. And, again, the great curtains parted and there before us were babies as far to the right, and as far to the left, and as far as one could see. Hundreds of them, thousands of them, perhaps, upwards of a million of them.

There were boy babies and girl babies and some in-betweens. Black ones, brown ones, white ones, yellow ones and red ones. Some were handicapped, some retarded, and a few with other great afflictions. I particularly noticed some with AIDS. And there were even a couple Siamese ones. Some had brown eyes, others had blues eyes, and still others had black eyes, and some had hazel eyes. And, yes, a few could not see. Some had big ears, while others had small ears, still others with pointed ears, and some had floppy ears. And, yes, a few could not hear. Some had a touch of brown hair, while others had black hair, still others had blond hair, still others had red hair, some had shiny hair, and some had frizzy hair. And, yes, a few had no hair. Some had curved noses, while others had straight noses, still others had flat noses, still others had wide noses, some had long noses, and a few others had pug noses. And, I could not tell if some could not smell.

Some were Americans, some were Germans, some were Mexicans, some were Russians, some were Japanese, some were Chinese, some were Puerto Ricans, some were Brazilians, while others were Indian, still others were African, even a couple of Aborigines, two Eskimos, and all by himself off to the right was a lone Pygmy. Each, crying, in his or her octave, as if to hint at the invisible presence of as many maestros. And way off behind them in the distanced horizon almost a speck was Paul. He seemed to be waiting there for his next instruction.

And the Father turning His back on us as to face them, said something softly, and all was quiet. Then addressing them He said, "Tomorrow, for each of you, is the first day of the rest of your life. Until now I have nurtured you, held you, protected you and loved you. Now you will be on your own. This is your chance," and pointing to the great theater behind Him, "at one of these seats. Tomorrow, all over creation, your cries will applaud my greatest work."

Then, He reached up and took two tears that remained balanced on the lid of each eye. And, holding them out, He said, "This evening, as I witnessed Paul's work, I wept two kinds of tears. Beautiful ones, and some not so beautiful. Those that left my heart full, and yet others that left my heart empty. I will take the first kind every time. But that is not my decision, it is not my power, for it is yours alone.

"Lucien and all the others behind me were once in your shoes," and then as if realizing His error, as they had no shoes, "your place. Yes, he gave me the first kind, as when Paul's great symphony reached into my heart, indeed, into the very depths of my soul, and brought forth the tears, something much greater was left in their place. But, yet, at the same time, I thought of all the others, of all my children who had not returned, and this also reached deep within me, and pulled forth the tears, but nothing, absolutely nothing, was left in their place.

"My rules are simple, you need not heed what others tell you, what all that has been written tells you. For I send you forward into the world with only two pieces of gold and with them the will to spend them on what you please.

"The first is the instinct of 'self survival'. This is a selfish one, it will drive your desire for materiality and self esteem. It has no concern for others. It has no heart. And listen to me," He said, lowering his voice as if whispering a secret, "This piece of gold cannot buy for you a seat in this great theater behind me. For it is, indeed, *fools gold*.

"And then," He offered, "I give you another great piece of gold, this one *real gold*. One that could, indeed, buy for you the very best seat in this house. This is a second basic instinct. It is called 'compassion'. This is the unselfish one, the one reserved for your work for others.

"And thirdly, I give you the free will to spend them as you please. As you proceed through life, you will benefit from the great knowledge that has been accumulated for endless millenniums before you. But, in the morning, you will posses only a single fragment of knowledge," and pausing as to excuse His vanity, He added, "Your God given sense to know right from wrong." And, with great instruction, He finished, "And this is your compass, the only thing you will need to guide you on your long journey through life back to this house.

"As you proceed through life," He went on, "the road will always take two paths, every year, every day, every hour, every minute, every second of your life.

"The road sign to the *right* will always read '*survival*.' At times it will mean *selfishness*, and at other times *mine*, and at other times *wealth*, and often it will read *take*, and then again it might read *hate*, and at other times it might read *murder*, and still other times it might read *betray ones loved one* or again it might read *molest a young one*. Selfishness, bigotry, hypocrisy, cowardliness and often even laziness will guide one down this path.

"And the one to the *left* will always read '*compassion*'. And this one will mean *unselfishness*, and at other times *yours*, and at other times *kindness*, and it will often mean *give*, and then again it might mean *sacrifice,* or sometimes *love*. Unselfishness, courage, bravery and gallantry, and often great effort will be necessary for one to take this path.

"And each time that the fork in the road comes up, sometimes only minutes apart, your choice of which path you take will count toward your place in the great room behind me. And, using your *compass*, your inherent sense to know right from wrong, you must always choose what is right. You must always go to the *left.*"

the candy and the paddle,

"I want you to look at the great room behind me for until you return you will not know it is there. All of your life this will remain a great mystery to you. And I do this for a very sound reason. For I do not want you to be motivated by reward, as all of your motivation must be solely for others. For if you do these things for reward you would be guilty of selfishness, the very thing I tell you not to be.

"Tomorrow," He went on, "you will be born into many different scriptures. Some of you will be born Christians, others Jews, Muslims, Hindus, Shintos, Buddhist and what are thousands of different beliefs. Sometimes these beliefs will lead you to me, but more often they will lead you away from me. These religions are inspired, sadly, by this great mystery, what happens to one after one dies?

"These beliefs are the invention of man's mortality, his lust for eternal life. These churches are full because it is man's dream that he can somehow live beyond the other side of the wall. And I give you circumstance here. For had I created man to be immortal there would be no churches, no scriptures and no adoration of the Magi. For man would assume that he, himself, was God.

"But these churches prosper, and the degree of prosperity depends on those who tell the best story or those that offer the best package, the greatest reward after death in exchange for the smallest possible sacrifice while on earth. Some go so far as to promise paradise for simply believing in a given emissary. For simply repenting for ones sins. And the most successful drive their business by fear and threaten a penalty for not believing, that there will be horror after death. Like offering a child candy in one hand, and the paddle in the other hand, sadly, they herd their flocks to satisfy whatever happens to be their whim.

"And the whim varies widely depending on the motivation of the founders of the particular scriptures involved. And one should not fool oneself for they, the founders, have all been men of motive as they all claimed to have had direct intercession with me. And each one knew that if he could convince his fellowman of this intercession it would make him a great man, and in most cases a leader of ones people. From the angakok of the Arctic, to the witchdoctor of the jungle, to all those who spoke from the mount.

"If a leader of a nation wanted to expand his empire he knew that the best motivation for his people would be to convince them that a message had come directly from me, that those who tilled the soil of the adjoining land were evil. Take Moses for example, *'And the Lord said unto Joshua, See, I have given into thy hand the promised land. Take all ye men of war and ye are to enter the gates of the many cities and take the silver and gold and palaces for yourself and take to the sword all the inhabitants thereof, every man, woman and child. Leave not a one alive.'* It saddens me greatly that so many of my children would think this of me, that I would tell them to murder their neighbors and take their land from them. "This is why I give you this," He pointed to His temple, "For it is common sense that had I intended the Israelites to have the Promised Land, I would have given it to them in the first place.

"So when you believe men of motive," He added, "believe me, you are taking great risk. For all of these men became wealthy men having many slaves including Joshua, himself, who as leader of the Israelite nation lived out his life in luxury in the silver and gold of the great palace of Jericho. And I tell you a story,

there is a mountain off in the distance

a small speck appears at the base of the mountain

much later the speck evolves into a man

the man approaches and tells us that

this is his mountain

> but there is a more splendid mountain yonder
>
> which view is hidden by his mountain
>
> so we go around his mountain
>
> which takes us on a long and difficult journey of faith
>
> and there is nothing there.

reason or belief,

"Tomorrow, as I have already told you, your cries will bear witness to my greatest work. Yet, I give to each of you the ability to improve on this work. For I have created each of you with a purpose in life. And it is my requirement that you complete this purpose no matter how great or how small. And your seat in the great house behind me will depend much on the degree to which you contribute to your fellowman. It is, indeed, a fool who believes otherwise. That I would create a human being without purpose as is set forth in western scriptures.

"You will come to know that you can choose of only two alternative mentors in life. Two alternative guides in everything you do along your long journey back to this house, *reason*, or *belief*. There are no alternatives. And believe me, these are exact opposites. As opposite as I am to Satan. They do not go hand in hand as some might want one to believe. Just think, if man *knew* all things he would *believe* nothing at all. He wouldn't have to *believe*, for he would *know* all things. And, on the other hand, if I was to create someone as an absolute imbecile, and I never have, he or she could only *believe*. For they could never *know*.

"If I had wanted you to be believers, I would have created all of you to be absolute imbeciles. But I gave you this," and He again pointed to His temple, "and, believe me, when you are out there on your own, I expect you to use it.

"The cumulation of knowledge depends upon great exercise of the mind, nothing more, nothing less. Whereas, man's *belief* has no dependence whatsoever upon the employment of the mind at all. As a matter of fact it is dependent on just the opposite. On ignoring this which I have given you," and He pointed to his temple once more, "and relying entirely on what others tell you. *Belief* is the way of laziness, of idleness and of sloth, the easy way. But, trust me, it is not the right way. Yes, *belief* is the great friend of those who falsely represent themselves as my emissaries, of those who make their livelihood in the way that preys upon the weakness of man to take the easy way out and simply believe.

"When you are out there you should strive toward Godliness, toward knowledge. For I know all things and believe nothing. And you should try to make yourself as much like I am as is possible. You should strive to know all things so that, like myself, you become independent of *belief*. Again, you should strive every day of your life toward Godliness, toward knowledge, toward knowing all things. For I am God and I know all things. For only then will you be able to make the contribution to your fellowman that I require of you.

"Each day as you come to the fork in the road, you should take the path to the *left*, not because you *believe* that it is the right path, but rather, because you *know* that it is the right path," He again pointed to His temple, "the path back to this house. Always keep in mind that '*Godliness*' has its synonymy in '*Knowledge*', in *reason*, not in *belief*. For, again, I *know* all things, and I *believe* nothing."

lions and sheep,

"In the morning, all of your cries will be the cry of the lion cub. There will not be a lamb among you. But during your lifetime you can so choose to be sheep.

"Lions are among the smartest of animals, whereas sheep are among the dumbest. Lions are among the most active of animals, whereas sheep are by far the laziest. In addition, sheep will believe most anything one tells them. They will follow a shepherd's direction or the sheep in front of them, right off of a cliff. The lion, on the other hand, is perhaps the world's most clever and cautious animal. Using great care he tests the waters or the grass with every single step.

"And there is still another major difference between these species. Lions are among the most courageous of animals. When the hyena pack attacks her young, the lioness, although she knows it means certain death, will fight to the end. The sheep, on the other hand, is a coward by nature, and when the wolf comes she will run for her life and leave her young behind.

"Believe me, in my house, there is no room for sheep, only lions. For I am *A God of Lions.*"

my own emissary,

"You will come to know that you possess something that is known as *common sense*. What some will come to know as *reason*. I give you this so that you will know that it makes no sense, whatsoever, that I would appear to literally thousands of different emissaries and give them as many different messages on how to get back to this house. And most of these so called emissaries will tell you that you are my chosen people."

And with great anger He added, "What kind of monster does one think I am that I would choose some of my children to be saved and cast away the others? That I would appear to one prophet in the east and give him a message and I would ignore my children in the west? That I would give another message to one in the west and ignore my children in the east? Even today, as we enter another millennium, there is a very slight chance that a child born in the Western Hemisphere will ever learn about Hinduism or become a Hindu. And, likewise, the child born in the Eastern Hemisphere has the same slight chance that he or she will ever learn about Christianity or become a Christian. In my creation all my children have an equal chance.

a point in time,

"And then we have the matter of time. This idea of a Savior. That I would choose to give all those who come after the time of a Savior a chance at eternity and yet deprive all my children who had come before that point in time of the same opportunity. Again, what fools these are, that they would think this of me. Believe me, all of my children from the beginning of time to the end of time have the same opportunity. Again common sense should tell one that. And, again, common sense should tell one quite clearly that it makes no sense that I would appear to thousands of individual emissaries and never once appear to two or more people at one time.

"And you will question the preacher, 'What happened to all of those children who were born and lived before the coming of the Savior?' And he will tell you, each and every one of you, 'God took care of those in another way.' And the believers will accept his word. But for those of you who use this it will mean something else," and He pointed to his temple, "For if I took care of the others in another way there would obviously be no point to a Savior. That is, other than making the preacher rich. For only a Savior can make the cash register ring, as most people already believe in me. The reason why religion is a multi-billion dollar business in the west and why it has no receipts in the east, as there are no Saviors in the east, only God.

"Whether or not you ever return to this house is solely your decision, your decision alone. It is not my decision. And you must make that decision because it is right, as I have told you it is right. You must make it independent of the candy or the paddle.

"Yes, you can choose to let it be someone else's decision. Yes, sometimes someone from the past, even someone from the ancient past. But when you so choose keep in mind that the past is still, only the present is moving ahead toward tomorrow. Remember that the past, particularly the ancient past, can never reach tomorrow. Can never reach this house.

"When *reason* speaks, listen to what it says, for it, and not *belief*, is the light in the darkness that will guide you back to this house. It is your ticket to eternal life. *Belief*, although, the easier way, the lazier way, is a blindfold. It will overpower *reason* and serve only to darken your journey.

born as sinners,

"And have no excuses. My powers are limited for I can only create what is good, I have never been able to and I have never wanted to create anything that was bad. Tomorrow you will all be born to be good.

"Once you are out there, out on the road, you will come to know, contrary to what some religions would want you to believe, that you were not born a sinner. For when you do what is right, you will know that it is right, and when you do what is wrong, you will know that it is wrong. If I were to create you to be sinful by nature, then when you did wrong you would think that you did right. And you will quickly find that this is not the case. Yet, I tell you this because I have lost many children, perhaps weaker ones, to this misconception. They try to excuse themselves by thinking it is my fault, that I created them to be evil, that I created them to be sinful by nature. That all they need do is repent. They only fool themselves. Believe me, you will all be born good. You will all be born lions. You can only choose to be bad. You can only choose to be sheep.

"These are all the tools you need, to be aware of the two basic instincts of life, the two pieces of gold, and your conscience, your compass, your inherent ability to know what is right from what is wrong. Let no one tell you different. Let no one, no matter how revered the speaker, no matter how eloquent the oratory, no matter how brilliant the rhetoric contradict what I say to you today. No matter how many claim to be my prophet, believe me, I am my own emissary and I come to you directly here today and I will be with you every day, every minute of your life *in that part of you, which is a part of me*," pointing to His temple, "which you will come to know as your conscience."

a role model,

"And I give you a role model, so to speak," and He looked to the box to his left, which was just a man's leap from the great stage. There sat a towering figure in a black suit, a bow tie and top hat. "Many years, ago, this great one came to a fork in the road. And all that he had learned in life told him that the correct path was to the *right*. His parents had told him, his preachers had told him, his peers had told him, even the very scriptures he had been born into told him that it was right. That slavery was God's will, that it was His way of life. His *Tenth Commandment* told him specifically '*Thou shalt not covet* (take from) *thy neighbor his slaves*.' Well, believe me," He said raising His voice, almost in a fit of anger, "slavery is not my way of life!

"This great one in the top hat took out the very same *compass* that I give to each of you today. And I will never forget watching him, as he looked first to the *right*, and there he saw great wealth and ease of living with his dark neighbors tilling his soil by day. With his dark neighbors shining his shoes by night. And then looking to the *left*, he saw a great struggle, war and bloodshed. He even saw his own end in the very box that houses him, today. And, again, looking to the *right*, and finally to the *left*, once more, he went bravely to the *left*, and an army of others soon followed him into this great theater tonight.

"This great army of men and women of good conscience and of great courage who defied what they *believed* was the only written word of their God as had been handed down from the mount in their scriptures. These great men and women who took from their southern neighbor all of his slaves, and, what's more, they took them away from him forever.

"Yet, despite the outcome of the war, the preacher was able to contain the blacks as a subordinate race for yet another century. Yes, for another hundred years, the preacher armed with his scripture was able to keep them in the hot and stuffy galleries of his churches, in the backs of buses and in unkempt toilets. He was able to use his scripture to create laws that put those who chose to violate his rules into chain gangs.

"If one cannot believe what is explicit in ones scripture, the only known written word of God, the *Ten Commandments*, that slavery is righteousness, then how can one even begin to believe in any of the other stories in scripture that were simply passed down through thousands of years simply by word of mouth?

put yourself in my place,

"Just stop and think for a minute. Put yourself in my place.

"Now, what would you want of your children? Would you want them to bring you gold, frankincense and myrrh? Would you want them to fall down on their knees and adore you? Would you want them to cut off their children's foreskins and offer them to you? Would you want them to hate one another? Would you want them to enslave *their dark neighbors to the south*? Would you want them to persecute the *strange little boy in the playground?* Would you want them to deprive him of equal human rights under the law? Would you want your sons to hold your daughters in servitude to themselves? Would you give your children the great gift of sex and tell them that it is shameful and sinful and evil? Would you go so far as to issue a directive to some of your children that they are your chosen few? That they are to invade the land of their neighbors, the Promised Land, and annihilate them, men, women and children? Your children?

"No, none of these things. Not a single one of these things," He concluded, "For a good Father, at the start of each day, when he sends His children on their way, would want only two things. That they love and contribute to each other as they go along their way and that they come back to His house at the end of the day. That is all. That is all that He would want. And that is all that I do want. For believe me," He resolved, "I am a good and just *Father*, regardless of what any scripture might say."

the great cathedral,

"And, as you go on through life you will find many who will fall on their knees in adoration of me, who will sing praises to me, who will build great edifices to honor me, to try to butter me up, so to speak. They only fool themselves. For they are playing with fools gold, for there is no substitute for my instruction. You will find that as long as you live, every single thing that you do will either be done for yourself, or it will be done for others. You will either take the road to the *right* or you will take the road to the *left*. That is the beginning, the whole, and the all of it.

"Just think, use the intelligence that I have given you. If I wanted you to adore me, to build great structures to my honor, I would be guilty of the very same thing I instruct you not to be. For that would be selfish of me. All that I ask of you, is that when you take the tear from my heart, that you leave something in its place.

"When you are out there you will quickly learn that all the wealth in creation cannot buy a single solitary life. That all the money, all the churches, all the songs, all the scientific progress of man combined cannot be exchanged for a single solitary human life. And, here, I am not dealing simply with lives. I am dealing with souls. And, believe me, all the golden images you place before me, all the magnificent cathedrals you build to my honor, and all the praise you may bestow upon me, all the songs you can sing, cannot save for me a single solitary soul. Cannot save me from the great sadness I feel when one of my children fails to return to my house. When one takes a tear from my heart and leaves nothing, nothing in its place."

enough for me,

"And I will tell you of a young golfer. This young man was widely traveled, including the great cities of the United States and Europe, on the one hand, and places like India, Uganda and Haiti, on the other. He was confused by the great cathedrals, the golden chalices and jeweled crucifixes, the pomp and pageantry and the immense wealth of religion and of the great mansions of the pope and cardinals and evangelists on the one side and the great extension of suffering and poverty on the other.

"One day, while waiting for the foursome ahead of him to leave the green, he laid down in the middle of the fairway and looked straight up. All was silent around him, and being a crystal clear day, all he could see was the blue sky, and he told me,

'I can offer you no great cathedral, no chant, no offering of gold. All I have to give is my promise that I will do what you have told me to do. To always take the path to the *left*, that one marked 'compassion'. I know not where this path leads. All that I know is that you have told me to take it, and that is all I need to know. And, if at its end, there is nothing there, it is enough for me that you have given me the great opportunity to walk this way. And I will always cherish having been given that privilege.

'I care not if it takes me over the highest mountains, or across the widest seas, or against the armaments of all the armies of the earth, or even through fire. I intend to do this thing with all the strength, courage and vigor that is in me, as if the very survival of every single child that you have ever created, depends on me alone.'

This was the prayer of Lucien, many years ago, who has followed his solemn pledge all the days of his life, even in giving up the violin bow, and is now back at my side."

Atom and Eve,

"Again, let *reason* be your guide. *Belief* will only tend to confuse you. Strive toward knowledge for it will give you the answer you seek. And, again, I will give you some role models. Men who, each time the fork in the road came up, took out their *compass* and did what was right, they went to the *left*. They always followed the sign that read "compassion". Some of the better seats in this house are occupied by men and women who never *believed* in me."

And glancing back a few rows back to the right, such as to acknowledge Albert Einstein and Charles Darwin, perhaps, the world's most acclaimed enemies of religion, sitting side by side. "When you get to earth you will come to know that an atheist is one who does not *believe* in me. And, concerning these two, this is correct. For these men did not *believe* in me, instead they *knew* me. Instead of simply accepting *belief* they strove toward *Knowledge*, toward *Godliness*. And they left enough behind them to evidence to each of you that I am, indeed, here.

"When you are there you will marvel at the perfection and harmony of what is before you. You will wonder how it all came about? You will hear from one end that I created it all in a few days. That like a fairy godmother of some kind I went from here to there touching my magic wand as I made my way and 'poof' it was there and 'poof', again, and man was there. That I touched a rib of man with my wand and 'poof' woman was there. Yet, from the other end, you will hear that it was all the result of a cosmic explosion.

"Common sense, *reason*, which I give to each of you today, will soon tell you that neither of these is so," and, again, referring to the two who sat side by side, "Because of these two great men you need no longer *believe* that I am here, for you will *know* that I am here.

"The first of these great men, proved beyond a shadow of a doubt that every physical thing in the universe, including each one of my children and even the hardest substance known diamond, is a composite of tiny atomic particles which are commonly referred to as 'energy'. And, what's more, that the tiniest bit of energy can multiple in itself to produce enormous, unlimited, energy. This man's followers demonstrated at Hiroshima and Nagasaki, what happens when a single atom of energy splits. Although, a very visible message, most ignored it and went back to their scriptures, their stories, their folklore, their fairy tales.

"Yes, what started it all, could have been, and I will not confirm this here, a cosmic happening? Yet, again, *common sense* will quickly tell you that *something* could not have come from *nothing*. That even a cosmic happening could not have come from *nothing*. And this is not conjecture. It is fact.

"You will know, therefore, that something had to be infinite in time. And this something had to be either a *conscious* being as I am or an *unconscious* being like a minuscule atomic particle of energy. There are no other possible alternatives. This is also not conjecture. It is fact.

"In order for one to not *know* that I am here, one would have to assume that the infinite being in time was an *unconscious* minuscule atomic particle of energy and that through time the composition of these *unconscious* particles somehow evolved into a *conscious* being. But an unconscious being cannot move. So *common sense*, again, will tell one that this could not be so. This would not be possible. This is also not conjecture. It is fact.

"Today one can look under the most powerful microscopes and can see these tiny particles. And one can see that they are all moving. Just as the great one in the long white hair had once theorized that all matter is made up of moving parts called 'energy'. They all have a job to do. So one knows that each and every one of them is a conscious being. And one knows this because one knows that an unconscious being cannot move. And this, again, is not conjecture. It is fact.

"And one also knows that each and every one of them has a purpose. Consider those which are involved in the building of the human body and brain. There are known to be over one hundred thousand different kinds of protein. One hundred thousand different armies of billions of tiny specks and every single one of them knows exactly what its job is. And protein is only one of more than one hundred different nutrients that are involved in the building of human life. And under a microscope today one can see these many armies going about their work in perfect formation. Some of them look like tiny spiders, others look like tiny worms, and still others look like tiny crabs, and there are some that look like tiny sea creatures, some like tiny fish and a few resemble tiny reptiles. And they all end up as one of you,

five of the 110,000 kinds of protein magnified a quarter million times.

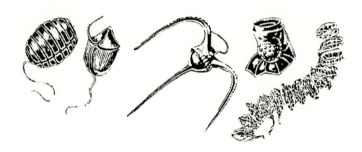

"And I might make it clear that every one of these tiny specs of protein has the very same beginning as does man. Each one of them has a mother and a father. Each one of them has a brain and a nervous system, a cardiovascular system, a respiratory system, a digestive system and a reproductive system. And that goes for every animal, every bird, every fish, every insect and every microcosm. For I have only one method of creation, for all of my children are equal,

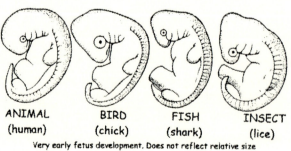

ANIMAL (human)   BIRD (chick)   FISH (shark)   INSECT (lice)

Very early fetus development. Does not reflect relative size

A God for Lions

"So *reason,* alone, will bring you this far. It will leave you with no doubt that the infinite being in time was a conscious one. Up to this point you will be dealing only with fact. But I will leave something for your judgment.

"The question whether this infinite conscious being is either an insignificant inferior being or a superior or what one might call a Supreme Being? Then I would ask you to look at the great organization, balance and symmetry of the world around you. For you to conclude that I am not here, you would have to conclude that all that is around you was created by another conscious being that was minuscule compared to man, himself. And I recommend that you look through a microscope for your answer rather than though a telescope at the cosmos. That all the tiny bits of energy that are responsible for the creation of human life and all the other armies responsible for the balance of creation are without a commanding general. That each of these billions of trillions of tiny creatures is going about its work entirely without direction. And *reason* will tell you that this could not be so. Scripture or *belief*, of course, will tell you something else. That I went about with my magic wand touching here and there as I made my way. And scripture tells you this because men wrote it before the time of the great one in the long white hair and the microscope. They had no way of telling how the job is actually done. So they had to guess.

"So you will *know* for all intents and purposes when you are out there that I am also there. In your conscious, your conscience, *that part of you, which is a part of me.*

"Again, let *reason,* the master of enlightenment, be your beacon. *Belief*, the master of darkness, will only bring you mystery.

"You will hear all kinds of theories, all kinds of claims. And, if you heed these theories, these claims, these things called religion, then you will have to resort to a position of weakness, one of *belief,* in the possibility of my existence. But I give to you, everyone of you, the ability to *know* me, to *know* that I am here. And at the risk of giving away some of my secrets," He concluded, "*common sense* will tell you that had I created *Atom*, then *Eve* and everything else would have eventually come along.

"That these two great men, in their respective works of '*relativity*' and '*natural selection*', have left behind them scientific proof of my existence. That these two men in their great genius prove my existence, Einstein providing the parts, and Darwin providing the path."

the chicken or the egg,

"Every religion in the world will tell you that the chicken came first. As a matter of fact it is on page one in all of the world's scriptures. And it is a story on which the credibility of all religions rest. And this includes Christianity, for had Adam and Eve never committed Original Sin then Christ would not be God. But one look under a microscope tells one quite conclusively that as a matter of fact, the egg came first. For it tells of that day when I sat in my great factory above and created the first part."

Phil,

"Look around you," He said, "Each time you show prejudice, persecute, or restrict the freedom of any of my children, your brothers and sisters, no matter how different they might seem to be, no matter who told you that it is the right thing to do. Whether it be your parents, your preachers, your peers, your political leaders or even your scriptures. You are taking a detour that will surely cause you to lose your way back into the great theater that stands behind me. And I give you a story,

"There was once a little boy. He came into the house one day and told his mother that the kids at school were calling his friend Jimmy a *fairy*. And he told her, 'They push him around and Jimmy

A God for Lions

cries.' And his mother told him, 'Phil, you must stay away from Jimmy.' And Phil replied, 'No, he needs me now more than ever, he needs a friend.' So, he stood by his friend and soon they began to call him, too, a *fairy,* and he carried this fear with him into his adult life. The fear that someone would think him, gay.

"And he grew up and went to college and he got into radio and into television and finally became what one might call a talk-show host. And he started to use his influence to help all those who appear to be different, all those who had occasion to be oppressed. And he brought them into his world, onto his stage. He talked to them, he listened to them, he talked to others about them, and he listened to others about them. And like a great chef he brought them all together in a mixing bowl and produced a cake with a face on it. But the face still had a slight frown. And he knew what was wrong. For he had left out a certain ingredient, and what's more, he had done it intentionally. For he was afraid that if he helped those like Jimmy now, the whole world would think him gay.

"So, the big fork in the road for him had come up and he had only two choices, cowardice or courage. And he first looked to the *right* and the road seemed clear. And then he looked down the road to the *left*, the one with the sign that says 'compassion', and off in the distance was his friend Jimmy. And Jimmy was in trouble, real trouble, for this time he had AIDS. And Jimmy was calling to him for help. But the road was lined on both sides with bigots, thousands of them on each side. Many evangelists and people like Jerry Falwell and Jessie Helms were there. And they were calling out names, all kinds of names, *'fruit, queer, fairy, faggot, pansy'* and what have you? And, what's more, they had sticks and stones and clubs and knives and guns. So he looked, again, to the *right* and this time a golden carriage stood there, and by the open door was an angel. And the angel commanded, 'Ignore him, for it is his punishment for having lived a sinful life, a life that is against God's will. Come here, hurry, we will be late for the *Bigot Ball*.' And, finally, he looked down to the *left*, once more. And without hesitation, without any concern for himself, with no fear of the sticks or stones, but still knowing that the names might bring him down, Phil valiantly turned and went down the road to the left and rescued his friend.

"So soon one forgets that it was this very same Christian preacher who inspired by Moses' slaughter of the Canaanites in the taking of the 'Holyland' roused the Crusades in which tens of millions of Muslim and Jewish men, women and children were put to the sword. This same preacher who armed with Moses' Tenth Commandment placed the black in bondage. And even after he was freed, it was this same preacher who employed Moses' white Aryan race edict to enact laws of subordination to keep the black in the back of buses, in unkempt toilets, in hot stuffy galleys of churches, and to grow up in slums. This same preacher who has kept woman in her place all these years. This same preacher whose teachings motivated Hitler in his murder of Jews in the Holocaust. This very same Christian preacher, who having had all these things taken from him, now unleashes his hate on those of my children who can only *fall in love* with one of their own sex."

the best remaining seats,

And glancing around Him throughout the great theater and coming to rest on the box on the other side of the theater which was also a man's leap from the great stage and resting on some empty seats that were marked '*vacant*', He said, "As you can see many of the better seats in this great house are still available. And great opportunity is out there for each of you. It is still possible, for you to even eclipse," and throwing a glancing smile back and pointing to the box to His left, "the works and the deeds of this great one in the top hat. For, in his time, the freedom of some of my children was at stake. But, today, you have even greater opportunity, even greater challenge. For, today, the equality of all my children and the very survival of civilization is at stake." Then, He raised His voice as if one could not help but get the message and He added with such force as if it were a command, "Now go for it!"

And in closing He beckoned to Paul who stood at the rear of the stage. And Paul turning away from us once more raised his violin and the bow and started walking off toward the seemingly endless stage. And once more we heard, very faintly, the hum of the bees, the song of whippoorwill, the blare of the trumpets, the roll of the drums, and finally the crash of the cymbals fading away into nothingness.

Off he went, with the babies following him, disappearing one after the other. The last one, a little Bushman, who turned and waived at us and had the biggest widest eyes and a most unforgettable smile that seemed to say, "See you later." This time, each and every one of them on their way to greatness.

Then, finally, with the curtains closing behind Him, turning and facing us, He said, "It is my dream, it has been my fervent dream, for a hundred, for a thousand millenniums, that one day I will send out my children, and that on another day all will return. Through the years I have tried, and tried, and tried again, but to little avail. But I refuse to give up and I will go on trying. For the challenge remains, the will is still there, the struggle goes on, for my dream must never die."

And, once again, I thought of all that had gone before me, I thought of Audrey, who now sat beside me clasping my hand and I thought of the old man of the pond, and of Paul and of his brother. And in my mind for all eternity, I knew that whenever the hand would touch the bow, that it would move across the strings of a thousand violins, that it would bring up the howling of the wind, that it would call forward the power of the brass, and that it would roll the drums, and that it would orchestrate all these things to the final crash of the cymbals. That the lighting would strike deep into the hearts of all that would be privileged to listen. And that it would gather up the tears from all their hearts and move them up to the corners of the eyes and would drain them dry. And in their place would be left something else, the very same thing that I had left in Paul's heart that day when he had left his tears in my shop. And that in the end, His dream would finally come true. That as each of His children would take a tear from His heart something much greater would be left in its place.

And then my thoughts turned to Audrey, my beloved Audrey. I knew her then, and I have never forgotten my last goodbye. As she lay there, the pallor of her lips seemed to eclipse the mystery of her smile. She was in death every bit as much as she had been in life. I had not known that a human face and form, if not translated into art by a great painter or sculptor, could be so beautiful. Mere mortal flesh, bones and hair, I reminded myself, trying to put aside the wonder one feels in witnessing perfection.

And, I thought back to that time, when I had reached over and touched her hand, so as to confirm to myself that this was indeed, forever, goodbye. And then, *not quite, yet, a man*, the tear, that I had held on the edge of my eyelid for so many years, suddenly, went over the cliff. First catching the light from the dazzling sun, and then, as if to attract attention to itself, it hovered in midair, glistening as a finely cut diamond, pausing, here and there, as if to afford each faucet a moment to bow. And, finally, plunging downwards it disappeared in a colorless blot. Its brother started right after it, and its sister and all the others came cascading down. All before I had a chance to look to the right, to look to the left, to look again to the right, and finally to the left, once more. They were all gone. And, in their place, I felt what I had never felt before, and I heard the hum of the bees, and the song of whippoorwill, and the blare of the trumpets, and the roar of the lions, and I realized the right of it all. And I thought of myself, "Yes, *not quite, yet, a man.* Perhaps, a God?"

about the bow.

Up until the time that the boy comes into the shop, *Not Quite, Yet a Man,* is a true story and is told precisely as it had occurred. The author, to this day, has never learned what the true market value of the bow is and he has no desire to do so. What he did know was that "IHS MDCCXLIV" was carved under the ivory casing which housed one end of the bow. This record was made when his household, together with its artwork, was inventoried by an insurance company in 1975. IHS, of course, is the Latin for *Jesus Christ*, and the author believed that the bow was of some sort of religious importance. Possibly of significant importance judging from the substantial offer that had been made for it.

However, after having given up the bow and having written the story, he gave a copy of it to a young student of the conservatory who told him that 'IHS', in the world of violins, stands for Iesus Hominum Salvator. This would evidence that the bow, referred to in this work, was made by Guarneri. That is, it was a *Guarnerius* bow dated 1744. That it was possibly the last bow that the great master made, as the accompanying violin with which it was to share its life was most likely never made. It is very rare for a bow to be separated from its violin, particular one made by one of the great master craftsmen.

That Guarneri died in January of the same year that the bow was made seems to support this theory. This is probably how, being an orphan, the bow happened to get matched up with one of the *Stradivarius* copies that were made around the turn of the nineteenth century.

The story of 'Phil' was inspired by Phil Donahue. The noted television personality has expressed the silent fear recounted in the story publicly. The childhood story of Phil is fabricated.

Although it was not my intent to make a case for reincarnation that is what to some extent has happened. For even the most doubtful of observers would place the likelihood of reincarnation well above the flip of a coin. And there are many I suppose who would come away with an absolute certainty of reincarnation. After all, that is what all of the circumstantial evidence that we have gathered to date seems to promise us, that we will indeed get a chance to do it over again.

Yet, for those of you who require a *sure bet* I leave you with the Hinayana, a one hundred percent chance at eternal life. And you will survive not only as a simply soul, but as a God, *that part of each of us that tells us right from wrong.* Not that you must rise to the level of a Lincoln or a Mother Teresa or a Ghandi, for I think that there is some room there for the little guy too.

And for those of you who are content with Christianity I have proved that Christianity and Einstein have the same thing to say,

God (Christ) is the infinite energy flow from which each of us had our beginning and to which each of us will eventually return.

And for those who must use their imagination, that God is some kind of a superman in princely garb, I leave you with,

A God for Lions

So we have covered the bases. We have left no one out, and we have left no questions unanswered, including the one at the end of your life.

the author

comments or gift or anonymous or signed copies of the author's books: email: <u>yourangel@att.net</u> or 410 625 9741
author's books can also be ordered on www.1stbooks.com

The Evolution of Belief in God

200000BC	earliest belief of survival of the sprit. Buried male dead at depths of up to ten feet suggesting fear of spirits, Neanderthals, Africa
75000BC	possibly the earliest belief in a Supreme Being, ritualistic shrine of bear skulls, Neanderthals, Africa
27000BC	ceremonial burial, Cro-Magnons, Europe
18000BC	earliest evidence of a religious ritual in America, Cro-Magnons, Monte Verde
13000BC	earliest evidence of belief in God in the Far East, pottery etchings, Japan
4261BC	earliest surviving calendar, Mesopotamia
4060BC	Adam and Eve are created according to *Bible*
3100BC	Pharaoh Naumer, earliest known hard evidence of belief in a heaven and hell. Earliest belief in resurrection, that the body will rise again, Egypt. First man to convince a population of his intercession with gods and this makes him the undisputed ruler of Egypt.
2500BC	Hinduism, believed to be the earliest time of belief in one God, a *Holy Trinity*

- The God Brahma, the Creator

	• Shiva, the Redeemer, provider of the afterlife
	• Vishnu, tells one what is right and wrong
2200BC	the earliest origin of a god who came to earth to die for the sins of mankind, the god Zagerus, Minoan culture, Greece
2050BC	in Sumeric culture the god Tammus comes to earth to die for the sins of mankind
1950BC	in Syrian culture the god Adonis comes to earth to die for the sins of mankind
1750BC	in Hittite culture the god Attis comes to earth to die for the sins of mankind, Turkey
1375BC	earliest known monolithic (one God) society in the west, Egyptians, the Sun God, 'Re'. Pharaoh Akhenaten declares that there is only one God.
1325BC	Moses 'writes' *Genesis* and *Exodus*. He founds a religion based on belief in one God. Like Pharaoh before him, he convinces the Israelites of his intercession with God which inspires them to engage in the first 'holy' wars.
960BC	Adam and Eve are created according to historical Bibliologists. See the following Biblical genealogy
950BC	The *Vedas*, Hindu scripture, reach their formality on silk
600BC	in Scandinavian culture the God Balder comes to earth to die for the sins of mankind

540BC	Buddhism begins in India. Buddha disclaims the existence of a *Holy Trinity* and declares that there is only one God, the God Brahma, and that His job ended with creation and that man is an extension of Brahma, that the rest of the job is up to man. He refutes the caste system of Hinduism and declares that all men and women are equal. He introduces the concept of 'love thy neighbor as thyself'
479BC	Taoism begins in China. Tao's ministry teaches that all of the God Brahma's creation is to be enjoyed equally by all of its creatures. He adopts Buddha's principle of 'love thy neighbor as thyself'
221BC	Qin, Prince Sheng is the first man to claim divinity. Origin of the idea that a man could be God.
4BC-27AD	Christ comes to earth to redeem mankind of Original Sin as foretold in the story of Adam and Eve. Christ rejects the Aryan race philosophy of His Father and teaches that all God's children are equal. He introduces the eastern concept of 'love thy neighbor as thyself' to the western world. His primary message is ignored by His Christian followers
50AD-75AD	East meets West. Those in the MidEast first become aware of the Indians and Hinduism and the Chinese and Taoism
53AD-96AD	The *New Testament* is believed to be written. It establishes the existence of a *Holy Trinity*, something that Moses had not

foreseen when he had established his religion of belief of one God,

- God the Father, the Creator
- Christ, the Redeemer, provider of the afterlife
- Holy Ghost, guides one in what is right and wrong

314AD — Constantine convinces the populace that he has had intercession with Christ which inspires the Romans to conduct the first Crusades in which tens of millions of Muslims who refuse to accept Christ are murdered

375AD — earliest surviving substantial text of the New Testament, British Museum

400AD — the *Vulgate*, the first complete *Bible* is believed to be written by St. Jerome

600AD — Islamism, Mohammed writes the *Koran*. He decrees that there is only one God, God the Father of the *Old Testament* who He calls 'Allah'. He convinces his people that God has ordered that they retaliate against their Christian conquerors. Christians are driven out of the Arab world.

975 AD — earliest surviving substantial text of the Old Testament, Jerusalem

1095AD — The Crusades in which Jews and Muslims are given the choice, *'convert or take to the sword.'* Tens of millions of unbelievers - men, women and children - are slaughtered in the name of Christ.

1858AD   Darwin's *Natural Selection* before the time of the first excavation of a prehistoric skeleton of a man. That archeology and, more so, genetics would eventually prove him right

1906AD   Einstein's theory before the development of modern day microscopes that eventually would prove him right. His theory claimed that man was not the single entity that he was believed to be but rather a composite of trillions of individual beings called 'energy'. That the method of creation is consistent to the tiniest of these individual beings, that every microcosm is the product of two others of different sexes, that the tiniest sub-atomic particle that exists has both a mother and a father.

1983AD   Jerry Falwell and Pat Robertson trade the Christian vote in exchange for Ronald Reagan's commitment that he will not approve funds for the new 'gay' disease. After almost a decade of delay, which in the end will cost millions of lives, Elizabeth Taylor leads an army of men and women of good conscience in establishing AIDS research.

1997AD   repeated DNA analysis proves the Cro-Magnon Man to be the direct ancestor of modern man with zero chance of error

Lucien Gregoire

From Adam to Christ

The authenticity of the *Bible* depends entirely upon the authenticity of its genealogy. This is why all major denominations universally agree that the time of Adam and Eve is around 4000 BC. This is why Darwin's theory was attacked so bitterly by Christianity, as the timing of Adam and Eve, which is explicit in the *Bible*, means that they could not have been created as caveman and cavewoman. That Darwin's Theory, which has since been proven true, meant that Christ was the Son that God the Father sent to save the world from Original Sin as was once foretold in a fairytale.

The *Old Testament's* genealogy is complete from Adam and Eve to Christ. The generation length for each of the patriarchs is explicit in the *Bible* except for three generations between Noah and Abraham. The 4060BC date for Adam and Eve assumes that these three men begot their offspring at the average age of the other patriarchs who came between Noah and Abraham. If they, in fact, begot their offspring in the last year of their lives, then the time of Adam and Eve would be 4192BC.

It should be noted that the earliest known hard evidence of a date etched in stone based on a 360 day calendar is 4261BC in Mesopotamia. This artifact is held by the British National Museum in London.

However, the great problem in the Bible's genealogy lies in the unusually long life spans of the early patriarchs, those between Adam and Noah having lived an average of 830 years and, those between Noah and Abraham, an average of 447 years, conceiving their offspring relatively late in life. Noah, for example, begot his first offspring at the age of 500. It should be noted that of the four hundred Egyptian mummies found to date that precede Noah's time, the median life span was twenty-eight and the oldest one lived to the age of fifty-four.

It is generally believed that when St. Jerome wrote the first *Bible* in 400AD that he substituted these unbelievable life spans, in order to push the date of Adam and Eve back to 4000BC, as if these men had lived normal life spans, he would have been looking at a time for Adam and Eve of about 1000BC. Since it was known even at his time that the great Egyptian civilization had thrived and the pyramids had been built long before 1000BC, this would have dealt a fatal blow to the validity of Christianity before it really had a chance to get off the ground. What Jerome did not know at the time was that it is not biologically possible for a human being to survive past the age of one hundred and fifty. The kidneys, filter about seventy five gallons of blood each day and will fail under perfect conditions between one hundred and forty and one hundred and fifty years. That had Adam actually lived the 950 years that the Bible says he lived, that he would have been of a different species, that is not of the human race.

On the average, the early patriarchs in the *Old Testament* fathered their firstborn at an average age of eighty eight. If one uses what is the current average generation period of twenty five years, the time of Adam would be 1400BC. If one uses what is know to have been the average generation periods of primitive societies, the time of Adam and Eve is 960BC or about five hundred years after the time of Moses. Probably substantiating the fact that what Moses had to say about the story of Adam and Eve had to have come from God, as at his time Adam and Eve had not yet been created.

The complete genealogy from Adam to Christ
↓

Adam 4060BC
Seth (Cain and Able were Seth's brothers)
Enos
Cainan
Mahalaleel
Jared
Enoch
Methuselah
Lamech
Noah
Shem (brother of Hamm, father of the Canaanites)
Arphaxad
Salah
Eber
Peleg
Reu
Serug
Terah
Abraham
Isaac
Jacob_____
   ↓   ↓
Judas   Levi
              ↓
  ↓   ___Eleazor___
         ↓   ↓
Phares Moses   Aaron father of the Aryan race
Esrom
Aram
Aminadab
Naasson

A God for Lions

Sakmon
Booz
Obed
Jesse
King Solomon   960BC approximate time of Adam and Eve
King David   if early patriarchs had lived normal
Roboam   life spans
Abia
Josaphat*
Joram
Ozias
Joatham
Achaz
Mahasses
Amon
Josias
Jechonias
Salathiel
Zorobable
Abiud
Eliakim
Azor
Sadoc
Achim
Eliud
Mattham
Jacob
Josep, husband of Mary, the mother of Christ

*the *Old Testament* ends with Josaphat. When Jerome put together the Bible he eliminated the books that spoke of those patriarchs from Joram through Josep possibly because these stories being more recent lacked credibility at the time. This is why this part of the genealogy of the Old Testament is summarized on the first page of the *New Testament*.

The Heavens

The Christian,

Reuniting of body and soul in the afterlife. The mind as one has known it to be in this life will not survive. That is, one will not survive with ones consciousness, freewill and the ability to make decisions. The soul will be focused for all time on a single thought, the adoration of Christ on His great white throne. For the definition of a 'soul', as opposed to a 'spirit', is that part of man that drives his adoration of his God. The 'spirit', on the other hand, is generally defined as what one is without ones body. The 'body' in the Christian afterlife will be asexual and not the biological body that one has had in this life. Its purpose will be to identify one from another, as all souls will be the same, as all souls will know all things. Reuniting with ones loved ones of this earth is not included in the deal as all of ones love will be for Christ alone. The environment is a great urbanization of sameness day after day. Specifically, a great city of gold where even the streets are paved with gold, where there are no pigeons or puppies to litter the streets, as there will be no plant, animal, air or sea life there. An existence of no change, no seasons, no rain, nor snow. Christians who are not saved will be cast into the fires of hell for all eternity. PRICE: believe in Christ and die in a state of repentance.

The Kingdom of Heaven,

The 'heaven' described by 'Johnny' as the *New Jerusalem* is explicitly described in the books of prophecy, *Jeremiah* and *Isaiah*. Therein God the Father promises a *New Jerusalem* for those who are to be saved and the *Book of Revelations* in the

New Testament confirms this prophecy giving the Christian a heaven limited to the eternal adoration of God.

When Christ grew up all Jews found their salvation in the *New Jerusalem* and whenever one referred to the afterlife they referred to the *'New Jerusalem'.*

Strangely, throughout His ministry, Christ never once mentions the *New Jerusalem'.* Instead He talks of the *'Kingdom of Heaven'* or *'His Father's Kingdom'* and there is no description of what He meant by the *'Kingdom of Heaven'* in the Gospels. Yet, it is reasonable to believe that since Christ did not use the words *'New Jerusalem',* that the *Kingdom of Heaven* was a place of great beauty and joy and one in which one will be rejoined with ones loved ones. A much more attractive heaven than is the *New Jerusalem* as has been sold by the preachers through the years. Of course, the price is much different. PRICE: accept that all of God's children are equal, whether they be men or women, or black or white, or Muslim or Chinese, or normal or handicapped, or straight or gay, or what have you. And live in a society driven by compassion rather than one driven by greed.

The Muslim,

Reuniting of the body and spirit much as the body and mind have been in this life including ones biological and sexual body and desires. One will survive with ones freewill and the ability to make independent decisions. Those who are saved will lead a life similar to what one has known on this earth except that each day will be a better day than the one before it. Although one will not be in sole admiration of Him, one will be continually thankful for everything that God the Father 'Allah' has given one. Reuniting of one with ones loved ones of this earth is a part of the deal. The environment is the Garden of Eden together with its plant, animal, air and sea life. Muslims who are not saved will be cast into the fires of hell for all time. PRICE: daily prayer and the weight of good versus evil.

The Buddhist,

Reuniting of ones mind with a new body. Similar to the Muslim, he gets a heaven of fresh air, of plants, of trees, of lakes, of rivers, of running brooks, of snow peaked mountains, of green valleys and cascading waterfalls. Of dogs and of cats and of our many friends in the forest. It is a land of marigolds and violets and tinker bells and buttercups and bees and butterflies which go from here to there. It is a land of reds, of greens, of blues, of yellows and of purples. Of Apples, of limes, of blueberries, of peaches, and of plums. Of the sun, of the moon, of the stars and of the sea. Where the creatures live in waters as deep, as high does the eagle soar. Not a perfect world. But, at least one where one can look forward to growing up, and taking the girl of ones dreams to the junior prom, of falling in love, and having children. Of hugging children. Of loving children. And, of watching ones child grow up, and take his girl of his dreams to the junior prom, and of falling in love, and having children. Yes, a land of ups and downs. One which gives one the opportunity to walk in the shadows of the deepest valleys and, yet, climb the tallest mountains. The Buddhists that are not saved cease to exist. PRICE: recognition of equality and contribution to others.

The Hinayana,

He goes to the same heaven as have Washington, Jefferson Lincoln, Einstein, Edison, Patton and some others, those who have made immense contribution to mankind. Instead of existing as a single mind, he will exist as a part of many minds, of many sprits, and will have many bodies, and as result he will live in eternity as a God, for he will tell one right from wrong. The environment is the earth, but not as we have known it. For by his contribution he has made it better each day for the world's future children. Hinayanas who are not saved cease to exist. PRICE: recognition of equality and great contribution to others.

The Hindu,

After a series of successful lives moving up the caste system the Hindu finally attains Nirvana. That is, the 'spirit', what one is without ones body, is taken to a place of great beauty and happiness. The environment is probably best described as being a combination of the Christian City of Gold and the Muslim Garden of Eden. Hindus who are not saved cease to exist. PRICE: redistribution of wealth and weight of good versus evil.

The Taoist,

He goes to a great Chinese restaurant where he uses chopsticks that, being too long to feed himself, he feeds others. And in return he is fed by others who likewise have chopsticks too long to feed themselves. And all is right. Those who are not saved go to another great Chinese restaurant. And again they have chopsticks that are too long to feed themselves. But not having learned to feed others in this life they are unable to feed each other. So they exist in a state of perpetual hunger and starvation for all time. PRICE: love thy neighbor as thyself.

The Jew,

He goes to the City of Brotherly Love best known as Philadelphia. If it is a nice day he gets to walk in the park. Jews who are not saved go to Jersey City. PRICE: live ones daily life according to the TORAH.

Printed in the United States
1303100004B/1-54